The Betting Game

Printed in the United States of America

First Printing, 2013
Second Printing, 2020

ISBN 978-0-9859752-1-0 Paperback
ISBN 978-0-9859752-4-1 E-Book

Bella Dama, LLC
PO Box 480677
Charlotte, NC 28269
www.labelladama.net

~Chapter 1~

Mango's Nightclub

It was late February and Spring Break came early in one of Miami's top destination spots…South Beach. It was the place to be with college kids letting off steam during their week long break from school. They flooded the streets looking for fun, thrills and excitement.

By day, these sun-drenched beaches were consumed with sun-bathers, noisemakers, nudists and drinkers. But when the sun went down, it was naughty hottie time. Nightclubs and bars were jam-packed and stayed open 'til the break of dawn. Women dressed scandalously and men looked delicious. Alcohol, drugs and sex all played a role during this dynamic time.

Mango's Nightclub was the hottest and sexiest Latin nightclub on South Beach. It sat on Ocean Drive between 9th and 10th street near one of the busiest corners on the strip. Its tropical-infused decor, exotic-looking servers and live entertaining shows always drew a crowd.

Saturday nights were regularly impenetrable and congested. So, this night wasn't any different. Onlookers blocked the entrance doors trying to catch a glimpse of the hoopla. And boy…she was mighty fine!

With *Que Bueno Baila Usted* by Oscar D'Leon blasting through the speakers, everyone stopped to watch as this sexy Latin woman, dancing on the bar, put on a show.

She exuded sexuality in her every step. Her smooth, vanilla mocha skin glistened with drops of sweat as she mixed fast turns, high kicks and body twisting moves to the beat with her partner. Her black, waist-length hair swung everywhere she did as she was whirled around in four-inch stilettos. The masses cheered, whistled and screamed as they watched this 5'7" salsa goddess gyrate her hourglass shape and heart-shaped butt in circular motions. With a dip and sliding through her partner's legs, the performance was over.

The woman heard her name being called as she was lowered off of the bar.

"Angelica!"

When she looked, it was her friend, Vivian.

Vivian was her 28-year old, Cuban and white friend. This petite-sized woman stood 5'5" with straight auburn-colored hair, green eyes, high cheekbones and big breasts.

"Hey, Mami! What's up?" said Angelica giving her a hug.

"Damn, Chica! You did yo' thang out there tonight! You goin' on again later?"

"Naw…I'm done for tonight. I'm ready to smoke."

"Yeah, well don't forget about me."

"I won't," said Angelica.

They walked over to the bar where the bartender had shots of

Patron waiting.

"Here you go…my two favorite ladies," he said passing each one their glass and pouring him one.

They toasted and tossed 'em back. Then, Angelica went to change.

Thirty minutes later, she came out wearing a very sexy, white halter jumpsuit. The front had a V neckline that stretched just passed her navel and was embellished with gold buckles. The backless one-piece was worn really low on her butt. She accessorized with large gold hoop earrings, lots of gold bangles on each wrist and a BCBG gold clutch. She sported white and gold-strapped Christian Louboutin heels and her hair was in a side bun with the front swept to the side.

Angelica made her way upstairs to VIP where her sister, Ariana, and her sister's husband, Falio, were sitting with his crew.

"Hey," said Angelica as she approached them.

"Hey," she heard throughout the group.

She kissed Ariana on the cheek, greeting her. Then, she went to greet Falio, but he sat her down on his lap. She kissed him on the cheek and tried to get up, but he wasn't letting that happen. So, she sat there and smoked with everyone.

Angelica looked over and saw the sour look on Ariana's face. She knew it was because of where she was sitting, but Ariana couldn't do anything about it. Falio was madly in love with Angelica and did anything for her. Angelica was the only female Falio behaved this way with, so Ariana had to just deal with it.

In the middle of their session, a waitress came over with a shot of Patron.

"Angelica…this is for you," said Candy, the waitress.

"From who?" she asked.

Candy pointed to a handsome, milk chocolate man with a low fade and goatee sitting at the corner of the bar. Angelica thought that was mighty bold of him since he didn't know if Falio was her man or not. Nonetheless, she was impressed. So, she raised her glass to thank him. He raised his as well. They tossed 'em back at the same time. She noticed an ornament sitting beside him, but dismissed her. She was going after him anyway.

Before leaving, she whispered in Falio's ear. He reached his hand back and his boy handed him a sandwich bag with four separate bags inside and a few blunts. He had just given her a quarter ounce of Purple Haze, Granddaddy Purp, Sour Diesel and AK47. She put the weed in her purse and kissed everyone goodbye.

When she got to the bottom of the steps, she felt a presence behind her. It was Falio.

"What's up, Lilo?" Angelica asked Falio, calling him by his nickname.

"Where you goin'?" he asked a little jealous.

"To mind my business."

"Angelica, te deseo. I want you so bad. Don't leave," he said real close to her face.

She caressed his face and popped kissed him on the lips. Then said, "Papi, you know that this…us…can't happen," and walked away.

Angelica was headed to meet her Prince Charming at the bar. She felt it was only right to thank him in person for her drink. But first, she stopped by the bar where Vivian was sitting to give her one of the bags of weed.

"Hi," said Angelica wedging her way between him and his ornament.

"Hello," he said laughing at her boldness.

"Excuse you," said his lady friend.

"I'm Angelica. Would you like to dance?" she asked totally ignoring the woman.

"I'm Austin…and sure," he said leaving the woman sitting there.

Austin held Angelica closely by the waist as they made their way to the dance floor. It felt like he was walking through a maze commented Austin.

Angelica was intoxicating. He couldn't take his eys off of her as they danced close. She made sure to pleasure him by rubbing her booty all over him, displaying sexual behaviors.

After groovin' through a few songs, she suggested they go out on the patio to talk and smoke. He agreed as she led the way.

She took a blunt out of her purse and lit it.

"So, are you enjoying yourself?" she asked barely able to talk.

"Yeah...it's cool, but I'm no stranger to Miami or South Beach."

"What do you mean?" she asked hitting the blunt one more time and then passing it to him.

"You're really gonna act like you don't who I am?" he asked arrogantly.

She frowned at his tone, but he assumed it was a look of confusion.

"NFL? Football? Professional athlete?"

Angelica turned her frown upside down as she schooled him real quick.

She stood up and sat on his lap, facing him. "I know exactly who you are. You're Austin Zachary, one of the best wide receivers to ever play in the NFL. You're 36, 6'3" and now weigh about… mmm…looks like about 225. You went to the University of North Carolina, Chapel Hill; you were drafted halfway through your sophomore year by the Carolina Cardinals; and you've played your entire 13-year career for that one team." She paused to take a hit. "You took the football world by storm…1,407 career receptions, 18,055 career receiving yards, 180 rushing and receiving touchdowns and averaged 70 yards per game that you played in. You're a four-time Super Bowl winner, was awarded NFL Super Bowl MVP twice and played in ten Pro Bowl games. You've done several endorsements, including Reebok, Pepsi, Dunkin Donuts, McDonalds and Mercedes-Benz, earning well over forty million. And…you made the Top 100 Best Football Player's list." She took another hit and passed it. "You called it quit four years ago when you tore your ACL and got a slight concussion after getting banged up playing against the Minnesota Loons, in what would be your last Super Bowl game. It was an intense game, but thank goodness it was towards the end and your team won. At least you went out with another ring."

He grinned from ear to ear showing off his deep dimples. He was truly impressed.

"Damn! I didn't take you for a football kind of girl."

"There's a lot about me you don't know," she said trying to get up, but he wouldn't let her.

"I'm impressed," he said staring into her deep-set, Paisley-shaped blue-green-gray eyes.

"Well, I'm not."

"What do you mean?" he asked confused.

"Being a professional athlete or "Ex" NFL player doesn't impress me," she said doing the quote sign with her fingers.

He stuck his hand in the back of her hair and pulled her close to his face. "Oh I get it. So it's my reputation with the ladies that impress you, huh? You want to be owned by me? You're one of those chicks that want to be taken care of, too. Is that it?"

After laughing hysterically, she looked into his brown eyes with hers barely open and said, "I don't want or need you to take care of me. I have plenty of other men to do that for me. Besides, your reputation with the ladies ain't that great, Sweetheart. You go through more women than I go through underwear. And no one will own me until there's a ring on this finger," she said wiggling the ring finger on her left hand. "So miss me with all that bullshit about you owning someone," she said pulling away from him.

He let her hair go and said, "I like you. You're feisty. I'm gonna enjoy breaking you down. 'Cause I will break you down and I will have you. I always do."

Angelica laughed again like she was at a Kevin Hart comedy show.

"You're funny. You make me laugh," she said dismissing his comment.

"Laugh now, cry later," he said confidently.

"You know…so far, you're really not impressing me. It's a shame, too. I thought you had true skills considering your reputation."

"Oh ok…Miss Angelica. Nothing I say seems to be working. So, I'm curious…what does impress you?"

Angelica softly touched the back of his head as she drew near his face. He thought she was going to kiss him. Instead, she whispered in his ear in the most sexual way, "Dick. A big, fat, chocolate dick." Then, licked his earlobe.

Austin wasn't expecting that, but she got his attention.

He whispered back in her ear, "Well, you're in luck. I just so happen to have one of those."

"Show me."

He pressed his smooth, brown lips against her full, pouty lips, kissing her while unbuttoning his pants. She was now impressed after seeing what he whipped out. Angelica tried wrapping her hand around his soul pole, but her fingertips were nowhere near touching.

They went to his limo and took care of business.

~Chapter 2~

Lunch at Clevelander's

Wake up…Wake up…

The next morning, Angelica woke up to her ringtone screaming in her ear.

"Hello," she answered half asleep.

"Hey, Sexy," said a male voice.

"Hey."

"You still sleepin'?" he asked loudly.

"Yep."

"Are we still on for lunch at Clevelanders?"

"Yeah…what time is it?"

"11:30."

"Ok. How long before you get there?" she asked yawning.

"Like thirty minutes."

"Ok…see you then."

She got up and took a quick shower.

Angelica decided to take her bike so she could maneuver through the streets of South Beach much faster. She could weave in and out of traffic better than in a car.

Clevelanders was one of South Beach's hottest and most upscale hotels with a chic sidewalk cafe, mega bar by the pool and plenty of live entertainment.

She cruised Ocean Drive on her black and lime green Suzuki GSX 600 until she reached her destination. She parked next to the valet.

Angelica saw her friend and walked towards him.

"Hey, Babe...you look good," said her male friend, Jaime, kissing her on the cheek.

"Thanks," she said placing her helmet and bag in the seat next to her. "This is a great table."

"I know. We get to see everyone and everything going by."

Jaime was Angelica's bartender friend from Mango's. He was a 27-year old, Argentinean hunk that stood 5'11" with green eyes and kind of lanky, but toned.

"So, tell me…what happened last night?" she anxiously asked.

Before he could get a word out, the waitress interrupted.

"Hi. My name is Monica. Can I get you something to drink?"

"Yes. I'd like two Caribbean Rum Punches with two shots of Cherry Grenade on the side," said Jaime.

"And two Purple Bomb shots…please," added Angelica.

"Ok. And would you like any appetizers?" asked Monica.

"Yes...the colossal nachos with chicken, ahi tuna sliders and two orders of Buffalo shrimp. Thank you," responded Angelica.

"And rush those drinks, Honey," said Jaime ready for his afternoon cocktail.

"Coming right up," said Monica laughing as she walked away.

"Ok…spill it," said Angelica.

Jaime's girlfriend was Vivian, Angelica's friend from Mango's. Vivian was a dancer at the club. She met a guy she wanted to have a threesome with and told Jaime. Jaime didn't mind since he was bi-sexual. So, the guy invited them back to his house to have sex.

"Y'all nasty!" shouted Angelica.

"So!" he said proudly.

"Are y'all gonna see him again?"

"I am. I'm meeting him after I leave here."

"So, is this guy gay? Straight? Bi?"

"I don't know, but I'm gonna find out," he said smiling hard. "But you've seen him before."

"Where?"

"He's a well-known artist, but I can't say any names."

"You lie!!!" exclaimed Angelica shocked.

Just then, Monica came back with their drinks.

"Here ya go," she said placing them on the table. Ten minutes later, the appetizers came out.

As they enjoyed their food, drinks and gossip session, they heard the roaring sound of motorcycles approaching. Angelica had a feeling she knew who it was. It was confirmed when a pack of fine, shirtless men drove up on their red and black Suzukis. Falio and his 20-man crew drove Hayabusas, GSX 1250 FAs, GSX 750s and GSX 1000s with "Miami's Finest" inscribed on them.

They parked diagonally across the street from Clevelanders. They packed the streets of South Beach being loud and wild while having fun. And their bikes were on display for all to admire.

Next, she told Jaime about Austin and how they got their freak on in the back of his limo.

"And you call me nasty! You just met him AND you screwed him," said Jaime laughing.

Angelica laughed and said, "Yeah, but it wasn't a threesome."

"Minor details," said Jaime downplaying his sexuality.

They continued trash talking as they ate. Jaime ordered another round of drinks. Again, Falio and his boys were distracting. This time, it was the whistling and yelling to get women's attention. It slightly annoyed Angelica.

"Do you ever think about it?" Jaime asked Angelica.

She sat there looking in Falio's direction. In a daze, she thought about Jaime's question. She knew how he felt about her, but she couldn't do anything about it.

"I do, but I just can't," she said.

"Girl…I wouldn't care about any of that if it were me. He is TOO fine!"

Falio was this scrumptious six-foot, Dominican and Puerto Rican man with a bald head. He had provocative hazel eyes with long lashes and lips that would make any woman, who was staring at them, lose track of what he was saying. And if anyone knew how to showcase a human male body, it was him. With his sculpted abs and tattoos everywhere, his body was like a piece of art on a human canvas. He was just beautiful and women flocked to him all the time.

Angelica didn't want Falio, but she did like stirring up trouble. So, she decided she would show all of his admirers who was really boss.

She stood up and said, "I'll be back. Lunch is on me."

"Don't hurt 'em, Baby," teased Jamie, cheering her on.

She fluffed up her hair and slowly strutted in Falio's direction. Nico saw her and tapped Falio, getting his attention. Angelica got looks and stares from all of them, including the women. She assumed it was her outfit.

Her sexy, black leather two-piece turned heads. The racerback, halter bra top had a high-collared neck and three gold snap buttons in the front that held it all together. The booty shorts had the same three gold snap button design on the sides. She wore black leather, peep toe ankle boots and her gold filigree jewelry set, which included double drop dangling earrings, a large cuff bracelet, a wide-banded dome ring and a long chain with a small, elaborate pendant on it.

Falio immediately let go of his girl and went to Angelica.

"Hey, Lilo," she said smiling.

"Hey, Mami," he said picking her up.

She wrapped her legs around him as he tongue kissed her.

Everyone in his crew greeted her. They all knew the deal with Falio loving Angelica.

"Lilo, I want money," she said innocently batting her eyes.

"How much?"

"Three."

"Aight," he said putting her down.

Angelica saw Nico and yelled, "I'm tellin'."

Nico laughed as she used Falio's phone to text Claudia.

Nico was Falio's best friend. He was Italian, white and black. He also stood six foot with a bald head and brown bedroom eyes. He was a solid combination of thick, muscular and ripped. He was sexy as hell.

Falio counted out three thousand dollars and handed it to Angelica.

"Thank you," she said pulling him towards her, kissing him again.

"Qué mala tú eres," he said.

"I'm not bad. Why did you say I'm bad?" she asked smiling.

"You know what you're doing."

She just winked at him and went back to the table.

Jaime wasn't surprised at what just happened. Angelica liked being the center of Falio's world, even though she wouldn't admit it.

From that point on, Falio didn't take his eyes off of Angelica. He didn't get next to another chick, let alone look at one.

A limo slowly cruised the street. Angelica saw it, but didn't pay it any attention…that was until it stopped and Austin got out with a look on his face.

He approached Angelica and Jaime and said, "Hello."

"Hi," said Angelica.

"Hello. My name is Austin," he said to Jaime, extending his hand out.

"Jaime. Nice to meet you," he said shaking his hand. "Please… sit," he said pointing to the available chair.

Jaime hated to leave and miss the fireworks, but he had some-where to be.

"Well, Austin…it was a pleasure meeting you, but I have to go," he said standing up, shaking his hand again.

"Likewise," said Austin.

"And you, my love…I'll talk to you later," said Jaime giving her a hug. He went to kiss her on the cheek, but she turned and pop kissed him on the lips. He knew what she was doing, so he added a slap on her butt for show.

"Have fun and be safe," she said smiling. "Call me…don't for-get!"

"Ok."

Jaime didn't even make it to valet when he heard Austin ques-tioning her.

"So, who was that? Your next victim?" Austin asked sarcastical-ly.

"You're funny," she said laughing. "He's just a friend."

"Friend, huh?" he said in disbelief and sounding jealous.

Angelica gave little importance to his behavior.

"Yes…friend."

"I didn't like what I just saw."

"So!"

"So?"

"Yeah…So!"

"So, I told you I don't like my women messing around."

"Well thank God I'm not one of those, huh?" she said standing up, throwing money on the table and walking away.

She almost made it to her bike when he gently grabbed her.

"Wait…please," he said.

She didn't have a chance to respond 'cause Falio was in his face real quick.

"Is there a problem here, Sweetheart?" Falio asked Angelica, ready to knock him out.

"It's cool, Lilo," she said knowing he didn't like the way Austin handled her.

"You sure?" Falio asked again giving her a look.

"Yeah, I'm sure," she said nodding up and down.

"Ok. Let me know if you need anything," Falio said in Austin's face, staring him down.

But Austin stood there and didn't even blink.

"I will," she said forcing her way between them.

Falio slowly backed away.

She jumped on her motorcycle and put her helmet on.

"Scoot back," said Austin so he could drive.

"No."

Once she started the bike, he jumped on in front of her, forcing her to scoot back.

"Excuse you!" she screamed, hitting him on the shoulder.

He didn't respond and took off.

~Chapter 3~

The Four Seasons Hotel

Austin finally stopped at the Four Seasons Hotel on Brickell Avenue in Downtown Miami. Angelica was furious.

"Give me my keys, Austin!" she angrily yelled.

"No! Not until we talk."

"I'm calling the cops," she said reaching for her phone.

"Fine! Here are your keys, but I just want to talk."

After hesitating, she put her phone away.

"Please come upstairs," he said. "Just to talk."

"Well…I'm not staying long," she assured him, getting off her bike.

"That's fine."

He reached for her hand and led her through the lobby.

Austin's Miami condo resided in the tallest and most glamorous building in Miami, The Four Seasons Hotel. This towering building had many unique features about it. It housed multiple office spaces, retail shops and six different restaurants on the first nine floors with its lobby on the first floor. The sophisticated hotel rooms and suites were occupied from the eleventh floor through the forty-fifth floor with its lobby on the tenth floor. And the luxurious customized residential units were occupied from the forty-sixth floor through the seventieth floor with their private lobby elevator on the ninth floor.

"I love Hernan Bas and Jose Bedia," said Angelica as they got on the private elevator.

"An art lover, are we?" he asked as he swiped his key card and pressed *70*.

"Yes."

The Four Seasons Hotel was also known for its vivacious, contemporary Caribbean and Latin American art collection showcased throughout the hotel. It spared no expense when it came to boasting the talents of Caribbean and Latin American artists, like Fernando Botero, Jesus Rafael Soto and Vik Muniz, through paintings, sculptures, installations, prints and photography. It made the Four Seasons the perfect place to vacation or live.

"I own several pieces of art myself."

"Like who?"

"Kris Lewis, Julio Larraz, and Felicity Aylieff…to name a few."

"Ok…" he said shaking his head and chuckling. "You never cease to amaze me."

When they exited the seventieth floor, there was a large, open foyer. On her left, she saw four doors. On her right, there was one…his.

He opened the door and invited her in.

"Would you like something to drink?" he asked.

"Water, thanks."

"There's a box on the living room table…look inside and light one," he said walking towards the kitchen.

She entered the living room passing through his gallery. His place was stunning.

It was a massive 7,500 square foot penthouse with four bedrooms, six and half bathrooms and an open floor plan between the living room, dining room and library. The Tuscan kitchen had Italian marble floors and countertops. And this unit was located on the best floor in the building, overlooking the entire city and bay.

Angelica stood next to an immensely large, wood-trimmed window looking out onto the water, daydreaming.

"Here you go," he said, breaking her concentration.

"Thank you," she said reaching for her glass.

"Are you ok? You looked a little spaced out."

"Yeah, I'm fine. Thanks. I was just admiring the view," she said taking a seat on the couch. "I like your place. It's very nice."

"Thanks," he said grabbing the box Angelica didn't get a chance to open. It was his weed box with all sorts of weed paraphernalia inside.

As he lit a blunt, he explained using the hotel's interior designers to deck out the place. He told them his ideas and she was looking at the results.

"I love what they did with it," she said, referring to the simple, but elegant African themed living room. She especially loved the enormous art wall near the fireplace that had large metal leaves and bamboo on it.

~Chapter 4~

New
Opportunity

"So, do you like working at the club?" Austin asked Angelica as they smoked.

"Mango's?"

"Yeah."

"What makes you think I work there?"

"I saw you dancing on the bar."

"I don't work there. I dance there for fun. The owner and I are good friends. He lets me get crazy whenever I want."

"Oh…ok. My apologies for making an assumption. So, what do you do?"

"I work in Human Resources," she said coughing a little.

"Oh yeah…doin' what?" he asked surprised and excited at the same time.

"I'm an Executive Recruiter, or headhunter if you will, at an employment agency on Miami Beach."

"Really? Do you like it?"

"It's okay, but I want to get back into management."

"Like what?"

"VP of Human Resources."

"That's a pretty big role. Do you think you can handle those types of responsibilities?"

Angelica looked at him and said, "Oh…so what…I can only handle dancing on bars? Is that what you're trying to say?"

"No. I'm not saying that. I'm just saying there's a lot that goes with that title."

"I know!" she said peeved.

"Angelica…please…can we talk without the sarcasm? I'm really trying to get to know you better and find out more about you."

She composed herself since he sounded sincere.

"Ok, Austin. Let's talk."

"Thank you. So why did you say get back into management?"

"I was the Director of HR for an international import/export company, but was laid off when they downsized."

"Sorry to hear that."

"It's ok. Things happen for a reason and it worked out in my favor."

"How?"

"The company closed six months after I left."

"Wow! That's crazy."

"Yep."

"So, where'd you go to school?"

"Well…I attended Florida International University where I received dual Bachelor's Degrees. The first in Business Administration with a concentration in Human Resources Management and the second in International Business, Honors Program. I also participated in a special track program called Leadership and

Change Management. I graduated Summa Cum Laude with a 4.0 GPA. Then, I received dual Master's Degrees. The first in Human Resources Management and the second by completing the International MBA program."

Angelica paused to hit the blunt and then continued.

"While in school, I was involved in the International Business Honors Society, ALPFA Honors, FBLA (Future Business Leaders Association), SIFE (Students in Free Enterprise), SGA (Student Government Association) and the student conduct committee. I was also a Peer Counselor for the Office of Orientation, Camp Facilitator, Student Ambassador, Recruiting Assistant for Student Media and Resident Assistant Selection Committee member. I am fluent in English, Spanish, French and Portuguese. I also speak a little Russian and German. And last, but not least…I am SPHR, GPHR and HRMP certified."

"Damn!!! I had you pegged all wrong!"

"Most do, but I'm very educated and experienced for my age. I've been working since high school; I've held executive level management positions; and I enjoy Human Resources. I feel as though I make a difference."

"Wow!!! That's amazing!!! How old are you if you don't mind me asking?"

"29."

"How did you work, go to school and participate in so many activities?"

"It was hard. Some days I didn't think I would make it. And the truth is that some of those extracurricular activities were only for a semester. I also networked my butt off. But what really helped me was dancing. It was my stress reliever right along with smoking."

"I understand."

"So what about you? What does the retired NFL player, Mr.

Austin Zachary, do these days?" she asked.

"Well…I own a successful retail franchise with its corporate office in Charlotte."

"Oh yeah…which one?"

"Sportie Fans."

"Aren't those stores like the Wal-Mart of licensed sports apparel?"

"Yes," he said laughing and then explained the history.

One day, Austin walked into Sports Authority looking for a specific jersey, but they didn't have it. He checked other stores around the Charlotte area, but no one carried it because it wasn't relative to the Carolinas. So, he decided to open up a store that carried all licensed sports apparel from every professional sports team, including NBA, NFL, NHL, MLB and NASCAR. It didn't matter the team he would carry it. He initially started off with clothes and shoes. Then expanded the store's merchandise to carry specific home good items, car accessories and office supplies. His stores also carried special event items like divisional playoff winners and national championship winners.

Recently, he added a special feature to the newer stores: a sports bar. It was a way to get people in the stores to shop while watching their favorite sports team and enjoying a beer.

"We're adding another thirty stores this year taking our store count to three hundred and seventy," said Austin.

"Nice! Congratulations," said Angelica excited for him.

"Thanks."

"You know…all this time I thought retired NBA player, Charles Bartley, owned those stores."

"Naw. We started them together in my last year of playing, but he pulled out after I got injured and retired. He didn't think I would stick with it after that. So, I bought him out. I kept his face and name."

"Why? Why not use your own?" she asked.

"I gave myself five years to see if things would work out. Besides…I couldn't have this pretty face all over a failed business venture," he said rubbing the sides of his face, laughing.

Angelica laughed too.

Then, he continued. "But seriously…I gave myself five years to grow the stores, expand throughout major cities and become a success. At the end of the five years, I would either revamp the company's image or shut it down."

"So, I guess you'll be revamping its image."

"Yes…I've already started. The corporate office just moved into its new and bigger location this year in January. I'm working on reorganizing the entire company, growing the profit margins, changing the face of the company and bringing on new people to help me do it all…especially if we go international."

"I know your HR Department is swamped as with any expansion. Recruiting is gearing up for more hiring. Payroll, benefits and training…they all have their part to do. And if you go global…you're talking management teams, currency exchange rates, taxation, operational impact in a new political and social climate, future profitability, location and infrastructure, suppliers, risk management issues and the country's culture. They tend to operate…" Angelica was explaining, but stopped in the middle of her sentence. Austin was just staring at her, smiling. "What's wrong with you? Why are you smiling like that?"

"Come here," he said, extending his hand out to her.

She reached for his hand and sat on his lap.

"You're amazing," he said, looking into her eyes. "And beautiful."

"I know," she said smiling.

"Come work for me."

"What do you mean?"

"I mean move to Charlotte and be my Regional Human Resources Director for the entire Eastern Region. I just promoted the man that had that position. So, I have an opening and I really need someone like you in it."

"Just like that? I'm supposed to move to Charlotte? Leave my family, my friends, my job? Just like that?"

"Yes. You wanted more responsibility…I'm giving it to you."

Angelica wasn't expecting Austin to offer her a job.

She got up and stared out of the window again.

"What do you want? Money? Car? Home? Me?" he asked seriously, but laughing at the last option.

She turned around and said, "Cute, but the question is what do you want from me? What are you expecting? Why are you really doing this?"

He stood up and went to her.

"Seriously? I'm offering you an employment opportunity. I heard every word you said. You sound like you know what you're talking about. You definitely have the education. I also believe you can get the job done. That's it," he said, pausing. "I understand we just met and it may seem unreal. And as much as I'd like you to be my sex slave, I honestly don't expect anything from you in terms of us…nothing! I expect you to do your job and step up to the plate."

Angelica got into thinking mode, which meant she began pacing the floor. "Ok…how much a year we talkin'?"

"Ok…here we go," said Austin taking a seat. "The position starts at $98K, but I'll pay you $110K because of your credentials. What else?"

"Housing? Relocation costs? Interview?"

"The company owns a condo building in Uptown Charlotte. It's used as corporate housing for executives that relocate and need time to look for their own place. You can stay in the available three-bedroom unit on the sixth floor for six months, free of charge. After that, you'll have the option of staying and paying rent or moving out, which the company pays for as well. The company arranges and pays for relocation up to $4,000. Plus, you'll receive a $3,000 signing bonus. And as far as the interview goes, we just had it. What else?"

"Transportation to Charlotte?"

"You'll be picked up from your residence here in Miami, fly to Charlotte and be picked up at the airport by transportation. The driver will take you to your new home, where your assistant will be waiting for you with further instructions. What else?"

"Office? Benefits? Amount of travel?"

"You'll have a big corner office with brand new furniture that you'll select yourself. My assistant will send you a catalog via e-mail with instructions. You'll have executive benefits. So that means full medical, dental, vision, 401K, life insurance, long-term and short-term disability, tuition reimbursement, free parking, car allowance and other perks that come with the position. You'll start off traveling about 30% of the time, but I'm sure it'll increase as business does. You're provided company credit cards for all of your expenses…hotels, cars, food, etc. What else?"

Angelica got quiet for a moment. So, Austin took the opportunity to point out some facts.

He walked over to her again. This time, he wrapped his arms around her and said, "Listen…you're coming to Charlotte as a single woman with no strings attached to me. It's strictly professional. I think you'll be a good fit. However, you'll have to work hard and prove yourself. But, I don't see that as a problem."

"It's not. I don't mind working my butt off to prove myself."

"Ok. So, you come to Charlotte, enjoy cheaper cost of living and enjoy a few of the other benefits."

"What?"

He picked her up and sat her on the recliner next to the window. He pulled the lever back, reclining it all the way. He unsnapped her shorts and spread her legs apart.

"You'll be closer for me to do this," he said as his long, hot tongue leaped inside of her moist, creamy pie. As he delighted himself in her juices, her body moved like rippling waves. He pushed his face further in, trying to devour her. He made her go crazy moaning and sex talking.

"This could possibly work," she said barely able to speak.

After he made her cum, he unsnapped her top to play with her breasts as he thrusted his chocolate penis deep inside.

"Fuck!" is all she could yell as he filled her up.

Austin sexed her slowly, savoring the feeling. He was gentle with spurts of roughness, making sure he touched every inch of her cavity. Then, he pounded her pussy, making her scream. She loved it and eventually got on top, straddling him in the chair. She made her booty pop while bucking on him. He pulled her hair as she rode him like a cowgirl.

He wasn't ready to cum yet. So, he helped her up and stood in front of the wall of windows with her naked backside pressed against one of them. He stood there delighting himself in her wetness.

For the next two hours, they sexed hot and heavy from the floor to the couch and then to the kitchen.

After catching their breaths, Austin said, "It'll be nice having you closer...I will admit."

"I bet," said Angelica as she went to the bathroom.

"So...I'm not sure how much time you needed, but I was thinking two weeks."

"Two weeks?" yelled Angelica quickly running out.

"I need more than two weeks."

"To do what?" Austin seriously asked.

"Inform my job…"

"Two weeks."

"Pack my things…"

"Two weeks."

"Handle some pending personal business…"

"Two weeks."

"My family…"

"Two weeks."

"At least give me four."

"Listen, Angelica. I can give you three…tops! But remember… this is business and I really do need someone in that position. I'm attempting to give you what you want, but you have to meet me halfway. Miami will always be here. You're just moving three states up and two hours on a plane."

According to Angelica, his arrogance was back.

"You're right. I'll deal with my personal issues. I'll be ready in three weeks," she said.

Austin reached for his wallet and gave her a business card. "Here's my card. Send your resume to the e-mail listed. I'll have my assistant contact you with further instructions," said Austin.

"Thank you for this opportunity," said Angelica, as she got dressed.

"Where are you going?" he asked.

"Thanks for the fuck," she hollered as she slammed his door closed.

"You're welcome," he said laughing, sparking up the blunt. "You're mine now, Angelica."

~*Chapter 5*~

51 Biscayne

Angelica literally made it to her building within seven minutes. Austin stayed about a mile from her.

She lived in one of the most prominent and recognizable buildings in Downtown Miami, 51 Biscayne. The 51 Biscayne building was a 54-story condo high-rise with its signature neon orange crown on the roof, illuminating the city.

51 Biscayne was her ideal place to live since it was located across the street from Bayfront Park, in walking distance to Bayside Marketplace, near most nightclubs, minutes from South Beach, in close proximity to the American Airline Arena and the Arsht Center and adjacent to many restaurants.

With all of the amenities it came with, the best part about her building was the 54th floor. She and Claudia were the only two that lived on it.

Angelica's unit was the largest. Six units were purchased and converted into a five bedroom, five and half bathroom residence with just over 7,000 square feet of space. She customized her unit to include a party room, circle bar with a liquor closet and a therapy room with a massage table and two pedicure stations like at a salon.

Claudia's home was converted from four units into a four bedroom, four-bathroom residence with 5,000 square feet of space.

There was one additional unit that was originally an 800-square foot one bedroom with a den that got converted into a storage space for their motorcycles.

When Angelica got upstairs, she didn't go straight home. She knocked on Claudia's door.

"Who is it?" yelled Claudia from inside.

"Me."

This Persian-Canadian woman that stood 5'7" with clear blue eyes and long, straight auburn-colored hair opened the door practically naked. She had on a red two-piece lingerie set with two thin vinyl strips covering her nipples and one thin strip covering her vagina. Everything else was hanging out, but looking good as she had a bad body.

Angelica just shook her head. She knew by the outfit who was inside.

"Hey, Nico!" she yelled.

"Hey, Angelica!" he yelled back.

"Where's Anthony?" whispered Angelica.

"Out of town," Claudia whispered back.

"Well, I'm giving y'all thirty minutes! Then, I'll be back! So, hurry up!" said Angelica loud enough for Nico to hear.

"Bye, Angelica!" yelled Nico, laughing.

"Bye, girl. Text me when you're done," said Angelica walking away, laughing.

Angelica's condo was every artist and designer's dream. She was a huge artsy person, but a minimalist at the same time. She loved color, drama and pizzazz mixed with simple elegance and femininity. So, she hired her interior designer friend, Jorge Carrillo, to create a concept that would give each room its own identity and fit her personality and style.

Her home was vibrant and full of designer brands, including Donna Karan, Roberto Ventura and Ralph Pucci. Decorative plaster molding beautified the ceilings and arches of the doorways. Large pieces of furniture, dramatic artwork and funky-shaped light fixtures glamorized the space. Italian marble and bamboo hardwood flooring could be seen throughout the home. And her spacious wrap-around balcony overlooked the gorgeous bay and beautifully lit city, allowing views from three hundred and sixty degrees.

After showering, she went into the dining room. She sat at the table and turned on her laptop. She reviewed her resume before sending it as Austin instructed. After, she checked her personal e-mail and social media accounts. Then, she sat back and looked around, reminiscing. She couldn't believe she was leaving.

Angelica thought about her home and all that she'd been through decorating it. For example, she cracked a smile remembering the bickering between her and Jorge when designing the dining room. She didn't think an espresso colored dining room table with chairs covered in a silk floral and bird fabric would match, but it went perfect together. It blended beautifully with the colored tableware, big floral centerpiece and layered glass ceiling light fixture. Then, she cracked an even bigger smile remembering the metallic silver wallpaper Jorge told her to purchase. Again, she didn't think an entire wall of shiny floral paisley wallpaper would go with the scheme of things, but she was wrong. It was toned down with white sheer curtains, an espresso colored console table with lots of glass candleholders and a huge painting by Rachel Moani. She remembered being speechless when she saw the end result.

Then, she thought about Claudia. They had been best friends and inseparable since their freshman year in college. Both attended Florida International University where they received dual Bachelor degrees and were smart, educated women. They've always lived in the same building or near each other. They both drove Infinitis. Angelica had a black Infiniti IPL G37 convertible with red leather interior. Claudia had a white Infiniti G37 coupe Convertible 6MT with camel leather interior. They dressed the same, loved to dance and were into the same things. They knew each other's secrets and had been through life's growing pains together. They were two peas in a pod.

About an hour later, Claudia texted her to come over.

Angelica walked in with a blunt in her mouth and made herself comfortable on the couch.

"So, I see your butt ran over here after I told on you," Angelica teased Nico.

"Yeah, well…I had to," he said laughing.

"He knows what's good for him," said Claudia, sitting beside him.

"I hope you got in trouble, too," said Angelica snickering.

"Oh…did I? I'm glad I was a bad boy," he said pulling Claudia on his lap.

As they kissed, Angelica said, "Cut that out!"

"You're just jealous," said Claudia in between tongue swapping.

Angelica lit the blunt and said, "So, I have some news."

"What's up, girl?" asked Claudia.

"I'm leaving in three weeks."

"Where are you going now?" asked Claudia assuming she meant vacation.

"Charlotte, North Carolina."

"For how long?"

"I'm moving," said Angelica.

"Moving?!?" yelled Claudia and Nico, surprised.

"Yes…moving! I just got a job offer I couldn't refuse."

"I'm telling Falio right now," said Nico moving Claudia off of his lap and calling his best friend.

Claudia and Angelica quietly went back and forth on the matter while Nico was on the phone.

"Charlotte? There's nothing there," said Claudia.

"You don't know that," said Angelica.

"It's not Miami."

"No, it's not."

"So, what's the deal? Is this Austin's doing? What does he get in return?"

"Yes, it is…and nothing! We're not a couple, I'm not his booty call and I'm not one of his women. He expects nothing!"

"If you say so."

"It's a job opportunity!"

Claudia tightly hugged her best friend as she teared up. "I am going to miss you, Bitch. You're my everything. You've always been just a knock away," said Claudia.

"Well, I'll be three states north and a phone call away."

"It's not the same."

"I know."

Then, Claudia asked about the details of the job.

"Damn! You'll be making as much as me now," said Claudia.

"I know. I'm finally going to do what I want to do."

"Ho!" said Claudia. "I'm happy for you, but I'm going to miss you so much." She hugged her again.

Then, Angelica's phone rang. It was Falio. She excused herself while they spoke. He invited her and Claudia out to celebrate. He knew they were a package deal.

"You're in trouble now," said Nico laughingly to Angelica when she returned.

"I can't get in trouble by someone who's not mine," she said laughing sarcastically.

"Yeah, but he is when you want something though," he said very serious.

She just looked at him

"Anyways…I'm out. I have to go, but I'll call you later," Nico told Claudia.

Claudia walked him to the door.

"Don't bring that clown with you tonight either," said Nico, referring to her boyfriend.

"He's not a clown and I won't. He's out of town," she said.

"Good…'cause I have a surprise for you," he said kissing her before leaving.

"Ok," said Claudia excited about her surprise.

~Chapter 6~

The
Bet

Once he left, they girl talked.

"So, what's really up between you two?" asked Claudia.

"Nothing! It's strictly professional."

"With a few extra benefits, huh?"

"Well…I can't lie. It'll be nice sleeping with the boss," said Angelica giggling.

"I bet," said Claudia. "Do you like him?"

"I don't know. He's much more of an ass than I thought he'd be. He's arrogant and cocky, but I know he's sweet and caring underneath it all. He just needs to let his guard down."

"So, what are you going to do? He's one of your three," said Claudia referring to one of three professional athletes that Angelica would ever date.

"I know, but for right now…nothing. He's more work than I

want to deal with."

"Oh…so is my girl losing her touch? Are you afraid of a little challenge?" asked Claudia condescendingly.

"Hell no!"

"Then put your money where your mouth is."

"Ok…you're on! I'll take that bet, but I want double the prize."

"Ok."

"And I want six months as oppose to our normal three."

"Why? Too much of a challenge?"

"That's not it. I'm moving to a new state. I want to check out the scene first. You never know who I'll find."

"You do realize that we just made a bet for you to settle down. You know…have one man, not many," said Claudia with a strange look on her face.

"I know."

"So, why would you keep looking?"

"Because the possibility exists that he doesn't really want to settle down. I'm telling you…he's a tough one."

"I understand. But just so that we're clear…the bet is to be in a monogamous relationship with Austin Zachary at the end of six months."

"Ok," said Angelica, shaking her hand.

"Besides you never know...he could very well be your future husband. Either way...it's time that you settle down, Angelica."

"I know. But I just want to be sure."

"You always say that. You're gonna have to let the past go and move on."

"I know, but it was painful. I gave that man my entire being and he shredded it to pieces."

"Stop using that as an excuse! Get over it."

"I know, but still…"

"And you know who is going to be very hurt once you do settle down?" stated Claudia with a face.

"Listen…I'm tired of hearing about him! You know the situation. He's married to my sister," said Angelica agitated, referring to Falio.

"Don't snap at me! I'm just telling you the truth! And you know Nico had a point earlier."

"I know," said Angelica calming down. "I shouldn't play with him the way I do, but it's easy because he loves me so much. I can get away with it."

"Well, karma's a bitch. Remember that."

Angelica didn't like that statement, but knew it was true.

"So, where are we going tonight?" asked Claudia. "Isn't that what that phone call was about?"

"Yeah. We're going to Mansions."

"Ok…he's big money baller tonight," said Claudia laughing. "What are you wearing?"

"I don't know."

Then, Angelica changed the subject and brought up Nico.

"So, what's up with you and Nico?"

"Nothing. The usual."

"I thought you weren't messing with him anymore."

"Nico is my kryptonite."

"Aren't you afraid you'll get caught?"

"No. I'm careful. Besides, you know our history."

"I know. But…"

"Don't say it. I know I have a good thing with Anthony. And I'm not going to mess it up."

"Ok…" said Angelica, shrugging her shoulders. "But remember…karma's a bitch."

Angelica was really happy for her. Claudia had been in a one-year relationship with her boyfriend, Anthony Christopher, the safety for the NFL team Miami Sharks. He was the first guy she'd

opened up to and taken a risk with since Nico. Claudia loved
Anthony and wanted to settle down with him. But Nico was her
drug. She had to have him.

They both realized the time and went to get ready.

~Chapter 7~

Pre-Club Party

The following weekend, Angelica was celebrating her move in a major way. The owner of Mango's Nightclub was throwing her a huge party. So, she decided to have a pre-club party at her house to start off the festivities.

It was scheduled to begin at 7:00 p.m. and go on until club time. She invited about fifty people, including her three sisters Ariana, Alina and Asila. So of course, Falio would be in attendance with his boys. Alina was coming with her boyfriend, Colin. Falio's older sister, Paula, was expected to arrive with her husband, John. Falio's younger sister, Gina and Nico's sister, Diamond, were bringing one of their many men. Falio's younger brother, Ricky, invited some of his friends. And Nico was coming, but so was Anthony.

Jaime and Vivian volunteered to bartend. She hired her friend,

Carlos Gutierrez, to cater. She also got one of Falio's friends to DJ.

Angelica came out looking very enticing in her red satin, burlesque corset dress. This short, strapless dress had a black ribbon lace up front, which she wore with a garter belt, black stockings and black satin Prada pumps. She accessorized with a black Victorian neck choker, Onyx droplet earrings and a black jeweled butterfly ring.

With a Ciroc peach lemonade in hand, Angelica stood near the front greeting her guests as they entered. When she saw Paula and John, the ladies yelled and hugged each other tight.

Paula Salis was also Dominican and Puerto Rican. She stood 5'9" with blue eyes and long, wavy auburn-colored hair. This 33-year old mother looked young for her age.

John Salis was her 35-year old Caucasian husband that stood 6'2" with brown eyes and short brown hair that he wore slicked back. He had an athletic build and stayed in shape to keep up with his wife and kids.

"Damn, Girl!!! You look good," said Paula to Angelica

"Gracias, Mami. You do, too." Then, Angelica turned to greet John. "Hi, John. How are you?"

"I'm good and you?"

Before Angelica could answer, Falio did.

"She's perfect," he said greeting his sister and brother-in-law, then stood behind Angelica.

"He's still chasing you?" Paula asked Angelica.

"Yes."

"Can I get a picture of you two?"

"Sure."

Falio winked at Paula, thanking her. Then, he tightly wrapped his arms around Angelica as Paula snapped a few pictures. Of course, Ariana stood there staring.

We run the night by Havana Brown came on and most of the people in the party room got up to dance. It gave Angelica a chance to smoke with Claudia and Anthony. She even saw her neighbor who lived beneath her in there.

Nico couldn't take his eyes off of Claudia. She was beautiful and sexy wearing a yellow one-shouldered mini dress. It was tight fitting with practically all of the sides out. She accessorized with black droplet earrings and black Giuseppe Zanotti pumps.

Mi Corazoncito by Aventura came on. Angelica and Claudia got up to dance. Falio and Nico saw them and joined them.

As they were dancing, the ladies remembered a routine they made up to the song years ago. So, they used Falio and Nico as their dance partners.

The ladies straddled the men's legs and got close. They mixed a 1-2-3-step pattern with popping and lots of turns. The ladies loved dancing Bachata.

Anthony kept looking at Claudia in disapproval. Towards the end of the dance, he got up and left. When Claudia realized it, she chased after him.

Angelica and Falio stayed on the floor, dancing Kizomba when *Mágico* by Mika Mendes played.

Kizomba was a soft, sensual dance with extreme closeness, gentle leans forward or to the side, fancy leg work, lots of butt gyration and smooth glides across the dance floor. It was an explosive and seducing good time.

Angelica's hands were around Falio's neck while his were around her waist. She began by slowly gyrating her hips on one of his legs. Slow dips of gyration were incorporated as they worked the floor. His body moved with such finesse as his feet slid and did tricks. They were cheek-to-cheek as they altered dancing front-to-front and side-by-side. Her body moved like a snake as she slowly gyrated on his leg again. Falio gently leaned back so she could lean forward and really grind on him. His hands were all over her and she didn't care. The music and dancing had taken over.

They looked so in love. He looked into her eyes, admiring her beauty. The more they stared, the closer they got…until he leaned in and kissed her. She kissed him back. He slowly moved them off the dance floor and into her bedroom.

He lifted her onto the dresser. He spread her legs apart and stood between them.

"I love you, mi Angel," he whispered.

"I know, Papi," she said kissing him.

His finger slid inside her steamy hot sea of wetness. It sent a chill down her spine. She quickly undid his pants, pulling out his monstrous dick. She jacked him off as he played with her clitoris. He got her so excited that she let go of his dick and held on to the edge of the dresser as she gyrated her hips. He made her feel so good. She wanted more.

"Oh My God! Falio…" she said breathing heavy.

"Give it to me, Mami," he said wanting her to cum.

"Oh Baby…what are you doing to me?" she asked going crazy.

"Dámelo, Mami…give it to me," he kept persisting.

"Baby…I'm about to cum," she said, moving like she was sexing.

She let out a big moan as she came. He quickly slid her off the dresser and said, "Now, I'm taking what's mine."

With his pants around his ankles, he shoved his dick deep inside of her with all his might.

"Fuck, Falio!" she said loudly.

"Yes! This is my pussy!"

Her legs wrapped tightly around him as he rocked her butt back and forth. She talked dirty to him in Spanish, driving him crazy. She even used him for support to bounce up and down.

He backed her up against the door to really stick it to her. She let out more screams mixed with moans and groans. He pulled her hair, kissing her at the same time.

"You're mine, Angelica! And no one else's," he said in a stern manner.

"Yes! I'm yours! Feed your pussy, Baby!" she said getting him more aroused.

He sucked on her breasts as he carried her to the bed. He laid her down and came out of his clothes. He spread her legs wide apart and was right back inside. He was on top, sexing her so good, when all of a sudden Gina came in.

Falio's sister, Gina, was 27-year old, stood 5'7" with light hazel eyes and long, wavy honey blonde hair. She was petite with big boobs.

"Falio…" said Gina, standing there.

"Get out!" said Falio still sexing Angelica.

"Ariana wants you," said Gina still standing there, watching them.

"I'm busy!" yelled Falio still beating it up.

"Get the FUCK out!" yelled Angelica wanting to cum again.

"But she said it was important," continued Gina.

Angelica pushed Falio off of her.

"Go see what the FUCK your wife wants," said Angelica, leaving him with a hard one.

"Sorry," said Gina with a smirk on her face.

"You're such a bitch when you want to be," Angelica told Gina as she went to take a shower.

As Gina watched Angelica walk away, Falio snatched her up by the throat.

"BITCH…don't you EVER fuckin' do that again!!! I WILL KILL YOU! You know damn well you don't give a fuck about Ariana!!! And you know how I feel about Angelica!" he yelled with his dick slanging around.

Paula and Ricky heard Gina's attempts to scream and Falio yell-ing. So, they ran to see what was going on.

"Falio…let her go! Let her go!" yelled Paula attempting to peel his fingers from around Gina's neck.

"We told you to leave him alone, but you didn't listen. You knew he was with Angelica, but you're always messing around for some money," Ricky said to Gina.

"Fuck you, Falio!" Gina screamed once freed.

"No, FUCK you Gina!" yelled Falio putting on his pants.

"Gina…why do mess with him like that?" asked Paula.

"I'm not one of your bitches or hoes!!! Don't talk to me like that or treat me that way!!" yelled Gina to Falio.

"I can talk to you any kind of way I want! I take care of you! I'm the reason you have what you have! And as long as you're running around here acting like one, I'll treat you like one," screamed Falio. "Every time Ariana throws money at you, you jump and say how high. But you better stay the fuck out of my business or I'll cut you off!"

Gina calmed down and said, "Ok…I'm sorry."

"How much did she give you this time?" Ricky asked Gina.

"$1,000," she said pulling out the money.

"It's my money," said Falio, snatching it back. "Now get the fuck out!"

Falio spent a lot of time on the streets. Often, he didn't go home. So, Ariana's main concern was who Falio was with. That's where Gina came in. For some extra cash, Gina would sing like a canary. She had everything to gain since Falio didn't care that she was doing it. Sometimes, he would encourage Gina to tell Ariana, hoping she'd divorce him. But she never did. She just argued with him when he did go home.

However, Gina knew her limits. She didn't snitch him out when it came to business or real important matters. Falio was her brother and her loyalty truly lied with him. She just used Ariana to get more money since she was giving it away. And when it came to Angelica, she was a hot ticket item according to Ariana's wallet. Gina would get paid big bucks. So, she did what was necessary to collect. Sometimes, Falio would let her slide. But this time, she crossed the line.

When Angelica walked into her bedroom, everyone was gone.

"Can I talk to you for a minute?" he asked waiting for her.

"Sure," she said standing there in her birthday suit, drying off.

"Mi Angel…" he said lusting over her body.

"What's up, Papi?"

"I'm sorry about Gina."

"It's cool. She was just being her."

"I know, but still…"

"So, how much did Ariana pay her this time?"

"$1,000."

Angelica laughed. "And let me guess…you got your money back?"

"Hell yeah! It's my money anyway and she ain't keeping it after what she did."

"That's Gina for you." said Angelica shaking her head.

Then, he changed the subject.

"Baby, don't leave. Let me take care of you," he said approaching her.

"Thank you, but no thanks."

"You felt so good, Mami," he said trying to hug her, but she pushed him away.

"Don't Falio. We should have never done what we did."

"Why not? Let me spend the night with you. Let's finish what we started."

"Naw…I'm good."

He got close to her and said, "Let me love you. Let me make love to you. I want to be inside of you so bad. Don't leave me like this," he said looking down at his dick. It had grown hard again.

"Falio…please don't start."

But he didn't want to hear that. So, he stuck his tongue down her throat.

She pulled away and said, "It's not going to happen."

"Why?"

"Your wife! My sister!"

"Fuck her!"

"No…that's your job!" she said walking towards her bathroom.

He jumped in front of her and said, "Mi Angel…wait!"

"What do want, Falio?"

"I just want to be with you. Why can't you understand that?"

"I get it, but you're married. You're the father of my two nephews. And you know how I feel about your lifestyle."

"But it's ok that my lifestyle takes care of you and gives you what you want, huh?"

Angelica slapped the shit out of him before walking away.

"I'm sorry! I didn't mean it," said Falio knowing he had fucked up.

Falio was one of the most notorious drug dealers, if not the biggest, in South Florida. He supplied whatever was desired: cocaine, E pills, weed, Meth. Whatever the crowd wanted, he had.

Falio left the $1,000 on her dresser and went back to the party. Ariana tried talking to him, but Falio ignored her. He continued talking and laughing with his boys.

Angelica came out looking ravishing as ever. This time, she wore a silver satin, two-piece skirt set. The sexy halter top had a rhinestone circle in the middle and the very short skirt gathered on the sides. Her jewelry was simple: large double hoop silver earrings, large wire cuff and a silver Calvin Klein clutch. She was rockin' her strapped Diego Dolcini plumed satin platform heels.

It was club time and she was ready to go.

"Hey, my Beautiful Queen," said a male voice behind her.

When she turned around, she smiled and hugged him.

"Victor…what are you doing here?" asked Angelica.

"Well…" he started to say.

"I called him. Surprise!" said Claudia who had changed as well.

"Yes. Claudia called me and told me the good news. So, I had the jet fueled and here I am. I couldn't miss my favorite girl's celebration," he said to Angelica.

"What will New York ever do without you for the night?"

"Oh...they'll manage," he said laughing.

Victor Celani was Angelica's older white/Italian male Billionaire friend, who Claudia called her sugar daddy. He resembled the handsome Patrick Dempsey. He stood six foot tall with blue eyes, jet black hair combed back and was very clean shaven. He looked like money.

Falio was mad as hell because Angelica left with Victor. He knew who he was and knew he didn't have another chance with her.

~Chapter 8~

Charlotte Bound

Two weeks later, Angelica was Charlotte bound.

It was bittersweet. She was excited about the professional opportunity, but sad she was moving away from her family and Claudia.

As her plane descended two and a half hours later, she looked out of the window at the vast patches of greenery. It seemed to have stretched for miles.

A man in a black suit was holding a sign with her name on it as she exited the terminal.

"Hi. I'm Angelica," she said walking up to him.

"Hi. My name is Bill. I'm your transportation."

He followed her to baggage claim and then escorted her to the car.

While driving, Angelica was even more amazed at the city from the ground. This Metropolitan area was clean with so many trees and lots of greenery. It was beautiful. She also saw lots of brick buildings, churches and Waffle Houses. She knew she was in the south.

"Here we are, ma'am," said the driver stopping in front of an eight-story building in Charlotte's Uptown Fourth Ward area. The gold metal plates on each side of the steps read *410 North Church.*

A brown-skinned woman with a briefcase stood outside awaiting Angelica's arrival.

"Hi. Miss Angelica Zambrano?" said the woman with a slight island accent.

"Yes," said Angelica shaking her hand.

"Hi. My name is Cherry Green. I'll be your assistant."

"Hi, Cherry Green," said Angelica wondering why her parents would name her two colors.

"Please follow me," said Cherry guiding her inside the building and into the elevator. The driver followed behind with Angelica's bags.

"So, where are you from, Cherry? I hear an accent," asked Angelica.

"I'm from Jamaica."

"Really? That's surprising."

"Why is that?"

"Most Jamaicans I know live in Miami," said Angelica.

"Well, there are some in North Carolina, too."

Angelica laughed. It wasn't what she said, but how she said it. However, Cherry looked at her wondering what was so funny.

"I apologize if I offended you," said Angelica.

"You didn't offend me. No worries."

Cherry was a skinny 28-year old with a bubble butt who wore braces and stood 5'6". She also wore small, squared glasses, had tiny twists and was an overall attractive young lady. However,

Cherry looked a little nerdy and was soft spoken.

"Wow! This is really nice," said Angelica opening the door to her new place.

The driver set her bags down in the living room while Cherry opened some windows.

"As you can see, your boxes have arrived. They came in early this morning and are all accounted for. Your car is parked in the garage in your assigned parking space, number 603," said Cherry handing her the keys to her vehicle.

As Cherry talked, Angelica stood there blown away, admiring the beautiful view. The unit was so modern and contemporary with coffered ceilings, marble floors, built-in wooden book-shelves, a marble fireplace, huge panoramic windows and beauti-ful furniture in the living room.

"Let me show you around."

Cherry gave her a tour of the fully furnished three-bedroom/three-bath, two-story end unit. It had two separate entrances, including a private, street-side entrance. The sleek designed kitchen had black cabinetry with stainless steel appliances, black marble countertops and a dining bar. The sitting room had curved windows; the media room had a wet bar; and there was surround sound on the main floor. The upstairs was carpeted and had an oversized master suite with a private balcony and two additional large bedrooms.

Angelica didn't have much to unpack because she didn't move all of her stuff. Miami would always be home and she knew she'd be traveling back and forth quite often. So, she didn't empty her place. Besides, she wanted a fresh start in Charlotte.

Just as they sat down to discuss business, Angelica's phone rang.

"Hello," she answered.

"Hey. How are you?" asked Austin.

"Just fine. Thank you. But I'm here with my assistant. Can I please call you back?"

"Yes. And welcome to Charlotte."

"Thank you."

Cherry opened the briefcase and took out some folders. One of them had all of her itemized receipts from the move.

Next, she discussed all of the building rules and leasing information. She also gave Angelica the number to a realtor. He could help her find a house, if she decided not to live in the condo.

Then, Cherry went over the rest of the items in the briefcase. Angelica had to sign equipment forms for receiving her laptop with wireless printing capability, I-Pad, wireless data card and company cell phone. She also received a temporary ID badge, garage remote with parking pass, a company credit card and other information.

"You'll take your picture tomorrow morning for your permanent ID badge. Here is your insurance information. Your benefits begin tomorrow. You also have orientation Tuesday morning. You'll meet with benefits, travel and legal, to name a few. They'll go over everything from insurance cards and physicians to hotels and expense reports," explained Cherry wasting no time.

"Ok," said Angelica.

Cherry went over some details about the company, like the company culture, roster, her schedule, the region she was in charge of, a list of her direct reports, the name and number of who she reported to and a map of the company building.

Angelica quickly glanced over the organizational chart, her list of direct reports and the roster. She quickly recognized two of the names and wondered if they were the same two people.

Last, Angelica needed to know where to find the non-work stuff, like hair and nail salons, where to shop and good restaurants. Cherry explained the different areas of Charlotte. She even provided her with a map and listings of restaurants, salons, clubs, shopping, entertainment and when the biggest events came into town.

Then, Angelica inquired about the men of the south.

"So, how are the men out here?"

"Well…it depends on what you're looking for."

"Fine, gorgeous, beautiful black men," expressed Angelica with enthusiasm.

"Well…drop dead gorgeous I haven't seen lately, but there are some nice looking professional men that will treat you well."

"Sounds boring."

Cherry laughed.

After working five hours straight, Angelica was hungry and ready to smoke.

"Well, Miss Angelica…I will see you in the office tomorrow bright and early," said Cherry collecting her things.

"Ok and thank you for all of your assistance this afternoon, Cherry," said Angelica walking her to the door.

"No problem. Have a good evening."

"I will. You, too."

Angelica opened one of the boxes that were neatly stacked in the living room. She grabbed the coffee can that said "Sour Diesel". She took out some bud and her bullet pipe and smoked outside on the balcony. So many thoughts ran through her head as she took in the city lights and view. She replayed everything Cherry went over in her head. She knew she had her work cut out for her, but knew she'd enjoy the challenge.

In the midst of her thoughts, she heard the doorbell. It was Austin. He came with food in hand.

"Hi," she said giving him a kiss on the lips.

"Hi. I thought you might be hungry, so I brought Chinese."

"Thank you. I'm starving," she said opening the bags.

"You're welcome," he said sorting out the food.

Austin went to P.F. Chang's. He didn't know what she liked, so he bought a variety of food. She saw egg rolls, crab wonton, Lo Mein combo, crab fried rice, beef with broccoli, sesame chicken, Kung Pao shrimp and crispy honey shrimp. For dessert, he got slices of red velvet and carrot cake.

"You got so much food," said Angelica smiling from ear to ear.

"I didn't know what you liked. So, I got a couple of appetizers and a few meats."

"It all looks so good."

They served their plates and then sat on the sofa.

"So, how do you like the place?" asked Austin.

"It's nice. I was pleasantly surprised."

"Why?"

"Honestly…I thought Charlotte would be more country. I thought floral patterns or fruit decor with lots of wood and plaid."

"Really?" he said laughing. "Well…Charlotte is country compared to Miami, but we have modern styles and city life."

"I see that."

"And there's plenty to do."

Austin quickly changed the subject and requested that she use discretion about them sleeping together at work. He didn't want rumors of favoritism. She agreed since it was no one's business who she slept with. Besides, she didn't want to make enemies or start rumors that she got the job because she slept with the boss.

After they ate, she invited him to a smoke session. She took out the other three cans and asked which one he'd like to smoke. The other choices were Orange Crush, Granddaddy Purp and Purple OG Kush.

"You're in my town now," he said hitting that OG Kush.

"So! What does that mean?" she asked in her usual sassy manner.

"You have no where to run."

And in true Angelica fashion, she said, "Oh, please. Don't start with that bullshit."

"I see you stay true to your feistiness and your ways."

"Am I supposed to change 'cause I'm in a new town?"

"No. But…just remember what I said. I will break you down and I will have my way with you. No woman can resist me."

Angelica laughed hysterically. "Don't you ever get tired of that line?"

"Ok. I'll show you better than I can tell you."

"Just remember something, Austin. I'm gonna do what I want to do and with whomever I want to do it with. And there's nothing you can do to stop me. K!"

Austin just looked at her and smiled. He heard the words coming out of her mouth, but he wasn't listening. He had his own agenda.

"Come here," he said.

She got on top of him and started kissing him.

"You're mine and don't forget that," he said.

"Whatever, Austin. Just fuck me already."

He did.

~Chapter 9~

The First
Day

It was Monday morning. Angelica was nervous, but eager about her first day at Sportie Fans corporate office.

She left at 7:00 a.m. even though her GPS gave an ETA of fifteen minutes. She figured it couldn't have factored in traffic.

As instructed, she merged onto I-77 north. She couldn't get over how beautiful all of the trees were and how clean the city looked as she drove down the highway. What was more impressive was that she was able to drive faster than two miles an hour in morning traffic, unlike Miami. Morning traffic there was hell.

She made it to Exit 18 in about twenty-five minutes and made a left off the exit ramp onto West WT Harris Blvd. Instantly, she became excited when she saw Northlake Mall on the right hand side and another plaza on the left. She couldn't believe she recognized all of the nearby eating establishments. She assumed Charlotte had predominantly NC-specific stores and restaurants, but was relieved the further she traveled.

Behind the mall sat a ten-story, moon-shaped office building that looked like it was made of glass with all of the windows. It had large steel beams in the front, lots of trees and the company's name centered on top.

Angelica followed Cherry's instructions to the letter. She drove into the garage and parked on the second level where she had a designated spot with her name already displayed.

"Good morning…good morning," was all she heard as people walked towards the building. She had to get used to the niceness. People weren't like that in Miami. Two people could be in an elevator and never say a word to one another in Miami.

Cherry was standing in front of the receptionist's desk when Angelica walked in.

"Good morning," said Angelica speaking to Cherry and the re-ceptionist.

"Good morning, ma'am," said the receptionist.

"Good morning, Miss Angelica," said Cherry.

The receptionist took Angelica's picture and immediately printed her new badge. Angelica returned the temporary one and accom-panied Cherry to the tenth floor.

"Here we are," said Cherry opening her office door.

"Very nice," said Angelica checking out her new workspace.

She had a beautiful and spacious corner office with enormous windows and a view of the mall. Her dark-colored office furniture in combination with glass and steel created a chic and sophisti-cated look. A white leather sofa and chaise lounge chair added contrast to the room. A glass conference table with steel chairs sat near the window. She even had her own powder room in her office. All of the executives did.

Angelica put her things down and gazed out of the window as

Cherry read off her schedule.

"You have a staff meeting at 9:00 a.m. with senior executives. Mr. Zachary will be down shortly to welcome you. You have a staff meeting at 1:00 with your corporate employees. Then at 2:30, you have a conference call with your regional managers and supervisors." Cherry paused. "Miss Angelica?" she said trying to get her attention.

"Yes. I apologize. I was just admiring the view," she said turning around and taking a seat. "I'm listening. Please continue."

Just then, Austin knocked on the door interrupting.

"Hello, Mr. Zachary. Please come in," said Cherry signaling him to enter. "Miss Angelica…we'll continue later," said Cherry closing the door as she left.

"You look beautiful," he said.

"Thank you," she said smiling.

He stopped by to make certain she was settling in okay.

"Be a good girl and you may just get a treat later," he whispered before leaving.

She thought to herself *'He can't be for real. What am I…a dog?'* She just shook her head thinking about his comment.

Cherry took her on a quick tour of the tenth floor. There were free sodas in the vending machine and all snacks cost fifty cents.

On their way back to her office, Angelica couldn't believe there weren't any cute guys. Not one! She saw a bald black man with a belly, a tall black man with glasses and a skinny, short white man with a military haircut. She saw the way they were dressed and heard the way they spoke. None of them interested her.

Angelica hurried to the large conference room for her 9:00. She arrived fifteen minutes early to make a good impression. But when she entered the room, everyone was seated except her. So, all eyes were on her.

"Good morning," she said to everyone.

They all said it back at staggering times.

She knew she was being watched as she went to her seat, but she didn't mind since she looked model perfect.

She wore an orange and purple fitted sheath dress with drape neck detail and cap sleeves. A thin, sleek gold belt and a pair of gold Jimmy Choo heels added that sparkle.

Everyone went around the table and introduced themselves. *'So this is where all the gorgeous men are'* Angelica thought to herself.

Damian Reid was the Recruiting Manager and one fine specimen of a black man. This light-skinned brotha had piercing green eyes, juicy lips, a low fade and a thin, well-manicured goatee with side burns. He had the damnedest smile and wearing the hell out of his suit. But he had on an unwanted piece of jewelry…a wedding band.

Then, there was the company attorney, Lance Gregory. He had velvety chocolate brown eyes, kissable lips, a baby Afro and well-groomed goatee. He had a brown sugar complexion with a tight, hard ass. She could tell that he worked out, even through his suit. He was possibly her next victim.

Austin spent the majority of the morning discussing corporate business. Then, he discussed entering the European market. His managers wrapped up the meeting discussing what was on their plates.

"Damian…Angelica…do you have a minute?" asked Austin before they left.

"Yes…yes, sir," said Angelica and Damian, respectively.

"I need to see you both in my office this afternoon. I need you two to go to Philadelphia and New York next week to resolve some issues we're having in some of the stores," said Austin.

"Yes, sir," said Damian in a deep and sexy voice.

"No problem, Mr. Zachary," said Angelica.

"My assistant will send you a meeting request."

The both nodded.

Angelica couldn't believe how appetizing Damian still sounded. It gave her butterflies.

Angelica went to see her boss, Max Williams, afterwards. He was one of the Regional Vice Presidents of Human Resources. He wanted to formally introduce himself, go over his expectations and discuss his management style. He also wanted to know a little more about her and her goals for career development.

By early afternoon, Cherry ordered lunch for Angelica seeing that she may not get a chance to get out. Angelica was grateful considering she had another meeting in twenty minutes.

~Chapter 10~

Shana's Office

Angelica's first day was very busy. She spent the afternoon in one meeting after another.

As she was leaving around 6:00 p.m., she saw Shana in her office. She stopped by to chit chat.

"Knock…knock," said Angelica.

"Hi. Come in. Have a seat," said Shana in a friendly and inviting manner.

Shana Reid was a light-skinned black woman who stood 5'6" with brown eyes, deep dimples and long, reddish-brown hair. She was beautiful and always well dressed.

"Working late?" Angelica asked, sitting in one of the chairs in front of her desk.

"Yes…as usual."

Then, they were briefly interrupted.

"Knock…knock…Sha…na," said Matthew Vaughn, Senior Director of Communications. "Sorry. I didn't know you were with someone. Hello, Angelica."

"Hi, Matthew."

"Matt…please," he said smiling and shaking her hand. "Well, Shana…here are those invoices you asked for."

"Thank you," said Shana.

"You ladies have a good evening."

"You too," they both said.

He left.

"So…how are you liking it so far?" Shana asked Angelica.

"It's great."

"Good."

"So, I have a question for you," said Angelica changing the subject.

"Ok."

"Aren't you from Miami?" asked Angelica confidently.

"Yes, I am. How did you know?"

"You attended FIU your freshman year and hung out with a girl named Alice?"

"Yes! Yes, I did. Do you know her?"

Angelica sat there looking at her, waiting for it to click.

"No! No way!!! Alice?" asked Shana, shocked and confused.

"Yep."

"Oh My God!!! It's been such a long time," said Shana getting up to give her a huge hug.

"I know...way too long."

"What happened to you? You look so different. You were so weird looking back then with blonde, orange and pink hair. And your eyes? I remember you had brown eyes when I left."

"Remember how I got teased a lot about my eyes our senior year of high school? So, I bought brown contacts to blend in and changed my hair color when we went to college. I didn't want the same thing to happen to me."

"Wow…that's right! I totally forgot about that. And you started calling yourself Alice to go with your new look."

"Yep!"

"Well, thank God you grew out of that stage."

"I know."

"Oh my God…wait 'til Damian hears…" Shana started to say.

"No…don't tell him yet! I want to surprise him, too."

"You're not plotting anything against my husband are you?"

"No! Of course not! Married men are off limits. But I see you two got married. How are you guys doing? Any kids?"

"Yes, we got married and things are great between us. We don't have kids, yet, but hopefully soon. What about you?"

"No…no kids. I'm single…looking to mingle," said Angelica laughing.

"Well, you just be careful mingling…okay?"

"Shana cut your crap! It's me! Time has passed, but I know you. Don't pretend with me. By saying that…you're saying stay the hell away from Damian, right?"

"Yes."

Angelica, Shana and Damian all went to Florida International University in Miami. Angelica remembered the first time she saw Damian with his frat brothers in the school's parking lot, steppin'. It was love at first sight, according to Angelica. He was the hottest and sexiest guy on the planet.

"Well, I'm not that same young female that was madly in love with him. That was freshman year of college. Or is it that he still cheats on you?"

"He changed after college! He stopped messing around and settled down with me."

"So, what's the problem then?"

"Well, you might want revenge for what he did to you?"

"You can't be serious right now! That incident was so long ago."

"I don't know."

Shana was referring to Damian's fraternity freshman prank. Every year, each member of the fraternity had to select two freshman girls that were best friends to play a prank called 'Duck and Fuck'. The ugly friend was the ugly duckling and would have an embarrassing prank played on her that would be blasted everywhere. The cute one got a dinner invitation, but only because he was trying to get in the panties and fuck. This prank was timed. The first guy to complete both tasks in the quickest time won the trophy and bragging rights.

Shana didn't really know the details of how the prank was played, but she volunteered her and Alice. She knew Alice was madly in love with Damian, but she secretly liked him, too. She figured it would be the perfect opportunity to get noticed or even screwed. Just her luck, Damian wound up selecting them.

One night, Damian invited Shana to dinner. But right before their date, he called Alice over to the frat house. He made her believe they were going on a date. They sat in his car talking for about five minutes. Then, he purposely dropped his keys on the floor. He asked her to pick them up since he'd gotten injured playing football, which was a lie. She didn't mind. All of sudden, there were flashing lights everywhere. His frat brothers were taking pictures of her bent over retrieving the keys, but it looked like she was giving him head. His facial expressions made it worse. When she realized what he'd done, she was outraged. She got out of his car and stormed off. Shana missed her by minutes.

Then, he took Shana to one of the many restaurants on Flagler Street. It was close to all of the motels that rented rooms by the hour. It turned out he didn't even need it. She gave it up in the restaurant's parking lot. Damian called the designated person and left his phone on. Everyone at the frat house heard them having sex. He won since he completed the mission in less than two hours. It was record breaking.

"Shana, I've definitely grown up since then. I don't have complex issues and can get any guy I want," said a smug Angelica.

"You sound pretty sure of yourself."

"I am."

"Well, there's one guy that's off limits…my husband."

"I don't want him…trust me. But if I did, I'd run circles around you. He'd be filing for a divorce in three months. I betcha that."

Shana laughed. "You think you're that good, huh?"

"Better!"

"Wow! That's pretty bold of you to tell me to my face that you can have my husband if you wanted him."

"It's the truth. But I don't want him and I don't have any pinned up anger. I just wanted to see his reaction when I told him who I was. That's why I didn't want you to tell him."

"Mmmm huh," said Shana looking at Angelica.

Angelica's phone rang. It was Austin, but she made it seem as though it was Claudia.

"You still talk to her?" asked Shana after she got off the phone.

"Yes! She's my best friend, my person, my female soul mate."

"That's good."

"Yeah. But I'll see you tomorrow, girl. I have some errands to run."

"Well, you better hurry up. Most places close by nine."

"Nine o'clock at night?"

"Yep."

"Oh my goodness! That's extremely early!"

"Welcome to Charlotte," said Shana laughing.

"Bye, girl…tomorrow," said Angelica leaving her office.

~Chapter 11~

Austin's House

Angelica called Claudia on her way to Austin's. She told her about her first day, the men in the office and how she saw Shana and Damian. She also told her about the conversation with Shana and how much finer Damian had gotten, if it were possible. She admitted he still gave her butterflies.

Angelica arrived to Austin's Lake Norman home within twenty-five minutes. She drove inside the garage since he left the door open for her.

"Hi," she said knocking on the slightly opened door that led inside the house.

"Hello," he said smiling.

He invited her in and took her things.

"How are you?" he asked closing the garage.

"I'm good now that I see you,"

It made him smile.

"Smells good in here," she said as they went into the kitchen.

"I'm making shrimp Alfredo with angel hair pasta."

"Nice."

His European Chateau sat on nearly four acres, had impeccable craftsmanship and timeless elegance. This prime waterfront estate mixed old world charm with sumptuous 21st century amenities. The main floor had a grand foyer, an opulent great room with vaulted ceilings, a towering fireplace and flowed effortlessly into the gourmet kitchen.

His kitchen was a customized chef's kitchen with commercial appliances, two islands and a seating area along the wall of windows that overlooked the rear deck. There was also a sweeping staircase led to the second floor.

"So, how was your first day?" he asked stirring the sauce.

"It was good. Everyone was so nice. I had lots of meetings, but overall I think it went well.

"Good. I'm really counting on you and Damian next week. We need to get those issues resolved in Philly and New York."

"Don't worry…I got yo' back," she said being sweet.

He winked and said, "That's good to know."

Angelica changed into something more comfortable before dinner. The plan was to not fight with him. She wanted to relax, get along and enjoy his company. After all, he was potentially her future husband.

He served their plates and then they adjourned to the dining room. He poured them each a glass of wine as they flirted some more. It was cute.

After dinner, they retreated to the backyard for a smoke session.

This open space had a heated 40,000-gallon pool with a cascading spa overlooking natural sandy beaches, an outdoor kitchen with lots of seating, a white wooded gazebo and a boat dock with a 17' boat sitting on the lift. It was simply beautiful.

They sat under the covered area near the pool. He got her a blanket, poured them a drink and lit a blunt.

"I have something for you," he said reaching for his wallet. "Here."

He handed her an AmEx black card with her name on it.

"What's this for?" she politely asked.

"It's for you. Buy whatever you want. It's on me."

"Thank you, Baby," she said kissing him.

"You're welcome. Enjoy it. You're one of my girls now," he said hitting the weed.

Angelica became livid. She couldn't believe how quickly he ruined the moment. She thought he was being sweet and sincere when in fact he was just being himself…an ASS!

She stood up and threw the card at him. "You can have that back. I'm out!"

She walked in the house and grabbed her things. He heard the garage door opening and chased after her.

He quickly closed the door and grabbed her. "Where do you think you're going?" he asked.

"Let me go, Asshole!" she said yanking her arm out of his hand.

She pushed the button to open the garage door again, but he closed it.

"You're not going anywhere," he said grabbing her again.

She slapped the shit out of him. "You don't know who you're fucking with, Austin! I'm not one of your hoes, bitches, chicks or women! And just because you're Austin Zachary doesn't mean you can treat people like shit!" she yelled mad and enraged. "Besides…I'm not for sale, Bitch!"

He attempted to kiss her, but she fought him off. In any case, Austin wasn't letting her go. He wanted her and was going to have her. She was the only woman who didn't put him on pedestal, always challenged him and didn't really care who he was. That turned him on! Most women were too afraid to piss him off because he'd cut them off.

"Angelica, I'm sorry," he whispered in her ear as he pinned her against his Benz. He lifted her dress and ripped off her panties. He sucked on her neck as he played with her clit. This roused her up. So, when he saw her less tense, he stuck his dick in her. He didn't want her to get away.

"Austin, st…o…p," she faintly uttered, enjoying his take charge attitude.

After a few pumps, she submitted to him and sexed him right back. He grabbed her thighs as she laid back on the hood. She was really mad at him, but he couldn't tell.

Twenty minutes later, they both came. It was evident they both enjoyed their quickie.

She went to the bathroom to clean up. Afterwards, she went to her car.

"Angelica, wait…please!" he said gently grabbing her this time.

She slapped the shit out of him again.

"I'm sorry. I shouldn't have said what I said and did what I did. But seriously, accept the card. It's yours," he said trying to hand it to her.

"Fuck off, Austin!!"

"Why are you being so difficult? I've never had to beg a woman to accept a credit card and be able to spend whatever she wanted!"

"You owe me a pair of underwear, Asshole!" she screamed before driving off.

Austin knew he had stuck his foot in his mouth again.

~Chapter 12~

The Next Day

"Good morning, Miss Angelica," said Cherry with a big smile on her face.

"Good morning, Cherry," said Angelica wondering what was up.

When Angelica walked into her office, she saw four large bouquets of white roses. There was also an envelope and gift box on her desk.

"Someone sure does love you," said Cherry.

"More like apologizing," mumbled Angelica.

"Huh?"

"Nothing. Can you please give me a minute before we begin, Cherry?"

"Ok."

Angelica smelled the roses and smiled. She sat down and read the note. It said:

I'm truly sorry about last night.
I shouldn't have handled you or the situation the way I did.
Please accept my apology and gifts.

Inside the box was a pair of underwear and her black card.

"Así me gusta," she said to herself smiling. "That's how I like it, Austin. You'll learn. It's not about you. It's about me."

Angelica sat back in her chair and thought about Austin. She knew he wasn't used to dealing with a woman like her, but he was going to have to get used to it if he wanted the sex. She knew how to play his game very well.

She reached in her desk and took out a black Sharpie. She wrote Austin's initials on the signature line next to "SEE ID". She wasn't stupid. She was keeping the card.

Then, she took out her wallet and made room for her third black card. She quickly glanced at the back of the other two. One had "V.C." while the other had "F.R.".

Her phone rang interrupting her thoughts.

"Miss Angelica…" said Cherry.

"Yes, " said Angelica.

"Mr. Zachary would like to see you in his office,"

"Thank you, Cherry"

Angelica put her wallet away and fixed herself. She opened one more button on her blouse and finger brushed her hair. She also made sure her bright red lipstick looked tantalizing before walking out.

She knocked on Austin's door.

"Come in," he said with his head down.

As she walked in, he said, "Hi. Please come in and close the door." Then, he looked up. He was speechless.

She stood there looking mouth watering with her white satin long-sleeve blouse and black satin form-fitting pencil skirt. It had a high-waist, small buttons along the sides and a bustled back that made her butt pop out even more. She wore it with two sleek red belts, Yves Saint Lauren red high heels and a chunky red turquoise necklace set.

"Hi. You wanted to see me?" she asked in a stern manner.

He stood up and said, "Please have a seat." He kept looking at her lips.

"Thank you."

"Did you like your flowers?"

"Yes, thank you. They were very nice."

"And the card? Are you going to keep it?"

"Yes, I will. I also accept your apology."

"Thank you, Baby. And by the way, you look absolutely beautiful."

"Thank you."

Austin jumped right into business. He advised her of more issues in Philly. She needed to get with Damian and strategize a plan. She assured him she would take care of it.

"So, I'll see you later?" he asked.

"No. I have other plans," she said lying through her teeth.

"Ok…"

Angelica hurried to orientation. On the way, she ran into Shana.

"Hey, girl," said Shana.

"Hey."

"So, what are you doing for dinner tonight?"

"I have no plans."

"Great! Dinner on me tonight…after work…"

"Ok," said Angelica hurrying off.

When she arrived to the conference room, a representative from each department was there. They asked her to sit in a designated seat, where she found a notepad, pen and a travel wallet on the table.

First up was payroll. They explained their systems and processes, how she approved her staff's timesheets, how she needed to submit her own time, how much leave time she earned and went over bank information. She also received her $3,000 bonus check.

Benefits went after. She received her insurance cards, a credit card for medical expenses only and pamphlets on medical, dental and vision plans. She needed to fill out other paperwork, including beneficiary forms and emergency contact information. She also received an additional insurance card for her travel wallet.

She was excited to see Lance. She sized up this 6'3" black man, contemplating her next move. She stared at his genitalia area as he explained all of the legal programs the company offered and their benefits. She also signed a gag agreement.

Travel was last. They had the most information. She received two more credit cards, Visa and MasterCard, to be used for all traveling expenses like rental cars, gas and meals. There was a specialized American Express card she received for hotels only. With it, she received four hotel reward program cards. She could stay at any of the hotels on the provided list for an exclusive rate and earn lots of reward points. She was also given a detailed list of business related expenses and a travel handbook.

Angelica advised the travel manager that she would always spend more than the allowed amount for a hotel room. So, she requested that a personal credit card remain on file for any extra charges.

Orientation was long, but not as bad as she thought.

"Cherry, can you see if Damian is available please," said Angelica returning to her office.

"Yes, ma'am."

Ten minutes later, he knocked on her door.

"Please come in," she said.

Before strategizing a plan for all of Austin's concerns, Angelica engaged in small talk.

"So, Damian…where did you go to school?" she asked knowing the answer.

"Florida International University. I wanted to get away from North Carolina and have my college experience somewhere else."

"I bet that was an experience, too…wasn't it?"

He grinned.

Once she saw he was a bit more comfortable, they began working.

Angelica decided to play with him before telling him who she was.

She got up and walked to her desk. She bent over and reached for a file. Through the monitor's reflection, she saw him looking. Then, she turned around and walked towards him. She got really close as she showed him what was inside. She could tell he wanted to flirt back, but didn't. So, she decided to finally tell him.

"Damian…" she said.

"Yes."

"Do you remember in college when you…"

Then, Cherry interrupted.

"Miss Angelica…"

"Yes," said Angelica.

"Thad from IT is here for your computer and telephone."

"Ok…please send him in."

Damian gathered his work.

"You were going to ask me something?" Damian asked Angelica.

"It can wait. Thank you."

She didn't get a chance to tell him.

Damian spoke to Thad and gave him some dap on his way out.

Thad Vaughn was a fine breed of a white man. He stood 6'2" tall with loud, penetrating green eyes; low, spiked light brown hair; a rugged jawline; thick eyebrows; and smooth tanned skin.

He was clean shaven, smelled good and was extremely sexy with a lean and toned athletic build.

"Hello, Ms. Zambrano," said Thad.

"Angelica, please."

"How are you today, Angelica?"

"I'm good. Thank you for asking. And yourself?"

"I'm good."

"I know," she mumbled.

He laughed 'cause he heard her.

As he installed all of the necessary software on her desktop and laptop, programmed her phone and set-up her voicemail, Thad had her in stitches laughing so hard from all of his jokes. He was a cool white boy in her book.

~Chapter 13~

Another
Bet

Shana went by Angelica's office around 5:30 p.m.

"Knock, knock…you ready to go?" asked Shana.

"Yes. I'm starved," said Angelica.

"We can take my car."

"Actually…I was going to follow you 'cause I'm not coming back afterwards," said Angelica pulling out her car keys.

"Ok. So what do you feel like eating?"

"Hmmm…a big, juicy burger."

"Ok. I know just the place."

Angelica followed behind Shana's black Lexus IS 350C until they reached Red Robin. They were seated in a corner booth towards the back.

"So, how was your day?" asked Shana looking at the menu.

"Good," said Angelica.

The waitress came and took their drink and meal order.

"I had orientation today," said Angelica.

"How did that go?" asked Shana.

"It went well. I'm all set for traveling next week."

"Damian, too. He's been working so hard. He's still at the office."

"There's a lot to do," said Angelica as the waitress set their drinks down.

"So I wanted to talk to you about Damian and I."

"Ok. What's up?"

"I lied yesterday. I think something's bothering him."

"Like what?"

"I'm not sure, but I thought about what you said last night."

"What are you talking about?" asked Angelica as she bit into her gourmet burger.

"About you taking Damian from me."

"Why would you think about that? I told you I'm not interested."

"Because I want to see if that's true. I want to test him."

"WHAT!!!" Angelica yelled in disbelief. "You want to use me to see if your husband will cheat on you? Have you lost your DAMN mind!?!" exclaimed Angelica.

"I'll pay you."

"You can't afford me!"

"Hear me out."

Shana wanted to know if Damian was having urges to sleep with other women again. He'd been a little distant lately, which was usually the first sign. For example, he wasn't concerned with having sex and preferred working late rather than coming home. He also changed the passwords on his cell phone and laptop. She feared the worst considering his infidelity issues from the past.

"At least I'll know with you I won't have to worry about you trying something behind my back," said Shana.

Angelica got upset and was offended. Then, she looked at Shana and started laughing.

"Shana…I told you I stay clear of married men. My men have to be single 'cause I demand ALL of their time, attention and money. So, your husband is of no use to me. But I know what's going on. I see you're still full of shit! What's his name?"

Shana looked disconcerted. "What's whose name?"

"Once a hood rat…always a hood rat! What's his name?" asked Angelica again.

"Fuck you, Angelica! I'm not a hood rat!" roared Shana offended.

Angelica laughed and said, "I know you, Shana. I know where you're from and what you're about. Although I commend you on how well you've done for yourself, you're still a five-dollar hoe. So, I'll ask you one last time. Who is he? What's his name?"

"I don't know what you're talking about, but you're gonna quit calling me a hoe," said Shana mad. "I guess I was wrong about you. I was under the impression you'd do anything for money. I guess not. My bad," said Shana now smiling.

"Oh…so you thought I was like you?"

"That was a low blow."

"I call 'em like I see 'em."

"Bitch!"

"The bottom line is that you want me to fuck your husband so you can fuck someone else. You need Damian distracted while you mess around with your boy toy," said Angelica.

"Stop saying that! And I didn't say anything about you having sex with Damian."

"You're a lie!!! 'Cause I'd fuck the shit out of him!"

Shana just looked at her.

"WHAT? Shana, I clearly remember how obsessed you were

when it came to Damian. Hell, you just told me yesterday to stay away from him. And now, all of a sudden, you're throwing him at me?"

Shana stayed quiet.

"I must say…whoever he is, he's good 'cause you're willing to lose your man and marriage," said Angelica.

"I don't want to lose Damian," said Shana wondering what she was talking about.

"Oh…don't you? Isn't that what all of this is about…getting a divorce?"

"Divorce!?!" yelled Shana. "No one said anything about a divorce!"

Angelica looked at her and laughed. "So, what did you honestly think, Shana? I'd flirt or sleep with your husband, get him out your hair for a week, a month and then return him? You're cute!"

Shana got serious. "Oh, so you do still want Damian? I knew it!"

"No! This is not about me wanting Damian! I'm actually looking at Lance, but it appears that I respect your marriage more than you do. So, if you don't want him, I'll surely take him off your hands. But not for a little while…forever!"

"That's not what I meant."

"Don't play big girl games then if your ass can't cash the check!"

"I got your yo' check…"

"As I said…you can't afford me," Angelica assured Shana.

"You know what, Angelica…I'm not worried about Damian. He can't leave me anyway. So, I know a divorce is out of the question. I just wanted to see if he was happy or not. But the more I think about it, the more I think I want to see your overly confident, overbearing ass squirm like you did in college," said Shana laughing.

"Shana, I'm not doing this with you 'cause this isn't about me. And let me be real with you for a second. You're stupid as hell! You can't possible believe the bullshit you're sitting here feeding me. You're sitting here playing with Damian's life, and your own as a matter of fact, like it's a game. You don't think that asking someone to sleep with your husband isn't dangerous? Feelings can develop, insecurities start flying around and it just doesn't work out." Angelica paused and then said, "Listen…you've made a good life for yourself. You have a beautiful husband, I'm sure a nice home, no kids yet so you can still travel and spend time together. Enjoy your life 'cause I can assure you that you'll lose it all if we make a bet. I'm not eighteen anymore. I can make Damian fall in love with me. The real question is do you want him as your husband or mine?"

"In your dreams, Angelica! He won't divorce me. But I see you're serious. So, what are you willing to lose to prove I'm right about Damian?"

Angelica laughed. "I have everything to gain, Sweetheart. Now… are YOU for real?"

"Yes," said Shana confidently.

"Ok," said Angelica sitting back. "What are the terms of the bet?"

After negotiating, Angelica had ninety days to get the three things Damian didn't like to share…love, money and Shana. They agreed to the following:

First, Damian had to tell Angelica he loved her. Shana knew that would be difficult since he avoided those words like the plague. Second, he had to take her on a $1,000 shopping spree. Damian was stingy and barely liked spending $100, let alone $1,000. Third, Angelica had to get Damian to sign the divorce papers. If she did, then she would get Damian, free and clear. Shana would sign the divorce papers without any questions asked.

Angelica would also receive Shana's secret savings of $20,000, all of Shana's shares in Sportie Fan and Shana's fifteen acres of land in Tennessee. Angelica had to teach her a lesson.

If Angelica lost, she had to match Shana's fifteen acres of land in Tennessee, paying an undisclosed amount. This would give Shana a total of thirty acres.

"That's a lot of land. What do you plan to do with it?" asked Angelica.

"Become a millionaire. I thought it was going to take me a few more years, but at this rate…I only have a few months," said Shana excitedly.

Shana explained what she planned to do with it. She also told Angelica where to purchase her future fifteen acres of land.

Just when Angelica was going to shake on the terms, she thought about how much she was in for. She wanted a little something extra to sweeten the pot.

"Since I have more at stake than you…" Angelica started to say.

"Excuse me! I'm betting my whole life here," said Shana interrupting her.

"Ok…fine. We both have a lot on the line. But I want something extra."

"What?"

"Sam."

"Sam?"

"Yes, Sam…from college!"

"You're nuts!!!"

"Take it or leave it."

"Fine! If you pull this off, I'll give you Sam. But I want something in return."

"What?"

"You have to get a picture with his signet ring on."

"Ok."

Damian NEVER let anyone wear his ring, not even Shana. Shana knew how important it was to him and his family. So, it was completely off limits.

They shook on it.

Angelica rubbed her hands together, anxiously. She was going to enjoy this. She just got the green light to do whatever she wanted to a man who she used to be in love with. Shana didn't realize what she'd just done. Angelica recorded the whole thing as a little insurance.

Angelica called Claudia on her way home to tell her what just transpired. She wondered if her emotions got the best of her. Now, she had two bets. The good thing was that Damian's was for three months. So, she still had time to win Austin over afterwards, if she wanted to. Nonetheless, she was going to concentrate on Damian for now.

~Chapter 14~

End of
the Week

It was finally Friday. Angelica had been playing this cat and mouse game with Damian all week. She'd wink at him, wear tight fitting clothes and smiled at him all the time. In turn, Damian would pass by her office for any reason, smiled a lot more and met about their upcoming trip as often as he could.

However, Angelica was ready to go out. She wanted to experience the town's nightlife, so she called Thad. She knew he'd know the happenings of Charlotte.

Thad told her about happy hour in Uptown. Afterwards, everyone was hitting up Club Halo. She was all in.

Before leaving for lunch, Angelica received an electronic invitation to Austin's surprise birthday celebration in the cafe at 2:00 p.m. A cake would be cut for staff to share. She accepted.

Angelica went to the mall on her lunch break. She wanted to find something for her outing and purchase Austin a birthday gift.

She entered Macy's through the handbag department. She immediately purchased four of them. Then, she walked over to the jewelry department. She went to look at watches for Austin. To her surprise, Damian was there.

"Hey you," said Angelica getting Damian's attention.

"Hey."

"For me…you shouldn't have," she said jokingly.

He laughed and said, "Shopping for the Mrs. It's our anniversary next Thursday. And since I won't be here, I wanted to get her something before I go."

Angelica looked around with him.

She pointed to a three-carat diamond bracelet, but he was interested in a necklace.

"What about this one?" she asked pointing to a gold necklace with a diamond heart.

"That's nice," he said asking the associate to see it.

They went back and forth a few more times before Damian decided on which one to purchase. Meanwhile, Angelica saw a gold Michael Kors watch she liked.

"Do you think Mr. Zachary would like this?" she asked Damian.

"Yes…it's nice," Damian said surprised.

"I'll take this one," she told the associate. Then turned to Damian and said, "I always buy watches for my boss's birthday. It's easy and impersonal."

"That's a lot to spend on a watch."

"Are you serious? That's nothing. I've spent way more on a previous boss."

"You're very generous 'cause I don't know anyone that would spend that kind of money for their boss."

"That's sad," said Angelica shaking her head.

She paid for it with her credit card. Then purchased some jewelry for herself on Austin's card.

She bought a silver necklace with a ruby and diamond pavé heart pendant; a gold necklace with a ruby and diamond key pendant; a white gold, three-row amethyst bracelet; a gold coin charm bracelet; and a Le Vian rose gold ring with garnets, chocolate diamonds and white diamonds.

"Wow! You sure do spoil yourself," he said.

"Yes, I do. I love jewelry. And by the looks of your ring, you do too. May I?" she said asking to see it.

"Yes, I do," he said extending out his hand.

"So…now that I've helped you, I need your assistance."

"Yes, ma'am. How can I help you?" he asked wondering what it was.

Her mind ran like a wildfire with sexual favors.

"I saw these dresses I want to try on, but I need help getting zipped in. Can you help me…please?" she asked hoping he'd say yes.

"Ok…sure."

Angelica was lying through her teeth. She hadn't seen any dresses. She'd just arrived when she saw Damian. However, she chose the two sexiest dresses she could find.

While he waited outside the dressing room, she made sure to leave the curtain cracked open for him to see her undress. And that he did. He salivated as her white lace bra with matching thong panties were revealed.

"Can you zip me up please?" she asked coming out in the first one.

"Sure."

"What do you think?" she asked doing a twirl.

"You look nice."

"Thanks."

He unzipped her so she could try on the second dress. This one was a little more revealing. This zipper started at her lower waist. He slowly zipped it trying to take in every part of her body. When he finished, she turned around.

"Ok…which one?" she asked twirling around in the second dress.

"Definitely this one."

"Perfect! I'll wear this one tonight."

"He's a lucky guy, whoever he is," said Damian fishing.

"Thad is the lucky one then," she said laughing.

"Thad?"

"Yeah. We're going to happy hour and then to the club. It's a bunch of people from work. You should come."

"I'll see," said Damian mesmerized by the dress. "So, am I done here? I really need to get back."

"Yes, after you unzip me…please," she said smiling.

Before he walked away, Angelica dropped the dress and walked up to him.

"Thank you for your help," she said kissing him on the cheek.

That afternoon in the break room, everyone sang "Happy Birthday" as Austin was presented with his favorite kind of cake…red velvet!!! He opened presents and had a good time.

Angelica went to get herself a Pepsi out of the vending machine. She overheard Damian and Thad talking and quietly stood where she could hear them.

"Man, she's sweet," said Damian describing Angelica.

"I can't believe you saw her naked," said Thad.

"Well not naked, but damn near. She is BAD-D-D-D!" exclaimed Damian excitedly.

"She's cool as hell, too. But you can't touch that."

"I know I'm not supposed to, but I sure as hell want to. My dick jumped when I saw all dat ass."

Thad laughed and said, "Shana will cut you if you cheat on her again."

"I know. I know. But I think I'm willing to get cut for this piece of ass."

"You stupid, man!" Thad said laughing again. "Listen, you have a wife. Let some of us other men have a shot."

"Hell no, man! You CANNOT have this one! No way, no how!"

"Damian, do you hear yourself? YOU ARE MARRIED!!!!"

"Shhh, man! Lower your voice. I know, but I have to have her."

"Man…you need Jesus! Why did you get married, then?"

"Man you know I had to."

The conversation was getting interesting. Angelica wanted to know more. But in being so nosey, she accidentally leaned in too far and hit the glass cabinet above her. They stopped talking assuming someone was coming.

She waited a few minutes and then walked around.

"Hello, gentlemen," she said in a flirty way when she saw them.

"Hey," they both said.

She got her soda and left.

Angelica was walking back to the party wondering why Damian had to marry Shana and how long ago he cheated on her.

Later that evening, Thad and Damian picked her up. Damian changed his mind after seeing her in that dress.

Damian stared at Angelica the entire night, but she stayed around Thad. Everyone knew Damian was married. She didn't want that reputation. Besides, she had big plans for Damian during their trip.

~Chapter 15~

Girls Day Out

Angelica had a shopping date with Cherry Saturday morning. She figured it was the perfect opportunity to get to know her new assistant and to see if she could be trusted. She needed a trusted confidant in town.

Before leaving, Austin invited Angelica to his house for dinner. He wanted to celebrate his birthday with her.

As the ladies traveled south towards South Park Mall, Angelica asked about R&B and Hip Hop radio stations. Cherry flipped through different channels showing her the good ones.

Then, Cherry stopped on a station and began singing the song.

"I didn't know you could sing," said Angelica afterwards.

"Yeah."

"So can I."

"Really? Let me hear," said Cherry as her eyes lit up.

They took turns singing a verse to the next song until it went off.

"Let's stop here first," said Cherry instructing her to turn on Cameron Valley Parkway.

"Ok, but where are we?"

"This is Phillips Place. It's a small and quaint shopping area with big name fashion and high end boutiques."

"That's right up my alley," said Angelica. "But I don't want to spend too much. I'm leaving early this coming Wednesday to shop in Philly."

They drove around the shopping center once looking at all of the stores. Then, Angelica parked in front of Caplin's. That was the first store they entered. Angelica's eyes glimmered when she saw Roberto Cavalli, Christian Louboutin and Oscar De La Renta. She purchased all of them, plus a few others.

Next, they went to Luna Estrella. They both tried on clothes.

"I like those jeans on you. You should get them," said Angelica as they came out of the dressing room.

"They're nice, but too much for me."

"$168.00 isn't a lot."

"Well…it's not in my budget. I can get the same look some-where cheaper."

"Where?"

Cherry's eyes twinkled when she said, "Kohl's! It's my favorite store, but I shop at Macy's as well."

"Well, I like those jeans on you. So, I'm getting them for you," said Angelica.

"No! You don't have to do that…really."

Angelica wasn't listening. She purchased all of the jeans they tried on and other name brands like BCBG, Juicy, Trina Turk and Theory.

They stopped at a few more stores picking up more popular and high end name brands, like Luciano Padovan, Badgley Mischka,

Giuseppe Zanotti and Christopher Blue.

Angelica treated Cherry to a frozen yogurt and a pedicure. Cherry was excited because she loved frozen yogurt. As a matter of fact, she loved food in general.

"Do you have a boyfriend?" asked Cherry as they sat in the chairs getting their feet done.

"No. I have friends," replied Angelica.

"Friends with benefits, huh?" asked Cherry giggling like a teen-ager.

Angelica couldn't help but laugh. She saw Cherry's innocence at that precise moment.

"You can say that," said Angelica. "What about you?"

"No. I don't have a boyfriend. I have a friend, but nothing more."

"Are you a virgin?"

Cherry was shocked and embarrassed at the question. It was so out in public and unfiltered.

"I'd rather not say," answered Cherry looking around hinting at how uncomfortable she was.

"My apologies if I embarrassed you. I didn't mean to put you on the spot like that."

"It's ok...and thank you."

Angelica could tell she was a little sheltered and a very private individual. So, she couldn't treat her like her friends in Miami.

After their pedicures, they stopped in Cafe Monte for a bite to eat. The yogurt was just a tease and Angelica didn't want mall food.

"Get whatever you want. It's on me," said Angelica.

"Are you sure because I can pay for myself."

"Yes, Cherry. I'm sure."

Angelica ordered the crab cake sandwich and lobster and crab crepe. Cherry ordered the herb-basted salmon with wild mushrooms.

Angelica was careful in how she approached Cherry. She didn't want to offend her again. Cherry saw that and broached the subject.

"Miss Angelica, I'm not as innocent as you think. I've had two boyfriends," said Cherry with a big smile. "So, I know about sex. It's just when you asked me earlier about being a virgin, you were loud and I wasn't expecting that question to be asked in front of everyone," said Cherry.

"Two boyfriends, huh?" said Angelica tickled. "Again, I apologize. That's just me. I ask questions straight up and don't sugar coat them. In Miami, you get it raw and uncut."

"I understand. I just have to get used to you."

"I as well," said Angelica. "So, you never answered my question. Are you a virgin?"

"No," whispered Cherry.

Angelica decided to change the subject. It appeared as if she was uncomfortable with the sex topic.

"So, tell me about yourself," said Angelica.

Cherry's family was from Winston-Salem. She was the oldest child of three and the first to go to college. She attended Salem College, a liberal arts women's college; moved to Charlotte after graduating; and was now pursuing her Master's Degree.

Angelica told her about being the oldest of four girls, where she went to school and all that she'd accomplished.

"Wow! You're really smart," said Cherry.

"Thank you. I've worked my butt off."

"Is that why you buy whatever you want?"

"Yes. I'm reaping the rewards by spoiling myself."

While they were eating, Angelica felt it was the perfect time to plant a seed of trust.

"So what do you think about Lance?" asked Angelica.

"Corporate's attorney?"

"Yes."

"Well…I think he's nice looking."

"That's it?"

"Well…"

"Cherry…loosen up. I understand I'm your boss, but I want us to be friends, too."

"Ok. Well, he's known for being a male whore. It's rumored that he has a lot of girlfriends and a new flavor each month. Did I say that right?" Cherry asked with a huge grin on her face. She was seriously asking.

"Yes, you did," said Angelica cracking up. Cherry really was a bookworm trying to be cool.

"See, I can be down. I know the lingo," said Cherry with the cheesiest smile.

Angelica lost it laughing.

"But as I was saying, Lance seems arrogant and into himself. He doesn't seem like the type that would ever settle down," said Cherry.

"What about Damian?"

"Reid?"

"Yes."

"No, Miss Angelica! He's married! Don't do that to yourself. Pick someone else. There are others out there."

"Like who…and how do you know? And call me Angelica."

"I be listening out for the news. Did I say it right?" said Cherry again with the cheesiest smile.

"Cherry…stick to English. Slang is not your thing."

"Well, I talk to a lot of people. They tell me things and I hear things."

"So who likes me?"

"Tony from marketing finds you attractive, Dan from IT thinks you're cute and Chuck from payroll really likes you."

"Ewww…Ewww…and Ewww," said Angelica making a face. "I wouldn't even let my dog lick on Chuck and I don't have one."

"That's not nice."

"Sorry, but true. I think I'll stick to Lance or Damian. I can make either one fall for me."

"How?" Cherry asked interested in hearing her plan.

"Work my mojo, girl."

"What is that?"

Angelica just looked at her and shook her head. "Let's go. I got money to blow," she said singing the song.

"Tell me what your mojo is?"

"I'll explain it in the car," laughed Angelica.

They made it to South Park Mall in five minutes. They didn't stay long because Angelica had to pick up Austin's cake from the bakery in Uptown before they closed. It was Austin's actual birthday.

Austin called Angelica, but she didn't answer because Cherry was in the car. Two minutes later, she received a text message reminding her about dinner at his place. She replied with an ETA.

Cherry collected all of her bags from Angelica's car.

"Thanks for everything, Cherry," said Angelica.

"You're welcome. Thank you for a great day. I had fun."

"You're welcome and so did I. We'll have to do this again."

"Anytime."

~Chapter 16~

Austin's Birthday

Angelica walked through his door singing *Happy Birthday*. She had his cake in hand with the candles lit.

"Thank you, Beautiful," he said blowing out the candles.

Austin hugged and kissed her like he missed her. Then, he took the cake and gave her a blunt. It was welcomed since she hadn't smoked all day.

"I didn't know you could sing," said Austin.

"I dabble here and there."

"You never cease to amaze me."

Austin was near the stove when Angelica went up behind him and said, "I need to take a shower."

"Can I join you?"

"Aren't you cooking?"

"I can stop."

"Ok."

His custom-made shower was enclosed in frameless glass with hues of color and etched glass doors. Unique shower heads sprayed from every angle. He also had fun features inside, like bars on the wall, a bench and special massagers.

Austin had her facing the wall with one foot mounted on the bench while she held onto a bar. He grabbed her by the waist and dicked her down from behind. Her moans became louder as it felt like he was in her stomach. He pulled her hair and slapped her ass, making it sting from the water. It was a good hurt and she begged for more. This turned Austin on. So, he turned off the water and laid her on the floor. With his feet supported by a bar, he did push-ups in the pussy. Angelica now knew how he stayed so physically fit.

They got out and went into the bedroom. Austin got close to Angelica. He whispered sweet nothings in her ear. He was rough, but gentle at the same time. He was pleasing her and showing emotion. She didn't know what came over him, but she took it all in.

After, they both took another quick shower. He held her the entire time.

"So…the credit card company called me. They wanted to make sure my card hadn't been stolen," laughed Austin as he finished cooking dinner.

"That bad, huh?"

"Yeah. But once they saw that I added a woman to my account, it explained today's $15,000 shopping spree."

"Was that all?"

"Ha ha."

"Well, thank you. Cherry and I went to Phillips Place and South Park Mall."

"Did you have a good time?"

"Yes! We spent most of the day shopping and snacking."

"Nice. A girl's day out."

"Yeah…and Cherry is funny, too. She's so innocent," said Angelica laughing and shaking her head thinking about some of the stuff she said.

"Well, I'm glad you had fun."

"I did." She paused and then continued. "I have presents for you."

"Thank you. That was nice of you to think about me," he said kissing her.

Angelica couldn't get over his demeanor. He was being extremely sweet. She wasn't used to it.

Austin escorted her to the dining room. He pulled out her chair and lit some candles to set the mood. He went into the kitchen and came back with bowls of salad and rolls first. Then, he served lobster tails with Shrimp Creole over white rice.

"I feel bad that you cooked on your birthday," said Angelica.

"It's ok. I'm doing exactly what I want to do."

Austin opened up over dinner. He talked about his family and how he was the older of two children. His mother was a retired school teacher and his father was a retired Lieutenant from the military. They traveled a lot when he was younger, but they settled in Raleigh when he was about thirteen. Austin talked about his love for playing ball, which started in high school and progressed in college.

Angelica was taken aback. He was being nice and acting human. She speculated it was from her infrequent visits during the week. She made it a point to stay away because of the stunt he pulled. She was teaching him a lesson. Also, she was concentrating on Damian.

After dinner, she showed him his gifts. He was surprised that she nailed his style.

She bought him three suits, seven ties, several dress shirts and cuff links. She also bought him a wallet, some underwear and a few casual outfits.

Next, she tried on her sexy outfit that she bought for him. He couldn't contain himself when she came out wearing a lace and leopard print push-up bra and a black lace thong.

"Come here," he said sitting on the floor with his back against the couch.

Angelica sat on him and kissed him. He quickly rose to the occasion. He popped her breasts out of the bra and began caressing them.

He looked at her and whispered, "I want to taste you."

He scooted down and leaned his head back on the couch. She stood up and kneeled on the edge of it. She leaned forward, holding on to the back as he gently kissed and separated her lips. He wrapped his arms around her thighs as he sucked hard making her move up and down. He spread her legs further apart, pulling her down closer to his face. He wanted all of it. He even grabbed her hair to sit her up so she could see him eating her out. She began sliding back and forth on his tongue.

"I'm about to cum, Baby," she said moving faster.

He held her and sucked to make it all come out. She quivered and screamed. Austin hurried and flipped her over. He wanted to feel her pussy pulsating as he melted in her warmness.

"You feel so good, Baby," said Austin.

"You, too, Baby. You too."

Austin didn't let her go all night. She fell asleep in his arms.

~Chapter 17~

Philadelphia
1st Night

Damian met Angelica at their departing gate Wednesday morning. They were scheduled to leave at 9 a.m. It was a full flight by the looks of the crowd.

"Hey…you made it," said Angelica.

"Yeah, of course," said Damian giving her a strange look.

"You don't have to look at me like that. I just wondered 'cause you weren't here yet."

"We still have ten minutes."

"I know, but you're cutting it close. I thought you might've changed your mind," she said flirtatiously.

"Now why would I do that?" he asked flirting back.

"Anything can happen in three days."

"Oh yeah…like what?" he said licking his lips.

"I don't know…use your imagination," she said licking her lips right back at him.

She was shocked at his behavior, but glad. She was going to see what he was really made of while away from home.

They boarded first since they were in first class.

During the flight, they discussed work and she flirted a little more. She was testing the waters as much as possible.

Damian was a bit nervous to be around Angelica alone. He was very attracted to her and she knew it. Also, there wouldn't be any interruptions like at the office. There was nothing stopping him from doing what he wanted to do. He just had to try and be good. However, Angelica had other plans.

It was early April and cool in Philly. The high was going to be fifty-six degrees. Angelica wasn't happy about it, but was pre-pared.

They landed around eleven and went straight to the hotel in downtown Philly.

"Welcome to the Hyatt at the Bellevue. My name is Megan. Do you have a reservation?" asked the black-haired woman at the registration counter.

"Yes…Angelica Zambrano."

"Damian Reid."

"Ok…let me see what we have here," said Megan looking up their reservation.

"Yes…Ms. Zambrano, I have you in the Arts Suite. And Mr. Reid…you're in a standard king room. Is this correct?" asked Megan.

"Yes…yes…"

"I see your room is ready Ms. Zambrano. Let me check on yours Mr. Reid," she said making a phone call.

"Ok...thank you," said Damian. Then turned to Angelica and said, "I see you like the best of everything, huh?"

"Yes. Why settle for less?"

"I guess you shouldn't."

Damian's room was also available. So, she gave each of them their room key and told them to enjoy their stay.

"I'm going shopping. You coming?" asked Angelica while they waited by the elevator.

"Sure. I'll go."

"Ok. Meet you back down here in like…fifteen minutes?" she asked, but stated.

"That's fine."

"Great."

Damian went to his room and called Shana to let her know he made it safely. Then, he sat there for a moment thinking about Angelica. He had to remember that she was his boss and that he was married. He couldn't behave like she was some random chick he wasn't going to see again. He had to tone down the flirting and have self-control. He didn't want to create any problems.

They met in the lobby and decided to grab a bite to eat before going shopping. They went to the hotel's restaurant, XXX Cafe, for lunch. Angelica had a Panini sandwich while Damian had a club sandwich.

With their stomachs full, she was ready to shop. They buttoned up their coats as they left the hotel. Angelica interlocked her arm with his trying to keep warm.

They exited on South Broad Street and turned onto Walnut Street. This was where Angelica wanted to be.

Ralph Lauren, Bebe and Kenneth Cole were a few stores they shopped in. Then, they stopped in Armani Exchange.

"This looks nice. You should try it on," Angelica told Damian as they looked around.

"Ok," he said still looking. "I'm gonna try these on, too."

Angelica sat right in front of Damian's dressing room so that she could see him when he came out.

"What do you think?" he asked stepping out in the first outfit.

"It's nice. Turn around."

Damian spun around.

"It looks good."

"I'm getting it," he said walking back into the dressing room.

After a few minutes, he came back out in the second outfit.

"Damn! That really looks good on you," she said smiling.

"Thank you. I like the shirt, but I saw a blue one. Do you mind grabbing it for me?" he asked.

"Nope. I'll be right back."

She left and came back.

"Here," she said barging into his dressing room.

He stood there with only his boxer briefs on showing all of his pectorals, biceps, triceps and six-pack. Then, she looked down and saw his V. She was speechless, biting her lip.

"Sorry," barely came out of her mouth.

"It's ok. Thank you," he said chuckling as he took the shirt.

She couldn't get the image of his body out of her mind as she sat back down.

After a few minutes, he came out wearing the second shirt with different pants. She thought both shirts looked equally nice. So, he got them both.

As they continued strolling down Walnut Street, Angelica saw Alma De Cuba. It was the famous Cuban restaurant she read about on the Internet. She stopped in to confirm her reservation. She was all set.

They went back to the hotel and got ready for their 3:00 meeting. She was upset she didn't get to finish shopping.

They arrived to Sportie Fans at exactly 2:55 p.m. and worked until nine that evening. They were thankful the hotel wasn't that far away.

~Chapter 18~

Philadelphia
2nd Night

They returned to the store at 7 a.m. They had meetings with the morning managers and a few employees. Damian had a brief training session to discuss new recruiting procedures and Angelica discussed pending disciplinary issues.

By 4:00 p.m., Angelica and Damian were finished with business. That gave Angelica two hours to shop. Damian went with her.

In the midst of shopping, Damian called Shana to wish her a happy anniversary and told her where her gift was. Shana was enthused with her necklace and started talking dirty as she normally would after receiving a gift. However, Damian cut her short and hung up when Angelica came around.

That night, they took a cab to Alma de Cuba for their seven o'clock dinner reservation. She knew they'd be drinking and didn't want to drive.

Damian pulled open the large white door. Angelica gave her name after being greeted by the hostess. The woman told them it would be about a fifteen minute wait. So, they opted to sit in the lounge area and have drinks while they waited.

The waitress came over with appetizer menus. Damian asked for a Corona, but Angelica quickly intervened.

"Hi. He will not be having a Corona," she told the waitress. "Please bring us two classic Mojitos."

"Ok...and can I start you off with an appetizer?" asked the waitress looking at Damian.

Damian put his hand out in Angelica's direction for her to continue ordering.

The women laughed as Angelica ordered the chorizo and cilantro sliders and the Cuba sampler.

"Your drinks are coming right up."

"Thank you," said Angelica, then she turned to Damian. "This is supposed to be an authentic Cuban restaurant. You have to experience Cuba and all of its essence."

"Ok," he said.

Angelica couldn't get over how beautiful the place was.

The walls projected black and white photos of Cuban people in sugar cane fields. The sleek, white furniture was accompanied by soft blue lighting, creating a sexy ambience. Several glass wall inlays with massive tobacco leaves hung behind a shiny Mahogany bar. A mix of old and new Latin hits commanded people to dance salsa wherever they could.

The waitress came back with their drinks.

"Damn, that's good!!" said Damian.

"Yes, it is," she agreed.

Shortly after, they were escorted upstairs and immediately seated. Their appetizers were on the table and she ordered two Cherry Caipirinhas.

Vaulted ceilings, whitewashed brick walls, classic decor, sheer canvases and seductive low lighting induced a spirit of Havana upstairs. The small, but contemporary cocktail tables afforded guests the opportunity to dine intimately. Three large picturesque windows provided a view of the night sky and Walnut Street. It was gorgeous.

Again, Damian allowed her to order since she was the expert at Cuban cuisine.

Angelica ordered the lechon asado for Damian, which was mouth-watering roasted pork, marinated and roasted with the skin until the outside was crispy and the inside was tender and juicy. It was served with congri rice (white rice and black beans cook together).

She ordered the vaca frita for herself, which was a succulent pan-seared skirt steak that was shredded, seasoned and fried to infuse a crispiness while topped with caramelized onions. It was served with white rice and black beans, separately.

No Cuban dish was complete without plantains. She ordered sides of tostones and maduros. Tostones were green plantains, sliced thick and fried. Then, they were flattened and fried again and served with a garlic mojo sauce. Maduros were ripened yellow plantains fried in its natural sugars, making them sweet.

She excused herself momentarily. As she went to the restroom, she pulled their waiter aside and slipped him a $50 bill. She ordered another round of drinks and asked him for a favor.

When she got back, the waiter arrived with their drinks.

"More drinks?" asked Damian feeling a buzz.

"Yes…why…you can't handle it?"

"I can handle whatever you give me," he said licking his lips.

These Mojitos were much stronger. She was trying to get Damian drunk to see how far he'd go.

Angelica took out her phone. She asked Damian to snap a few pictures of her in the restaurant. When their waiter passed by, she asked him to take a picture of them. Damian didn't hesitate. They got real close as she sat on his lap.

Then, the waiter insisted the couple kiss. So, Damian gently pulled Angelica's face in and did it. This was no peck on the lips either. He stuck his tongue down her throat with a longing desire. His head moved. Her head moved. It was like they forgot where they were. All the while, the waiter was snapping away.

They were interrupted when their food came out. Angelica got off of his lap and returned to her seat.

"The food looks great," she said trying to break the awkwardness she saw on his face.

"Yes, it does."

They enjoyed their dinner and left room for dessert. She had to try the famous Chocolate cigar. This chocolate almond cake was wrapped in chocolate mousse, dusted with cocoa and served with Dulce de Leche ice cream and edible matches that light on fire.

When the waiter came with the bill, Damian insisted on paying. But Angelica wouldn't have it. She paid and told him it was her pleasure taking him to Cuba.

"I got the next one," he said.

"Ok."

The bill was almost $200 and she tipped the waiter another $100. As they walked out, she winked at him and thanked him for everything.

"Have a good night," said the waiter winking back.

Besides adding more liquor to their last drinks, Angelica paid the waiter to insist that they kiss for a photograph. She wanted to show Shana her progress.

It was about 9:30 p.m. and they decided to walk back to the hotel. It was cold, but they were liquored up and full. So, the walk would do them some good.

They talked and laughed all the way to Angelica's suite. She invited him in, but he declined. He didn't think it was appropriate considering what he wanted to do to her. She understood and respected that.

She went to give him a goodnight kiss on the cheek, but he had to taste her one last time. Fueled by lust, he pressed his mouth against hers. As they kissed, she backed him into the room. He hadn't noticed because he was so enthralled with her. She took off her coat so he could really embrace her. As she pressed against him, his dick got harder than steel. Once he felt her hands touching him, he backed away.

"I'm sorry I can't do this," he said.

"Ok," she said, nonchalantly. "Good night, Damian. See you in the morning," she said opening the door for him to leave.

After a slight hesitation, "Ok. Good night," came out of his mouth.

She closed the door behind him.

Angelica wasn't really upset and had no worries. She knew he'd crack in New York.

~Chapter 19~

New
York

Early the next morning, Angelica and Damian caught their flight to New York. They dreaded the day because it would be a long one, considering they had a 9:30 a.m. meeting scheduled. They didn't anticipate getting out of there until late.

Before takeoff, Angelica sent Shana some of the pictures from the night before.

"Angelica, can we talk?" asked Damian seated next to her on the plane.

He wanted to address what happened so it wouldn't be weird between them.

"Yeah…sure. What's on your mind?" she asked.

"Well, I want to talk to you about last night."

"Damian…let me ease your mind. We drank too much and things got a little heated, but we're good. I'm not some psycho chick that's gonna tell your wife. So…relax. Besides, it wouldn't look professional if this got out. So, no one will know."

"Ok," he said more at ease.

Angelica couldn't very well tell him the truth.

She took out her laptop and went over their game plan, discussing their strategy to tackle New York's issues.

A car picked them up from the airport and took them straight to the store for their early morning meeting.

By 1:00 p.m., they left to check into the hotel.

"Hi. Welcome to the Sheraton Hotel & Towers, Manhattan. Do you have a reservation?" asked a blonde-haired woman behind the desk.

"Damian Reid and…"

"Angelica Zambrano."

She typed in their names and found their reservation. She removed two envelopes from a binder.

"Here you go, sir. You're in one of the Sheraton Club Suites, Room 4810," she told Damian.

"And you ma'am are in one of the Penthouse Suites, Room PH51A," she said to Angelica.

Damian wasn't surprised anymore.

"The hotel attendants will help you with your luggage. Please enjoy your stay."

They tipped the attendants to take their bags to each of their rooms while they grabbed lunch. They had to get back to work.

They finished around 8:00 p.m. They were tired and starving. Damian instructed the driver to take them to West 44th Street between 7th and 8th Avenue.

"Do you like Italian?" asked Damian.

"I love Italian," said Angelica.

They stopped in front of Marcelini's Ristorante. It was five minutes from the hotel.

"Hi. Two, please…" Damian told the host.

"Please follow me," said a tall, thin man with glasses grabbing two menus.

A sultry, red glow illuminated the white and black themed dining area. White sheer paneling crisscrossed throughout the soft globe lighting on the ceiling. Black leather walls, red uplighting on the brick columns and red lamps on each table accentuated the inside. Red leather, high back booths were lined perpendicular along the walls while all of the dining tables were centered and dressed in crisp white linens with high back black chairs.

"Here we are," said the host holding his hand out to help Angelica up to their booth.

"Thank you," she told him. Then turned to Damian and said, "This is really nice."

"Thanks."

Just as they opened the menus, their waitress came over.

"Hi. My name is Patty. Welcome to Marcelini's. Can I start you off with something to drink?"

"May I?" Damian asked Angelica, wanting to order for them.

"Please."

"Yes, Patty. I'd like to order the Tour D'Italiano," said Damian in his best Italian voice.

It made the ladies laugh.

"Yes, sir. House specialties or choice selections?"

"House specialties, please."

"No problem, sir," said Patty reaching for their menus. "Your first course is coming right up."

The Tour D'Italiano was the American version of a 5-course authentic Italian dining experience. It consisted of Antipasto (or appetizer), "Primo" (or first course), second course (or meat course), Contorni (or vegetable serving) and coffee with Dolce (or dessert) as the fifth course. All courses were proportioned and served with red or white wine, depending on the meat selection.

This meal was in no way rushed. This was the type of meal ordered when on a date, allowing the couple time to enjoy the food and each other's company.

Two plates of Antipasto were served with two glasses of Chianti Classico. The first plate had cured meats (prosciutto, salami and mortadella), three cheeses (pecorino Romano, Parmigiano Reggiano and Taleggio) and a selection of garnishments (a variety of olives, cipolline onions and sun-dried tomatoes). The second plate had Ensalate Capresa, which was sliced mozzarella cheese on tomatoes topped with basil, olive oil and salt and pepper.

When Damian selected house specialties, it meant the food was pre-selected. So, they could sit back and enjoy.

Twenty minutes later, the first course was served. It mainly consisted of risottos, pastas or soups. One plate had Tortellini Bolognese served with glass of Cabernet Sauvignon. The other had Risotto Al' Seafood cooked with shrimp and crab and served with a glass of Chardonnay.

Angelica tasted both plates of food.

"This one is really good," she said referring to the risotto. So, she kept that plate.

They conversed about birthdays, sports, current events and work. They talked about family, Shana and the dynamic of their relationship. The more he spoke, the more she could hear the desperation in his voice of not wanting to cheat. So, she eased his mind.

"Maybe my boyfriend and I can join you two for dinner some time," she said eating more food.

"You have a boyfriend?" he asked baffled.

"Yes. Why is that surprising?"

"No…no reason. Sure…that sounds great."

Damian was kind of relieved that she wasn't available.

"So what's his name?"

"Aus…Lem," she stuttered almost saying Austin's name.

"Auslem?"

"Yes. He's from Dubai," she said lying through her teeth.

Damian asked many questions. She answered them referring to Austin. She was trying to throw him off. She succeeded.

The second course came next. They were presented with a tower of deliciousness. The top level had the seafood: shrimp Parmigiana, salmon in mustard sauce and Lobster Carbonara. The middle tray had poultry: Sicilian Chicken, Chicken Parmigiana, Chicken Florentine and Chicken Piccata. The bottom had the red meats: Veal Marsala, Old-Fashioned Sicilian Succo, Filet Mignon Marsala, rosemary-braised Lamb and Spintini a la Sicilana (meat roll). Two glasses of red wine and two glasses of white wine were served with this tower.

"Oh my God! Damian…this is a lot of food," said Angelica.

"You can handle it. I've seen you eat," he said laughing.

She scooted closer to him feeling frisky from all of the wine. Once again, they sat quite cozy.

"You are so beautiful, Angelica," he blurted out.

"Thank you, Damian. And you're very handsome."

"Thank you."

He reached over and kissed her. It was like everything he said earlier went out the window.

Once again, the kissing was interrupted by the fourth course. One plate had zucchini frittata and the other had stuffed eggplant. No wine was served with this course since they each received two glasses previously.

Angelica was feeling tipsy and full. So, she asked Damian the question.

"So, just out of curiosity…have you ever cheated on your wife?"

Damian lightly choked on his food. "That's a bit personal, don't you think?"

"It's ok. I got my answer."

"Not really."

Yes, really. Any man that hasn't cheated on his wife would've instantly said no. You choked and are avoiding the question. Come on…its textbook."

"Ok…yes I have. But I'm not proud of it."

"Of course, you're not. You have to tell yourself that so it's ok in your mind."

"No…that's not it."

"If you say so."

"Oh…so you're one of those men bashing type of women?"

"No, I'm not. I love men. Maybe too much," she whispered that last part. "But I don't believe in excuses. Don't put yourself in a position to cheat. For example, you know I find you very attractive. And honestly, I'd love to fuck the shit out of you. So in knowing that, would you come to my room late at night?"

"If invited, yes."

"Exactly! Now you've put yourself in a position to cheat."

"Not necessarily."

"You're more stupid than I thought if you don't think I'd take advantage of you."

Damian stayed quiet before he dug himself into a deeper hole.

The last course was coffee and dessert. The waiter served them two cups of espresso and one plate of Dolce, which consisted of stuffed cannoli topped with chocolate, Italian gelato and peaches with mascarpone.

It was close to 11:00 p.m. when they finished. It was Friday night and Angelica was ready to hit up the club.

"I'm going to my friend's club. You comin'?"

"What time do we have to be at the new store tomorrow?" he asked paying a $250 tab.

"2:30 p.m."
Damian decided to go.

~Chapter 20~

The Club

Damian knocked on Angelica's hotel door before walking in. She left it cracked open since she knew he was on his way.

"Angelica!" he called out.

"Come in!" she shouted from the bedroom.

When she came out, Damian's dick jumped.

"Damn! You look nice!" he said trying not to stare.

"Thank you," she said smiling.

"You ready to go?"

"Yep," she said grabbing her silver Emilio Pucci clutch.

Angelica wore a strapless, silver metallic and jeweled Sherry Hill dress. She wore diamond chandelier earrings, chunky diamond bracelets and Christian Louboutin silver studded platform pumps.

They made it to Club Saavy on Broadway and W 26th Street by

12:30 a.m. This Hip Hop/R&B club played mixed music including: Reggae, Salsa and Reggaeton. She knew the club very well
considering it belonged to her friend, Victor.

"Hey, Rick. How are you?" Angelica asked the bouncer, hugging him.

"Damn, Shorty! Long time no see. I'm good. How are you?"
asked Rick in a thick NY accent.

"I'm good," she said laughing. "Rick…this is my co-worker
Damian. Damian…this is Rick."

"Nice to meet you, man," said Rick shaking his hand.

"Likewise."

"You lookin' good as ever," Rick told Angelica.

"Thank you."

"Enjoy yourselves," said Rick, opening the door and letting
them in.

"Heyyyy!!!!" screamed Angelica approaching the bar.

Everyone there had that same thick New York.

"Oh my God…Angelica!!!" screamed Roxy, the bartender.
"When did you get into town?" she asked giving her a hug.

"Today, but we leave tomorrow."

"We who?"

"Oh…I'm sorry. This is my co-worker Damian. Damian…
Roxy."

"Nice to meet you," he said shaking her hand.

"Damn! He's fine, girl!" exclaimed Roxy.

"We're here on company business," said Angelica.

"I've heard that one before," said Roxy, making them laugh.

Another waitress friend approached them screaming.

"Angelica!!! When did you get in?" yelled Maggie, giving her a
hug.

"Today," said Angelica. Then, she turned Damian towards her.
"Damian…Maggie. Maggie…Damian," she said introducing

them.

"Damn! You're a cutie," said Maggie.

"Thank you. It's nice to meet you," said Damian, smiling and shaking her hand.

"It's just work, girl," said Angelica.

"I've heard that before," said Maggie making them laugh. "Come on. Victor has your area ready."

They followed her to a private, enclosed area upstairs in VIP. It was decorated with white sheer curtains, a white leather sofa, a cocktail table and a bottle of champagne with a note that said *To my Queen'*.

"Does everyone always give you what you want?" Damian asked Angelica amazed.

"Yes."

Angelica told Maggie she wanted two of her "special" drinks, winking at her. Maggie winked back and said, "Coming right up."

Angelica excused herself momentarily to greet Victor. Damian watched as Victor carried her off behind a black curtain.

Minutes later, she came back high as hell with Maggie on her trail with those drinks.

"Here you go. Two lemon shots and two waters. Enjoy," said Maggie placing them on the table.

"Thanks, girl," said Angelica tipping her $100.

Angelica handed Damian one of the glasses. They toasted and drank up.

Everyday Birthday by Swizz Beatz came on. Angelica stood up and started dancing. Damian took off his jacket and escorted her to the dance floor.

His hands were all over Angelica, touching her as he pleased. And she didn't care.

"I feel so good and free," said Damian once they made it back to VIP.

Angelica laughed knowing why he felt so good. He was rolling. She whispered in his ear, "Do you feel like you're in ecstasy?"

He just turned and kissed her. He was very touchy-feely. He also performed libidinous acts like undoing his pants and pulling out his dick. He had Angelica rub it as he unzipped the back of her dress, fondling her breasts.

She was glad he had the type of dick she liked: long, thick and brown. Nonetheless, she performed the building blocks test with her hands. She went up at least three times and was unable to touch her fingertips.

"I want to taste her," he said looking into her eyes.

She got up and lifted her dress to her waist. She laid back on the table and spread her legs into the widest V possible. He scooted her to the edge like it was dinner time and dove right in. He kept up with her as her hips moved uncontrollably. He wasn't letting that sweet tasting pussy go anywhere. He deliciously pleased her until she came.

He stood up, allowing his pants to fall to the floor.

"I want to fuck you so bad," he said rubbing on himself, getting ready for her.

"Then do it."

He obliged.

"Shit!" she said as they became one. "Fuck!"

"Yes! Oh yes!" said Damian craving Angelica. "Give it to me, Baby!"

Angelica melted hearing his deep, sexy voice in her ear.

"Take it, Baby," she told him.

Damian lifted her legs onto his shoulders as he pounded. He told her how good she felt. Then, he picked her up, penetrating deeper. He sexed her faster, wanting more. She wrapped her arms around his neck and gave him what he wanted.

She got down and pushed him against the back wall. She raised one leg onto the sofa and stood on the other. She bent over in front of him and fucked him like a wild horse. He held onto her waist, slapping her on the ass. Then, he grabbed her hair as they were like two dogs in heat.

She had one more trick up her sleeve. She lifted her one leg onto his shoulders, doing the splits standing up. Damian got very excited and rammed his dick back inside. She jumped and screamed as he touched everything with his magic stick. But she showed good sportsmanship by letting him tear it up like it was his.

Angelica knew he wasn't cumming anytime soon. She had her friend crush an E-pill in his shot. She wanted him and knew that was the only way to get him.

She was ready to go back to the hotel and get down right nasty with him. So, they got dressed and left.

While in the car, she asked him to take a little blue pill to enhance his high. He agreed. Now, he was on ViX (a Viagra and Ecstasy combination). She couldn't wait.

Back at Angelica's suite, Damian took off his clothes.

"Come here," he said standing there naked.

"Take off your wedding band," she demanded.

He threw it and then undressed her. Damian released all his demons on Angelica, pleasuring her for almost four hours. She loved every minute of it.

~Chapter 21~

Saturday

Angelica's alarm went off about noon. Damian lifted his head and looked around. He was trying to gauge his surroundings when he saw Angelica and instantly smiled, remembering their early morning sex session.

"Good morning, sleepy head," he said scooting closer to her.

"Good morning," she said scooting backwards into his arms.

"Damn…I'm so sore," he said not wanting it touched.

"Me, too."

"I had a great time."

"So did I, but we have to get up."

"I don't want to. I want to lie in bed with you all day.

"Well, too bad. Let's go," said Angelica getting up and going to the bathroom.

She turned on the shower and lit a blunt. Damian smelled weed and got up.

"Here…hit this," she said handing it to him. "It'll take the edge off."

He sucked it up and then started coughing.

"Damn! You alright?" she asked.

"Yeah…I'm fine," he said barely able to talk.

She hit it one last time before putting it out.

"You're incredible," he told her as the hot water hit his back.

"I know," she said laughing flirtatiously.

"You brought out the beast in me last night. You stretched him beyond the point of no return."

"That's a good thing, isn't it?"

"It is, but I can't recall the last time I felt like that."

"That's too bad."

The weed mellowed him out, but he needed a Red Bull to wake him up.

They both requested late checkouts, so they didn't have to be gone until 3:00 p.m. However, Damian cleared out his room since he knew he'd be hanging with her until they left.

Angelica ordered room service.

"I'm not flying back with you after today's meeting," Angelica told Damian as they ate lunch.

"Why not?"

"I have to go to Chicago. It's my best friend's birthday."

Damian had a disappointing look on his face.

"I'll be back in Charlotte Monday morning," she told him.

"I guess…"

"I'd ask you if you want to come, but…"

"I'd go if you're extending an invitation."

"You sure?"

Angelica gave him the flight information for Chicago. He gladly paid the additional cost. He wasn't ready to go home. He wasn't ready to leave Angelica.

"I'm all set," he said full of smiles, hanging up the phone.

"You're crazy…you know that?" Angelica said laughing.

"For you."

"That's the cheesiest line ever," she said making them laugh.

Damian excused himself to call Shana. He wasn't sure what she was going to say, but he wouldn't be back until Monday morning.

Angelica called Claudia and told her Damian would be joining them. Claudia didn't care. She just wanted her there already.

Before checking out, they searched for Damian's wedding ring. He threw it so fast and didn't pay attention to where. He wound up finding it near the living room. He wasn't sure how it made it that far.

During the meeting, he kept staring at her. He kept thinking about the most wonderful night he'd ever had. He knew it was wrong to feel the way he did, but he couldn't help it. She rocked his world and all he wanted to do was keep playing house. He'd deal with the real world once they got back.

They demonstrated true professionalism and kicked ass during the two-hour tour/meeting. Damian was able to concentrate long enough to conduct business. Angelica definitely showed out.

They rushed out of there to catch their 6:00 evening flight. They barely made it.

"So, what happens with us," Damian asked sitting next to her in first class.

"There is no us, Sweetheart. You're married remember? We're just two adults enjoying each other's company."

Damian nodded in agreement, but still looked bewildered.

"Damian…I like you, but I'm not one of those women that will allow herself to be a glorified booty call or second in any man's life. I don't have to."

"You sure don't," he mumbled under his breath.

She laughed 'cause she heard him.

"You can't have your cake and eat it too. We may have a good time occasionally, but I'm not one of your women," she further clarified.

Damian understood and agreed, but didn't like it. He wanted Angelica in his life, but wasn't sure where she'd fit in his equation.

Damian decided to be honest with Angelica. He admitted that he had no excuse for his actions. He wasn't going to lie and say he didn't want his wife or they were having problems in order to justify what he did. Shana was a great woman, wife and lover. But Angelica took his breath away. She put him on a high that he'd never been on before.

"You sure it wasn't the X," joked Angelica, but then realized she hadn't told him what she did to get him in bed.

However, Damian was quite familiar with Ecstasy and knew he was on it after drinking his shot. That was also the reason he agreed to take the Viagra. He wanted a good hard on to tackle Angelica.

"So, you're not mad at me for what I did?" asked Angelica.

"Mad? Hell naw I'm not mad! I'm glad you did it. I wouldn't have had the nerve otherwise," he said kissing her hand.

Angelica changed the subject.

She asked if Shana knew he smoked. She did, but not as frequently as he does. He confessed that he smokes with Thad all the time, but asked her to be discreet. No one knew about Thad smoking weed.

They landed in Chicago around 7:30 p.m. central time. So, they gained an hour.

Anthony had a limo waiting at the airport to take them to his penthouse at The Legacy in downtown Chicago.

~Chapter 22~

Chicago

Damian woke up Sunday morning to his phone vibrating. It was Shana calling, but he didn't answer. Instead, he laid there looking at Angelica sleep. He played back the past few days in his head and found himself in a peculiar situation. For the first time, he wasn't concerned that he cheated on Shana. He was having a good time.

Angelica awoke to Damian's eyes beaming down on her.

"Good morning," she said.

"Good morning, Sweetheart."

He hugged her and whispered, "I want to be inside of you again."

So, she rolled on top of him and rode him for their morning quickie.

"Knock, knock…" said Claudia.

"Come in," said Angelica.

Claudia hopped in the bed with them, lying next to Angelica.

"Anthony has this whole day planned for us," said Claudia.

"It's so early," yawned Angelica.

"It's almost 10."

"Yeah, but we just got home from Excalibur not even five hours ago," said Angelica referring to the club they partied at on Saturday night, her actual birthday.

"So…" said Claudia with attitude.

"What time are we leaving?"

"Now."

Damian was under the covers the entire time the ladies talked.

"Damian!" screamed Claudia, messing with him.

"Yes, ma'am," he answered.

"Wake up! And enough of this ma'am shit."

"I'm up."

Claudia jumped up and down on their bed before leaving. She did it until Angelica chased her out. Her and Angelica always played around like that.

"Y'all nasty," teased Claudia from the other side of the door 'cause Angelica was naked.

"Are you two always this way?" asked Damian laughing as she returned to bed.

"Yes," she replied. "I do the same thing to them. Anthony is used to me though."

"Y'all crazy," he said shaking his head.

They got up and took a shower. The smell of breakfast awakened their taste buds.

Anthony made homemade waffles with fresh strawberries, blueberries and whip cream. He scrambled eggs and grilled turkey bacon and sausage. There was a platter of sliced fresh fruit on the table and he juiced fresh oranges, apples and carrots to drink.

Claudia always referred to her man as sexy when he was in the kitchen. But that's because he really was.

Anthony Christopher was a 32-year old Korean, Puerto Rican and black man. He stood 6'2" with a naturally tanned complexion, short and wavy black hair, slanted eyes and sexy lips. He was from Chicago, but lived in Miami during the season. Off-season, he spent lots of time in his hometown with his family.

The Legacy was prime real estate in the heart of downtown Chicago. Anthony resided in a four-bedroom, five-bathroom penthouse on the 69th floor. His 5,000 square feet of living space included an open floor plan between the living room and dining room, large family room, master suite with sitting room, game room and lakefront view of Lake Michigan.

Anthony was excited to get the day started, which began at the Peninsula Hotel. Each couple was being treated to a half-day spa package. Anthony chose the one for him and Claudia. Angelica let Damian choose theirs.

After two hours of de-stressing and relaxing, they went on a horse carriage ride. It was cool out, but they bundled up as they toured Michigan Avenue. Claudia and Angelica were happy that Damian and Anthony were getting along.

Shopping was the next planned activity on the agenda. They strolled down Magnificent Mile beginning at E Illinois Street. They shopped until they reached Water Tower Mall. They spent the duration of their day there.

Damian and Angelica acted like Anthony and Claudia: holding hands, kissing in public and being very considerate of one another. Damian spent $1,500 on Angelica and treated her like his girl.

Last, Anthony planned a special dinner for Claudia. He knew how much she missed her best friend. So, he rented a 75' Sunseeker Manhattan to host an upscale dinner cruise. This luxury, private yacht was scheduled to cruise around beautiful Lake Michigan and the surrounding area for four hours as a private chef prepared an intimate and romantic dinner for four.

As they boarded, the crew welcomed them with glasses of champagne. They were escorted to the top deck to enjoy more cocktails and appetizers.

Anthony was a Remy Martin man. So, him and Damian drank on that while the ladies sipped on Nuvo.

The fellas left the ladies alone to catch up and girl talk. About an hour later, dinner was ready.

The dining area was a very romantic scene with lots of lit candles, flowers and jazz music playing in the background.

The chef started them off with a spicy lobster and pineapple salad served in halves of pineapples topped with basil, mint and a Thai chili sauce on the side.

Next, three entrees were served for everyone to relish in. The first was Churrasco (grilled skirt steak) with a Cuban chimichurri sauce and roasted asparagus. The second was stuffed chicken breasts with a mango curry sauce over rice pilaf. The third was sesame-crusted salmon steaks with a maple glaze over fettuccine pasta.

After dinner, they adjourned back upstairs to the top deck.

"Angelica…" said Anthony.

"What's up, Baby?"

"You know I love this woman, don't you?"

"Yes, I do. And you better love her forever."

"I will…I promise."

Claudia's cake came out just the way she liked it…Chocolate! She had a chocolate cake with fudge filling and milk chocolate frosting. Chocolate chips and swirls of chocolate syrup embellished the cake while topped with a glass slipper.

Anthony took the glass slipper and got on one knee.

"I love you, Claudia Victorsen. Will you do me the honor of becoming Mrs. Christopher?" he asked opening the glass slipper.

She yelled, screamed and hugged him so hard they both fell to the floor.

"Yes! Absolutely, 100% YES!" she said kissing him as he slid the ring on.

Claudia's ring was a 10-carat diamond platinum ring. The flawless radiant cut center stone was mounted in a pavé diamond setting with a knife-edge style going around the stone. The same knife-edge design went halfway down the shank with round pavé diamonds.

Angelica couldn't contain her excitement. She jumped on top of them hugging, kissing and congratulating them.

Claudia was on cloud nine the rest of the night.

Once they made it back to Navy Pier, they were off to Studio Paris on W. Hubbard. They stayed until 2 a.m.

Damian and Angelica didn't sleep at all. They had sex while in the shower before going to the airport. They barely caught their 5:45 a.m. flight back home. Needless to say, they slept on the plane.

~Chapter 23~

Yet Another Bet

"Good morning, Miss Angelica," said Cherry.

"Good morning, Cherry," said Angelica strutting her stuff like a runway model.

"Welcome back."

"Thanks."

Cherry followed Angelica into her office. She ran down Angelica's schedule, meetings and told her about any good gossip she heard while Angelica was away.

Angelica had a meeting with Austin, Max and Damian to go over the details of their trip. So, she took a moment to make certain she looked fabulous.

Angelica and Damian were on the ball. Most of the issues were resolved. However, the next action items for those facilities were discussed and planned.

As Angelica and Damian approached her office, a guy was standing at Cherry's desk with two bouquets of flowers. Angelica overheard her name.

"Hi…I'm Angelica Zambrano," she said to the guy.

"These are for you, ma'am. Where should I put them?'

"Please follow me."

He placed the arrangement of Birds of Paradise on her conference table and the orchids on her desk.

"Thank you," she said, tipping him.

"You're welcome, ma'am. Have a great day."

"You, too."

Five minutes later, her phone rang.

"You look beautiful today," said Austin.

"Thank you, Love."

"Do you like the flowers?"

"Yes. They're beautiful. Thank you."

"You're welcome. Can you please come to my office?"

"Ok…bye," she said.

Damian had a look on his face as she hung up the phone.

"Nice flowers. Who are they from?" he asked a little jealous.

Angelica played on the boyfriend lie.

"The boyfriend."

Damian got real close and said, "We just got back and I can't stop thinking about you. I want you right now."

"Oh yeah…"

"Yeah. I want you all to myself, Angelica."

"I do, too, Baby. I want you in me every night, wake up in your arms and do it all over again. But you have to get divorced first."

Damian jumped back. He was caught off guard with the "divorce" word. He hadn't thought about divorcing Shana while he was pretending to be single.

"What's wrong, Sweetheart?" asked Angelica knowing it was

what she said.

"Nothing. I'll talk to you later," he said storming out of there.

She'd thrown him for a loop.

Angelica went to Austin's office and closed the door behind her.

"Yes...how can I help you?" she asked.

"I want some of my pussy, Angelica."

"Your pussy?"

"Yes! I haven't seen you since my birthday. I've called and text while you were away, but you were either too busy or didn't respond. Then, I get a text saying you're going to Chicago to see Claudia…"

"I did!"

"Do you think I'm some kind of fool? Who's in Chicago? And why do you play so many fuckin' games?"

"I'll talk to you later," she said getting up from her seat.

"Wait, please! I'm sorry."

"You act like I haven't been working my ass off while I was away! Did I not produce results? Aren't we back on track?"

"Yes and again I'm sorry. Let me make it up to you. Come over."

"No, I have a date," she said walking out of his office, pissed off.

Angelica went to the mini garden in the back of the building. She paced as she tried to calm herself down.

As she passed by the wooden fence to the patio, she overheard male voices. It sounded like Damian and Thad. So, she got closer.

"Calm down, Damian! There's nothing you can do about that. She has a boyfriend…and YOU'RE MARRIED!" Thad shouted.

"Shhhh! I know that, but I still don't like it," said Damian.

"Man, you're acting like a jealous boyfriend or lover. What's up with that?"

Damian hesitated and then told him. "Man, me and Angelica…
in New York, Chicago…we…you know."

"What?"

"We hooked up."

"Aww naw, man!!! I was gonna try to get at her."

"You can't handle that."

"You don't know what I can handle."

"Thad, come on. You're a white boy. That says it all," said Damian laughing.

"My dick is bigger than yours, Mutha Fucker! Ask yo' wife."

"Yeah, in your dreams."

"Whatever, man!"

"Man, she's amazing and her sex game is crazy. I spent $1,500
on her when we went shopping," Damian admitted.

"You did what?" yelled Thad.

"Shhh! I did, man…I did."

Angelica smiled from ear to ear.

"What about Shana?" asked Thad.

"What about her?"

"Man, what are you gonna do about this situation?"

"I don't know, but I have to break Angelica down. She has to
fall madly in love with me and stay with me being married."

"Man, you're stupid! Do you honestly think she's gonna stay
with someone married? She can have anyone she wants…like
me."

"Man, don't even think about fucking her. You hear me?"

"It's not your choice. It's hers."

"She won't fuck you. So, I'm not worried."

"She might."

"Put your money where your mouth is then."

"What are you talking about, Damian?"

"I bet you can't," said Damian confidently.

"I'm not betting you. You're MARRIED!!!"

"Shhh…will you stop saying that?" Damian said getting agitated.

"But it's the truth. You want to bet on someone that's not yours."

"She will be. I'm gonna break her down, if it's the last thing I do."

"Man…she's not having that. You're gonna have to divorce Shana to be with her."

"She mentioned divorce earlier. It kind of freaked me out."

"Why? You usually laugh at females when they say that."

"I know, but it was different with her."

Thad intentionally ruffled Damian's feathers.

"Sounds like you're in a tough spot. I can help you out with Angelica," said Thad laughing.

"BITCH…you're not fucking my girl! Bet $1,000!"

"Calm down, BITCH!!! She's not yours. Besides, I don't think she'll fall for your bullshit. She doesn't need you, Dame. She's not one of those silly ass bitches you're used to messing with."

"That's my Bitch! I'll have her without getting a divorce!"

"Yeah right! I'll fuck her before that happens."

"Is this a bet I hear, Thad?"

"Whatcha talking?" asked Thad giving in to the bet.

"Triple or nothing," said Damian confidently.

"I accept that bet," said Thad shaking on it.

Within a month's time, either Damian would have Angelica wrapped around his finger and still be married or Thad would have sex with her. Whichever came first.

"You won't get none of that pussy. I'll make sure of it," Damian assured Thad.

"This is going to be like talking candy from a baby," said Thad rubbing his hands together.

Angelica's blood was boiling. She couldn't believe her ears. Her and Damian just got back from having the time of their lives. She let her guard down and believed everything he told her. But it turned out to be a game for him. So, she took her head out of the clouds and put her game face on. It was time she pulled out some serious artillery.

She went straight back to Austin's office. She changed her mind about going over. However, when she got there, she overheard Austin ask his assistant, Marla, what her plans were for the evening. She knew what that meant and left.

Angelica was furious. Nothing was going her way. She needed to get out of the building, so she escaped for lunch.

She got on I-77 heading north, made a left off of Exit 25 and drove until she saw some commercial property. Then, she made a right and drove around, eventually parking near a restaurant called Red Rock Cafe.

She entered the restaurant and was seated in a booth. Angelica wasn't that hungry, so she ordered Buffalo wings and a Pepsi.

She sat there thinking about what had just transpired. On one hand, she had Austin who was a chauvinistic male pig. On the other, there was Damian who was a washed up, married player.

Then, she had to laugh. Karma was kicking her in the ass. She made a bet on someone and that same person betted on her. *'No honor amongst thieves'* quickly came to mind.

Angelica's phone rang. It was her friend, Victor. He had impeccable timing.

Victor was a significantly important person in Angelica's life. He was very smart, educated, refined and someone Angelica trusted. When they dated, he introduced her to art, Wall Street, traveling and some of the finer things in life. He taught her how to value herself and know her worth. He even schooled her on men. He taught her how to get what she wanted from them; to never,

ever settle for less; and explained how men think. They eventually became really good friends.

He was convinced that Angelica was the love of his life and would do anything for her, except settle down. Victor absolutely loved women too much for that. This was the reason they weren't together. However, if he were to ever get married, she'd be the one.

Angelica opened up to him about her men issues. She explained everything, including all of the bets. He reminded her of who she was and gave her some really good advice. Then, he told her to go on another shopping spree on him. He knew it would make her feel better. Shopping always made women feel better. That was his philosophy.

Angelica was calm after her phone conversation. Victor reminded her of what she needed to keep in prospective. She was back to her cool, calm, collective self again.

Driving back to the office, she thought about Damian and Austin. Then, she thought about Thad. Thad seemed cool. So, she decided to add him to the equation. She felt it was only right he get his money. Besides, Damian had to learn his lesson about playing with fire.

~Chapter 24~

Angelica and Damian

Damian saw Angelica by the elevator when she returned from lunch. He grabbed her in a non-obvious way and led her down the hall, through the building and next door to the Distribution Center. He took her to a conference room near the file room in the back of the building. He locked the door and kissed her with a hungry urgency.

"Baby, I can't stand it. I miss you," said Damian taking off her panties.

"I miss you, too."

"Baby, I want you for myself."

"I know, Baby…but you know what you have to do," she said innocently.

"Leave him. Leave your man and be with me," he said taking off his pants.

"But Baby…" she faintly said as he made his way in.

"I want you. I need you, Angelica," is all she heard as he pumped away.

Things got very hot and heavy. She removed her dress so it wouldn't smell like sex.

After some serious pounding, Damian came. His body quivered.

"Damn, Baby. You feel so good," he said.

"Thank you."

"Baby, can I come over tonight?" asked Damian.

"I don't know. What time can you get out 'cause I was going out with Thad to have drinks after work," she said lying.

"How about I come with you guys and then go home with you after."

"Ok."

Angelica didn't believe a word he said anymore. Everything that came out of his mouth was a lie, in her opinion. Her only concern was winning the bet. So, she was going to do what she had to in order to collect.

She called Thad once she made it back to her office. He agreed to go out for drinks. He also invited other people to join them, making it a work social.

Angelica made an excuse to go back to Austin's office. She didn't like him thinking about anyone other than her.

On the way, she stopped and asked Cherry to book her flight to Miami for Memorial weekend.

Angelica walked in Austin's office and closed the door. He was sitting at his conference table. She walked up to him and grabbed his penis. She massaged it through his pants, turning him on.

"That's how he better be for me when I grab him," she said in a sexual tone.

"Angelica…come over tonight."

"But I thought you had plans."

"With who?"

"Your assistant."

Austin didn't know what she was talking about. So, she told him what she overheard. He clarified why he asked that question and then realized what she was doing. She came to protect her territory.

"Oh…I see. So, you thought I was going to fuck someone else?" he asked her.

"Yes."

"And you're honest. I like that."

"Why lie?"

"No need. But I thought you were forgetting about me."

"I couldn't do that. You know I like my way with you, especially in the bed."

"As do I."

"Well since my job here is done, I'm gonna go."

"That's fine, but I'm onto your game. You should know that's still my pussy and I'm coming tonight to get what's mine."

"Call first, Darling," she said walking out. "Someone else might be in it."

"Not if you know what's good for you," he said laughing, but serious.

Angelica was glad that things were back to normal. She felt in control again.

Whiskey River in Uptown Charlotte was the meeting spot. Angelica invited all that attended to a tequila shot. After, the rounds of drinks kept coming.

Damian kept looking at Angelica as she sat next to Thad. He noticed her being a little too friendly. He didn't like it, but couldn't say anything. She was just having fun.

Throughout the evening, they texted back and forth right across from one other without anyone suspecting a thing. After a couple of hours, Damian was ready to go.

"Aite y'all. I'm outta here. Everyone have a great evening."

He gave Thad some daps before heading out.

"I'm with you," said a couple of other people.

"Bye," everyone said at staggering times.

"Well, I have to go, too," said Angelica.

"Not yet," said one of the girls from Finance.

"Maybe we can all hang out this weekend," said Angelica.

"Ok."

Angelica asked to speak to Thad alone.

"Hey, so do you want to go out this weekend? Just me and you?"

"Sure."

"No girlfriends to worry about, right?"

"No, ma'am."

"Good 'cause I have big plans for us," she said winking at him.

He smiled as she planted the seed.

As Damian followed her home, she was trying to figure out who she really wanted to be with. However, fate decided for her.

She received a text from Austin saying he couldn't make it. He was still at work. It was like the sound of sweet music. She could handle her business with Damian.

~Chapter 25~

Austin and Angelica

"Miss Angelica," said Cherry.

"Yes, ma'am," said Angelica trying to sound like a Southerner.

"The meeting with Marsh Developers Group has been re-scheduled to 9:00 this morning instead of 10. Also, Mr. Zachary would like to see you. He asked that you bring the information regarding the Virginia and Florida stores."

"Ok. Thank you, Cherry."

As she printed Austin's report, Angelica was glad Friday had arrived. It had been a crazy week with all of the preparations for this meeting. She was so busy she hadn't had time to sex Austin or Damian since Monday.

Austin was standing at Marla's desk when Angelica approached, handing him the information he requested. He briefly reviewed it and asked that Cherry send Marla the electronic file so it could be merged into one document. They were leaving in thirty minutes and it had to be done before then.

Angelica went back to her office with instructions. Cherry immediately sent the file to Marla.

"I've also cleared your calendar for this afternoon per Mr. Zachary," said Cherry.

"Thank you."

She called Damian back, but hung up when Shana walked into her office.

"Hi," said Angelica.

"Hello," said Shana.

"How can I help you? I'm sort of in a hurry," said Angelica gathering her things.

"Well…I must admit I didn't think you had it in you, but you're better than I thought."

"What are you talking about?"

"I'm talking about my husband."

"Aren't I giving you what you want?"

"Yes…you are. I just came to thank you. See, I needed proof of Damian's infidelity. You've given me that by sending those pictures. Now I have a stronger case in court."

"Whatever, Shana. Do what you want with those pictures. I just want my end of the deal when it's all over. Now if you'll excuse me…" said Angelica rushing out of the door.

Several executives from Sportie Fans attended this important meeting scheduled at the Hilton Hotel on J.M. Keynes Drive.

"Austin," said a male's voice as the group entered the hotel.

"Ted. How are you?"

Austin introduced everyone.

Ted was the President of Marsh Developers Group. This Virginia-based software development company was number one on the East Coast. Customizing software for big corporations was their specialty.

They convened in one of the hotel conference rooms where they got down to business. Austin expressed his interest in stream-lining all aspects of the company's software to make it less cumbersome. Ted and his five-member team discussed their list of services, the different ways to incorporate his ideas and suggested some easy fixes. Austin was pleased with the outcome.

The meeting lasted three hours. Afterwards, Ted and his staff left for the airport. Everyone else returned to the office, except Austin and Angelica.

They rode the elevator up to the tenth floor and stopped in front of a door that Austin had the key to.

"Austin…what's going on?" she asked.

Before she knew what was happening, his tongue was down her throat.

"I haven't felt my pussy in so long. I miss her," he said.

"She misses you, too."

He ripped her clothes off and threw her on the bed. He dove head first between her legs. Austin was in rare form as he drove her mad. She was gonna have to starve him more often she thought to herself.

After the second time, they rested.

"Move in with me," he blurted out lying next to her.

"Are you crazy?"

"Why not?"

"We barely get along now. Live with you? Hell no!"

"You mean you don't want to wake up to all of this everyday?"

"You want the truth, Austin?"

"Yes."

Angelica sat up and explained.

She wanted to wake up next to a man that would take care of her physically, emotionally, financially and sexually. She didn't want someone that did a half-ass job. She wanted a husband, a partner, a supporter; not a fuck man that she occasionally had a good time with. She wanted love, depth, intensity and passion in her relationship. Her Prince Charming had to sweep her off of her feet and she had to trust him with her whole heart. She wanted a man she could love for a lifetime like her parents.

"Besides, how can you live with someone you don't love?" she asked.

"Understood," said Austin not pushing the issue.

"But I do need to find a permanent place to live."

"You know where you can stay."

"Thank you, but I'll start looking soon."

Austin wanted more sex. This time, he was very loving and caring. He demonstrated some of that passion she desired and depth by going in deep.

They'd spent all afternoon having sex.

"I'm starving, Austin. You've sucked me dry," teased Angelica.

He looked at his watch and said, "Ok…let's go grab some food."

The Shoppes at University Place was the closest shopping plaza. She ran inside T.J. Maxx to purchase another shirt since Austin ripped hers. Then, they stopped at Panera Bread. They got their food to go because they had an appointment.

"Are you staying with me tonight?" he asked as they drove north on I-77 in his platinum Mercedes Benz CL65 AMG.

"I don't know. I'm supposed to go out," she said thinking about Thad.

"Yeah. I've heard the talk."

"What do you mean?"

"Angelica is so cool. Angelica is so nice. She's this or that. People like you."

"That's good."

"I'm just waiting to hear who you're fucking."

She just laughed.

He exited on Gilead Road and made a left. She watched as commercial property turned into residential homes. As they navigated along a winding road, the homes became more spaced out with trees everywhere. It really looked like the country.

After traveling about three miles, they turned into a subdivision called Tillwell. They drove on a small two-lane street with a grassy median. Angelica could barely see the homes through the plethora of trees.

Austin drove slowly looking for an address. Once he found it, he turned into the driveway. They stopped in front of a massive brick veneer and stone home with a six-car garage off to the side. Angelica couldn't believe what sat behind what she called a forest.

There was a woman standing next to a parked car with a folder in her hand. She walked over and introduced herself. She was Austin's real estate agent, Lina. Lina escorted them inside.

This breathtaking five-bedroom, seven-bath home sat on three acres with over 7,000 square feet of amenities, like a two-story foyer, gorgeous walls of windows, Swarovski crystal chandeliers and exquisite crown molding. And that was just the living room.

The dining room had luxurious wood flooring, partial wainscoting walls and recessed lighting. The kitchen was breathtaking with its rich walnut-stained cabinets, light-colored marble countertops and glass tile backsplash. The secluded master suite had a sitting room, an enormous closet and oversized master bath. Other features were a 6-seat theater, wine cellar and a sunroom. And the backyard had a swimming pool, Jacuzzi and a circled trek deck with a fireplace and seating area.

As they inspected every inch of the house, Angelica's stomach started cramping. It was mild, but annoying.

"So what do you think?" asked Lina.

Angelica loved the home. She pictured herself in it along with the upgrades she'd make. That was until she was told the price tag…$1 million.

Angelica felt more cramping as they drove back towards the highway.

"You ok?" he asked really concerned.

"My stomach keeps cramping. I think my period is about to start."

"I'm taking you home with me. We'll get your car tomorrow," he said going north on I-77 towards his house rather than south towards the office.

She kept asking was he sure about hanging out. She knew there was nothing sexy about a menstrual. But he was sure.

Austin dropped her off in front of his place. He told her where the spare key was and the code to his alarm. She waited inside while he stopped by CVS.

Thad texted her, but she asked for a rain check. She wasn't feeling well. Then, Damian called to check on her. She told him about her period and wished him a good night.

Austin emerged bearing gifts: Tylenol, Advil, Aleve, Pamprin, Midol, Bayer, ThermaCare heat wraps and water caplets. He also had regular and super maxi pads, regular and super tampons, pantyliners, feminine wash, hypo-allergenic intimate wipes, a box of douche and anti-itch cream. He didn't know what she used, so he got them all. He even got some K-Y warming gel, but for a later time.

Angelica couldn't help but laugh at him. It was very sweet, but funny as hell.

She immediately popped two Advil and took a shower. He set a T-shirt and a pair of his sweats on the bed for her. When she came out, she couldn't believe her eyes.

"What's all of this?" asked Angelica.

Austin waited for her to go the bathroom before bringing out the rest of the stuff he bought while he was out. He prepared a buffet spread on the floor.

"I didn't know what you liked during your woman time, so I got food and snacks for any of your cravings."

He bought butter popcorn, Twizzlers, potato chips, nuts, cookies, Goldfish crackers, vanilla pudding, sunflower seeds, trial mix, cereal bars, Combos, Cheez-it crackers, beef jerky, prunes, chocolate-covered pretzels, mints and all sorts of chocolate candy when he went to CVS. Then stopped by Brooklyn Pizzeria and ordered a double meat extra large pizza, chicken wings, garlic knots with Mozzarella cheese and a Pepsi for dinner.

"You did good. Thank you," she said joining him on the floor and kissing him. "But you know I can't eat all of this, right?"

"I know, but I got some stuff I like too," he said smiling.

They ate and then cuddled to watch the movie Friends With Benefits.

~*Chapter 26*~

Back in
Action

Angelica chilled out on the fellas for the week. It was her "me" time as Mother Nature took its course. Yet her and Austin seemed to have gotten closer during this time. They hung a lot.

As a new week began, Angelica came bearing gifts. It was Cherry's birthday, so she planned a special day for her.

Cherry received a bouquet of flowers every hour beginning at eight o'clock in the morning until noon. Each time a bouquet of flowers arrived, Angelica put a gift on her desk. She also treated her to breakfast and bought her a cake.

Angelica went to the break room to get a drink from the vending machine. Damian happened to walk in at the same time for a snack. When he saw her, he couldn't contain himself. He took her by the hand and drug her down the side stairwell to the third floor. There were empty offices in the back. They went in one and locked the door.

"I missed you, Baby," he said rubbing on her breasts.

"I missed you too," she said all over him.

They got partially undressed as Damian sat in a chair holding her legs as she rode him. He was in hog heaven after not being with her for a couple of weeks.

"Angelica, I have something to tell you, but I'm scared," he said afterwards, getting dressed.

"Hablame."

"What does that mean?"

"Talk to me."

He pulled her extra close, hugging her waist. "I love you. I'm in love with you. Like I want to be with you all the time. I think about you all the time. And for the first time, I'm questioning my marriage."

"I love you, too, Sweetheart. I've loved you for a long time," she said catching herself. "I mean since New York. I think I knew then."

Damian told her about his attitude problems and being short with people since he hadn't seen her. Shana even questioned him.

"So, does this mean you want a divorce?" asked Angelica.

"I don't know…maybe. All I know is that I need you in my life."

Angelica seized the opportunity.

"I'm single again. I broke up with my boyfriend for you," she said.

Damian hugged her and got real sentimental. She played along with him.

That afternoon, Thad passed by her office. He extended a dinner invitation after their meeting. She accepted.

Then, Cherry buzzed her because Austin wanted to see her. So, she excused herself and went to his office.

"Angelica, please come in and close the door."

She did as instructed and sat down.

"Do you have a valid passport?" asked Austin.

"Yes."

"Good. Me and you are going to Europe this Saturday."

"Really? Like in five days Saturday?"

"Yes."

"Ok," she said wondering what that was about.

He explained that it was business and pleasure.

They and several other executives were traveling to France and the UK to meet with consultants about opening stores in their respective countries. Everyone was scheduled to arrive on Monday morning. He, on the other hand, wanted to go early to spend some alone time with her.

"Oh my God! Seriously?" she asked elated.

"Yes, but we actually depart on Thursday," he said with a smile on his face.

"Like in three days Thursday?"

"Yes," he said laughing at her.

"But I thought you said Saturday?"

"I said we'd be in Europe on Saturday. But we're leaving sooner than that."

"Ok," said Angelica not even questioning him anymore. "Just let me know when and where you want me."

"Right here…right now."

"Austin!" she said not taking him seriously.

"Will I see you later?"

"Probably not. I have a few conference calls with some of the managers in California and Ohio. Josh is asking for my assistance resolving some issues he's having in his regions. Then, I'm meeting with Thad about IT issues for some of my facilities," she said truthfully.

"Ok. Well tomorrow."

"Definitely."

"Come here," he said wanting a kiss.

She got up and stood next to him. Just as he was going for it, Marla busted through the door.

"Mr. Zachary…oh, I'm sorry. I didn't realize Ms. Zambrano was in here. I'll come back."

"No, please…stay. We're done here right, Mr. Zachary?" asked Angelica winking at him.

"Yes, thank you," he said to Angelica. Then turned to Marla and asked, "What do you need?"

Angelica was ecstatic about the trip. She decided Europe was the perfect place to take Victor up on his shopping spree offer.

~Chapter 27~

Angelica and Thad

After dinner, Angelica invited Thad over to her house for a smoke session.

"You know you got that boy going crazy over you, don't you?" asked Thad laughing.

"Who?"

"Damian."

"You think so?"

"I know so. He was talking about getting a divorce. That's huge for him, but that's what he gets."

"Why do you say that?"

"He was certain you'd fall for him and he'd be able to keep you and Shana both. But now look at him…he doesn't know what to do with himself."

Angelica laughed.

"Angelica…we're cool right? I can talk to you without you acting funny?" asked Thad.

"Yeah."

"Ok…so I'm gonna tell you something, but don't get mad."

Thad told her about the bet between him and Damian. He told her everything she overheard. So, she knew she could trust him 'cause he was telling the truth.

"I already knew," she confessed since they were being honest.

"How?" he asked with a confused look on his face.

She explained how she overheard them talking the day the bet was made. It pissed her off because she had kind of fallen for Damian in New York and Chicago. But after what she heard, she hasn't believed a word out of his mouth since.

"He's not lying to you. He's telling you the truth. It's just Damian acts like a bitch sometimes. He wants to seem all suave with women and then act hard with his boys. He said all that stuff, but I know him. He seriously likes you!"

"He told me he loves me," said Angelica smiling.

"He does."

"Who else knows about us?"

"Just me."

They took their smoking session to the balcony.

"So, how long y'all been friends?" she asked.

"Since he moved back from college."

"And what do you think of Shana?"

"Honestly…I tried to get at her before I knew she was married," he said making them laugh.

"She's a piece of work," said Angelica hitting the blunt.

"You telling me? I know first hand."

"What do you mean?"

"She's fucking my brother, Matt."

"WHAT?!?!?!"

"Yep…" he said hitting the blunt.

"I knew she was fucking someone else! I knew it!"

"Man, she's trifling and my brother is in love with her. But I can't really blame her though. Damian has done her wrong on several occasions."

Thad told their story.

Damian wasn't sure about Shana in the beginning, but married her anyway. Eventually, he fell in love with her. After some time, she became jealous and overbearing. She wouldn't let him breathe. He got fed up with her bullshit.

So one night, they went out to a club and Damian met this woman. She seemed cool and liked Damian. Little did he know, she was crazy. She turned out to be a real nightmare and the reason Shana lost their baby.

"What happened?" asked Angelica into the story.

Shana found out she was eight weeks pregnant. She was going to surprise Damian with the news. That same day, the chick called Shana warning her to stay away from her man. Damian found out, argued with the chick and rushed home to Shana. When he walked through the door, Shana was cursing him out from upstairs. In trying to rush downstairs, she missed a step and tumbled down, losing the baby. She blamed Damian for it.

'So that's what she meant' Angelica thought to herself.

"Damian swore he'd never cheat on her again," said Thad.

"Did he?"

"Yes. He messed around with this girl named Monique, but she was married, too. It lasted about two months. Monique and her husband relocated to Washington DC."

"Did Shana ever find out?"

"No, but she suspected."

"So, now she's ready for a divorce, huh?"

"I guess so. She says she loves Matt and wants to be with him.

She definitely has been spending more time with him lately…ever since you came into the picture."

"Well, do you think she knows it's me?"

"Naw. She doesn't know who it is, but she acts like she doesn't even care."

"Have you said something to him?"

"No. I'm not getting in the middle of it."

"Why? He's your friend."

"I tried telling him something one time. He didn't believe me. So, I left it alone. Besides, I fucked her, too."

Thad told Angelica how he went to Matt's place one night drunk. Matt wasn't there, but he was. They drank some more and he wound up fucking her. The next day, she made excuses about how she thought he was Matt.

"That bitch knew who you were. She just wanted to try you," said Angelica.

"I know. I'm not stupid."

"Dirty Bitch!!! She's so conniving."

"Man, you don't know. Her and Matt are always in this secret room at the office."

"Where?"

Thad told her exactly where it was and then changed the subject.

"So, you know Austin is my best friend, too right?" he asked winking at her.

Angelica just looked at him. "So you know?" she asked.

"Yeah. But it's all good," he said smiling.

Thad asked if he could take a shower and freshen up. She didn't mind and showed him where the bathroom was.

After she heard the water running for a few minutes, she got naked and joined him.

She lusted after him harder than she imagined she would after seeing his body. It was perfectly chiseled. His abs reminded her of Falio's...firm and toned.

She rubbed soap on his back, slightly massaging his shoulder blades. Then, she massaged his chest, embracing all of his per- fectness. Her hands massaged downward until she held his dick in her hands. The myth about white men certainly wasn't true. Thad was equally as big or bigger than what she was used to deal- ing with. The anticipation radiated chills through her body.

With every touch, stroke and pull she performed, he grew bigger and bigger. She kissed his back, arousing him more. Thad made sure he was stretched to the limit. He wanted to satisfy her real good.

"Can I have you?" he turned around and asked.

"Yes," she said with no hesitation.

Thad was truly a lady's man. He handled Angelica with care. Their kisses were passionate and intimate. His touch was gentle, but powerful. The tongue movements he performed on her breasts were electrifying. She came just from that.

Then, she felt like she couldn't breath from the way he licked down on her stomach. It was in knots waiting for the unexpected.

"Lay down and spread your legs," he told her, moving the show- er head over her vagina.

The water rained down on her clit, tickling her until she came. It felt amazing. She couldn't believe she came twice and he hadn't done anything yet.

Thad turned the water off and got out. He reached for her hand and led her to the bed, wet and all. It was time for him to show out.

He spread her legs apart and stuck his smoldering, hot tongue between her lips. He sucked, licked and did tricks that made her grab the bed sheets as she hollered. Then, he slowly penetrated her, asserting all of himself inside. She accidentally scratched him trying to hold on. Thad didn't mind. He was going to have her his way.

He eventually sped things up and gave it to her. Thad made her body react to his while in different positions and slapping her ass. She came multiple times.

"How do you feel?" he asked Angelica after their two-hour session.

"You're bad! I mean like BAD ASS!" she said lying there drained.

He laughed.

"Where in the HELL did you learn to do all of that? Never mind…I don't want to know," she said.

He ran downstairs and got water, the liquor and the blunt.

"I don't do this with everyone," he said climbing back in the bed. "But I knew I had to come correct with you."

They laughed and smoked again.

"To be honest, I wasn't expecting all of that," she said.

"I know," he said laughing.

They talked for about forty-five minutes. Angelica asked Thad not to tell Damian he won the bet just yet. She wanted to wait for the right time. He agreed.

She went in the nightstand, took out a scarf and climbed on top of him. She practically sat on his face as she tied his hands. It was purposely done so he could wet her up some more.

She slid down to his nipples, whirling and twirling her tongue around, making him moan. He quickly rose to the occasion.

She poured rum on his lower stomach, slurping it off of him. The touch of her tongue made him squirm. Then, she licked all the way down to his V, partially tickling him. Thad couldn't take it anymore. He broke his hands free and threw her on her stomach. He wanted to dig deep from behind. He demonstrated more of his skills as he unleashed his wrath. Thad knew he was bad for a white boy.

~Chapter 28~

Atlanta

Austin called Angelica.

"Are you ready?"

"Yes."

"Come down."

"Ok."

It was 5:00 p.m. on Thursday evening and they were headed to the airport.

When she got downstairs, Angelica wasn't expecting to see Austin standing next to a black Rolls Royce Phantom with a dozen of red roses in his hand.

"Thank you," she said accepting the flowers.

"You're welcome," he said helping her inside the car.

He poured them each a glass of champagne as she lit the weed pipe.

Angelica wasn't sure what Austin was up to, but she promised herself she wouldn't ruin it. Austin had been different lately, so she was going to let her guard down. She would avoid sarcasm at all cost and try to conquer his heart. She was determined to break down his walls, even if it meant being submissive.

The car parked next to a Cessna CJ4. Austin got out first and then assisted Angelica since she had the roses in her hand. They boarded the private jet. Next stop…Atlanta, GA.

The plane arrived to Dekalb-Peachtree Airport in about an hour. A white Bentley GTC Convertible drove up as they parked. Inside were another dozen of red roses.

Austin had a car rental company meet him at the airport with the vehicle. He signed the necessary paperwork and left.

"Thank you for my roses," said Angelica.

"You're welcome," he said smiling.

Austin drove to his condo in the Sovereign Tower on Peachtree Road. It was the tallest building and the most elaborate, architectural-designed high-rise in Buckhead. His three-bedroom, three-bath unit was on the 42nd floor and exhibited fine living. There were tall ceilings, imported wood flooring, travertine backsplashes, signature cabinetry and a panoramic view of the city.

When they walked inside, there were dozens of red roses.

"Are you trying to get in my panties?" she asked jokingly because of everything he'd done thus far.

"Yes," he said laughing.

"Well…it's working."

She set her roses down and threw her arms around him. She melted as they kissed passionately. Being submissive was going to be easy if he kept this up.

Minutes later, he said, "Come on. I have a surprise for you."

Austin sent someone a text message as they headed for the elevator.

"Where are we going?" she asked excitedly.

"You'll see," he said taking her by the hand.

They exited on the ground floor. Despite everything being closed, they continued walking until they saw a beautiful, white woman with long blonde hair and a tall, sexy black man standing in front of a store called Sasha Elise.

"Devin Williams!" said a surprised Angelica when she saw him.

"Angelica Zambrano!" said Devin copying her excitement, giving her a hug.

Angelica was surprised he knew who she was.

"This is my wife, Sasha," said Devin introducing them.

"It's so nice to finally meet you," said Sasha giving her a hug too.

Devin was Austin's best friend and former NFL colleague. He stood 6'1", brown skinned, slanted brown eyes with a short fade. This 34-year old wide receiver for the Atlanta Eagles had a goatee and devilish smile.

The fashionable, blonde-haired woman with him was Sasha Vaughn-Williams. She was 32 years old, stood 5'8" with clear blue eyes, a petite frame and killer smile. She was a cross between Charlize Theron and Amber Leigh Lancaster.

Sasha's boutique, Sasha Elise, carried high-end, exclusive designer brands, like Gucci, Prada and Vera Wang. It carried men and women's clothing and accessories. Sasha also had her own couture and lingerie line in the store. Devin's line was coming soon.

Sasha guided Angelica through the store selecting items for her special dinner date with Austin. Austin grabbed a couple of things, too. Then, Angelica got ready at Sasha and Devin's place while the fellas went to Austin's.

Sasha and Devin lived on the 45th floor of the same building. Their unit was a plush and spacious four-bedroom, four-bath condo similar to Austin's. The exception was the Italian marble flooring, colored natural stone and a custom made kitchen.

Angelica had Sasha pegged all wrong. Angelica thought Sasha was this sophisticated, snooty female trying to get along with her to make Austin happy. But she wasn't like that at all. Sasha was really down to Earth, funny and caring. She made Angelica feel very comfortable.

As they talked about Austin, Sasha gave Angelica some insider information. She asked Angelica to be patient. Austin really was a nice guy. He just hadn't had the best luck in love.

Meanwhile upstairs, the fellas gossiped.

"DAMN, Man!!! She's BAD!" affirmed Devin.

"Yes, she is and she's different. She doesn't care who I am or who I used to be," said Austin.

"That's cool."

"I mean she speaks her mind, quick to cuss me out and doesn't hold back. She's this feisty, spicy, gorgeous Cuban woman that fights with me and I love it," said Austin getting excited.

"Have you told her about any of your plans?"

"No. Everything is a surprise."

"All I can say is you must really like her."

"I do and I'm gonna show her just how much."

It was almost 8:00 p.m. and time for Austin to pick up his date.

"Wow…you're truly beautiful," said Austin when he saw her.

Angelica was stunning! She wore a Sasha original. It was a very sexy and revealing red dress with a plunging neckline, center split and open back that flowed into a cascading train. She wore red Giuseppe Zanotti rhinestone-encrusted, ankle-strapped heels, platinum diamond earrings and a three-diamond cuff bracelet. Her hair was up in a neat high bun and her makeup was flawless with bright, red lipstick.

"Thank you. You look nice as well," Angelica told Austin.

Austin was in a black Prada suit with a black shirt, red tie and red handkerchief. He sparkled with a diamond watch, bracelet and ring. He was freshly shaved and smelling good.

"You're missing something," said Austin opening a black velvet jewelry box. It was a single-strand diamond necklace with over twenty carats. She covered her mouth in shock as he fastened it around her neck.

He escorted her to the roof for a breathtaking candlelight dinner on the Sky Terrace.

"This is beautiful," said Angelica with such emotion.

The entire terrace twinkled and sparkled as every tree and shrub was covered in outdoor tree lights. The crystal chandeliers hanging from the trees and multitudes of candles heightened the elegance. A fresh black tablecloth with champagne and many more candles adorned the table. A saxophonist belted out soothing tunes. There was even a uniformed server and bartender. It was like a fairytale.

They started with mussels in white wine with shallots, cream and parsley. Next, their garden salads were topped with bleu cheese, walnuts and apples. Angelica had the braised lamb shank with dried apricots and candied ginger. Austin had cracked pepper crusted beef tenderloins cooked with brandied cream mushrooms.

The night was perfect, but not over. Austin had another surprise for her.

Around 10:00 p.m., they drove down the street to Miami Circle NE. They stopped in front of Piner Fine Art Gallery. Angelica couldn't believe he remembered how much she loved art. She anxiously went inside.

A middle-aged white woman named Gabrielle greeted them as they walked through the door.

"Knock yourself out," he whispered in her ear, treating her to whatever she wanted.

As they maneuvered around the building, Angelica rambled on

and on about artists such as Kim Frohsin, Rebecca Kinkead and Kim Schuessler. Austin listened as she praised their artwork. But all he kept thinking about was how beautiful she looked and how his surprise made her happy.

An hour later, she ended up with thirteen pieces of artwork, including Jeff Cohen, Mark Perlman and Ryan Coleman.

He had one more surprise for her. They drove to another nearby gallery, Katy Kegan Art Gallery. A brown-haired woman named Ana patiently awaited their arrival.

Angelica did the same thing and picked out whatever she wanted.

She ended with eleven pieces of artwork, including some from Frank d'Antignac, John Michael Torino and Gustavo Torres.

Angelica was so happy. So, she felt it was only right to return the favor.

She didn't say a word when they got back to his place. She simply untied the dress and let it fall to the floor. Austin had no complaints as she stood there in red heels and diamond jewelry. He picked her up and carried her to the bedroom. Angelica treated Austin like never before.

The next morning, they smoked and got real high before ordering food from the restaurant downstairs.

"Babe…our flight to Paris leaves at 6:00 this evening. So we have to be there by 5," said Austin.

"What about clothes?"

"I know," was all he said.

So, she didn't say another word.

They munched out on breakfast. Then, they went to Phipps Plaza Mall and Lenox Square Mall, which were right across the street from one another. He told her to buy a few things, but not too much. After all, they were going to the fashion empire of the world.

They made it to the airport on time. They pulled up next to a white Falcon 900EX. A representative from the rental car company was there to receive the Bentley before they left.

~Chapter 29~

Paris

Austin and Angelica landed in the City for Lovers…PARIS!
Between the time difference and flight time, they arrived at 8:30 a.m. Saturday morning.

Austin had big plans for Angelica on this trip. He felt it was time to show her the real him. It was the perfect opportunity to open up, reveal his true feelings and throw lots of money around. She'd have the best, be treated like a queen and be catered to at all times when they weren't working. He spared no expense.

Austin rented a silver and black 1962 Maybach as their transportation around the city until Monday. It picked them up from the airport and took them to their prestigious hotel.

When Angelica stepped out of the car, she was instantly reminded of the final episode of Sex in the City when Carrie went to Paris with "The Russian".

They were staying at the Hotel Plaza Athénée on Avenue Montaigne. Its signature red awnings and red geranium flower boxes fancied each window. The lobby was just as elegant and royal in person as it was on TV with gold embellishments, decorative marble floors, large crystal chandeliers and an Art Deco wrought iron staircase.

Austin specifically chose this hotel because it resided on the most famous shopping avenue with luxury boutiques in walking distance. It was also located between the Avenue des Champs Elysées and the Eiffel Tower. Ultimately, this five-star luxury hotel was said to be very romantic and Austin was all about the romance.

He reserved the Eiffel Tower Suite, which was known for its spectacular view of the Eiffel Tower through the large living room window. But there was more beauty to this signature suite. It was spacious and lavishly decorated in a classical Parisian theme with a color palette of pinks, silver grays and golds. There were tall ceilings with decorative crown molding, Victorian-style furniture and beautiful crystal chandeliers throughout the rooms. There was even a baby grand piano in the sitting area. It was phenomenal!

"It's so beautiful," said Angelica after touring the suite.

"I thought you'd like it."

Angelica opened her bag and retrieved her marijuana. She wasted no time in smoking. There was no way she'd be in Paris and not be high. So, they smoked out on the balcony and took in the sights.

She was already feeling the love as Austin led her to the bedroom. There was nothing like morning sex in the "City of Love" while being zooted.

"So, I was thinking…we could grab some breakfast, do a little sightseeing and go shopping," said Austin.

"I love the way you think," said Angelica kissing him.

The hotel's restaurant offered an American version of breakfast. Their Continental breakfast consisted of croissants with butter and marmalade, coffee and freshly squeezed juice. It was accompanied with eggs (any style), choice of bacon or sausage and a serving of yogurt.

Angelica had an omelet with sausage, mushrooms and tomatoes. Austin ordered the same, but with both meats.

After breakfast, he escorted her outside the hotel.

"I have another surprise for you," said Austin as they stood next to the car.

"Ok…what is it?"

"An all-expense paid shopping excursion," he said inter-locking her arm with his as they walked.

"What do you mean?"

"We must shop in Paris," he said in a girly voice imitating Sasha. They both laughed.

He told her how he reached out to Sasha for help. She gave him some good ideas and mentioned that he had to shop big while there.

"So we're going to walk this entire avenue with the car following us so that we can buy whatever we want and as much as we want," he said.

"You paid to have a Maybach follow us as we walk and shop?"

"Yes. We can't carry everything."

Angelica jumped in his arms, hugging and kissing him.

"Who are you?" she asked teasing.

"Your Prince Charming," he said winking at her.

They walked all the way down to Chez Francois restaurant. Then, they turned around and shopped on the other side. They went into practically every shop, beginning at Valentino and ending at Gucci.

Austin planned a relaxing and entertaining evening. They were having dinner at Le Jules Vernes restaurant in the Eiffel Tower, touring Paris by boat and taking in a Moulin Rouge show.

Angelica wore a white shimmery gown by Dolce & Gabbana, crystal-embellished Jimmy Choo heels, Harry Winston platinum drop earrings and a black 3/4 length Chinchilla coat.

Austin wore Salvatore Ferragamo from head to toe and his jewelry was from Harry Winston as well.

Le Jules Vernes was a very cozy and romantic place to dine. Dim lighting, gourmet cuisine and the remarkable window view of the city made it worth every penny.

Angelica asked Austin about his relationship with Sasha as she ate her poached blue lobster. He explained a little of Devin and Sasha's story as he dined on pan-seared beef tournedos.

Devin and Sasha were friends first. They met at a football game about ten year ago when Devin and Austin played for the Carolina Cardinals. Sasha's family was from North Carolina and her brother was also his best friend. So, she went to the games quite often. Devin liked her cause she was into cars, football and riding motorcycles. But Sasha saw through his womanizing ways and wasn't interested.

Fast forward five years…she finally gave him a chance. Sasha felt they'd matured and she was always Devin's biggest supporter. He realized that when he got cut from the Cardinals and went to Atlanta. She moved with him without asking questions, never doubted him and stayed by his side not knowing what the future held. They've been together ever since.

"You know whose sister she is, don't you?" asked Austin.

"No."

"Thad's."

"Vaughn-Williams," said Angelica recognizing the name.

"Thad and Sasha were always at my games. That's where Devin first saw her. But she's a little fireball that doesn't take crap."

"At first, I thought she was one of those fake white women living off of her husband…"

"No!" exclaimed Austin laughing. "Sasha would fight you if she heard you say that. She's not like that at all. She's really sweet and caring, but raised with boys. So, she likes what the boys like and knows how to hold her own."

"Yeah, I noticed that she was cool when we were in Atlanta. She made me feel really comfortable and she adores you."

"She's like my sister. We've been there for one another. Devin slightly fucked up and I've gotten fucked over," said Austin getting quiet. "But she's about to blow up. Her clothing and lingerie lines are about to hit mainstream. She's working on Devin's clothing line now. And she's opening a boutique in Charlotte soon. So, things are going well for them."

They finished dinner and went to meet their group for the "Tour of Paris" boat ride. They departed from the Eiffel Tower to embark on a two and half hour tour around the Seine River showcasing sights like Notre Dame Cathedral, Musee du Louvre, Musee d'Orsay, Assemblée Nationale and Hotel des Invalides.

"So what happened?" asked Angelica hugged up to him.

"What are you talking about?" asked Austin.

"Who hurt you? Or fucked you over as you so eloquently put it earlier?" she asked making him chuckle.

"My fiancée, Lacey. She left me when I got hurt and retired. She thought I was going to blow my money and not have shit since I wasn't playing anymore."

"I'm sorry to hear that. Have you seen or heard from her again?"

"When I made my first million with the store. I went to her and still tried to make it work. I told her my plans for the stores and she laughed at me. That's when I found out it was all about the Benjamins. She told me it wasn't the same kind of money as NFL and the endorsements. So, she dismissed me. But payback was sweet."

"What do you mean?" asked Angelica.

"I saw her last year in Atlanta. Devin and I were at a club and she was sweatin' me hard. I didn't pay her much attention though. I was with another chick. But she kept coming at me. She heard how well I was doing and all of a sudden wanted me back."

"I hope you didn't fall for that bullshit."

"No, but that night I took her back to my mansion that I had at the time. I fucked the shit out of her and wore dat ass out. Then, called her a cab and told her to find her way home," he said laughing.

"Why do guys always think sex fixes things or is the sweetest revenge?"

"Cause it does! And it is!" he said laughing. "It's a guy thing. Women will never understand."

"Try me."

"It's not really about the sex…although it's an added bonus and an excuse to get that ass one last time. It's about power over the person that had power over you. At one point in time, she had control over me. I was up her butt chasing her hard. But I wasn't good enough. Now…it was different. I treated her however I wanted to, and didn't care about her feelings or fall for her tricks. It was about the exchange of power. I needed to see if she still had control over me. She didn't. She had no affect on me what so ever. So, I got my closure and it was over."

"So then you became a hoe?"

"Honestly….yes. I figured chicks wanted cash and I wanted ass. So, I gave a little, they gave a little. Even exchange. And if I wanted to be bothered, I would be. If I didn't, I wouldn't. If I wanted to be nice, I would be. If I wanted a late night booty call, I would have that too. The choice was mine and I promised myself to never let another woman do that to me."

"I understand, but not all women are the same. Yet you treat every one of us like we are," said Angelica.

"You have to remember something. I was in the limelight all the time. My face is known and people still want a piece of me. Women throw their panties, phone numbers, ass, you name it at me. None have shown me that they're any different. Then, you come along. I knew you weren't like the others when you recited my stats to me the first night we met. And I couldn't believe it when you threw my credit card back at me that night," said Austin making Angelica snicker. "You talk back. You don't care who I am or used to be. You look at me as a person…a man, not a trophy or a bank."

"You are a person."

"I know, but I haven't always been treated that way."

Angelica understood Austin better after their emotional conversation.

The last activity for the night was the world-renowned Moulin Rouge Show at the most legendary cabaret. The hour long show was filled with original music, beautiful women, sequin, feathered costumes and stage settings with lots of color, glitz and glam.

That night, they made passionate and sexy love. Austin stayed close to Angelica. He was gentle and soft. He got to know every inch of her body.

He rolled on top of her and swept her hair away from her face. He got really close and whispered, "I love you and don't want to ever let you go." She looked at him with watery eyes and replied, "I love you, too and don't let me go."

The next day, Austin got Angelica up early to go to Spa Dior. Their shop-weary feet could use the rejuvenation considering what was still on the itinerary.

Austin was taking her shopping again. This time, they were headed towards Avenue des Champs Elysées. They started at the Arc de Triomphe and visited each side of the avenue. They drove down Rue du Faub Saint-Honoré and visited Place Vendôme. They shopped at stores like Elie Saab, Stefano Ricci, Givenchy, Christian Louboutin and Missoni. They also snacked on foods like Chouquettes, chocolate-filled croissants, apple tarts and a variety of crepes.

Angelica felt the magic. She was with the man she loved, doing what she loved. She blamed it on Paris.

~*Chapter 30*~

London
Thursday

Austin and Angelica were finally alone again early Thursday afternoon.

Monday and Tuesday were extremely busy days in Paris. The staff came in and it was business as usual. Tuesday evening they flew to London for their meetings on Wednesday and Thursday. Everyone left on Thursday.

Austin rented a silver Rolls Royce Phantom to pick them up from the Sheraton Heathrow Hotel and drive them to the Mandarin Oriental Hotel Hyde Park. Once again, Austin planned to spoil his queen.

He reserved the 3-bedroom Royal Suite. It was elegant and chic with a contemporary style that had a color palette of creams, golds and powder blues. This spacious suite had stylish details ranging from Romanoff wall designs and a marble fireplace to beautiful double-tiered crystal chandeliers and decorative wall mold-ings. The master bedroom had a large walk-in closet, the master bath had a steam room and there was a private bar. The balcony wrapped around the entire suite overlooking Hyde Park. But the best part was that guests could purchase any of the artwork dis-played throughout the suite. Austin did good again.

"I can get used to you spoiling me like this. You better watch out," said Angelica as she looked around.

"Good 'cause I could get used to spoiling you," said Austin hug-ging her.

"You say that now..."

"I know what I'm getting myself into," he said kissing her. "Come on...we have to go."

As they rode down Knightsbridge, Angelica admired the city. She gazed out at the buildings, stores, double-decker buses, peo-ple and Hyde Park. She looked at everything.

They made their way to Old Bond Street. Austin asked the driv-er to wait while they went inside Georg Jensen.

"More shopping?" she asked.

"Yes...jewelry shopping," he said with a smile.

Angelica perked up assuming they were ring shopping.

They entered several stores, like De Grisogono, Asprey and Chopard, purchasing jewelry. They continued down to Van Cleef & Arpels. But there were two specific jewelry stores he wanted to visit.

The first one was Graff Jewellers. He had her try on some en-gagement rings.

"This one is really pretty," she said holding out her hand.

Austin requested to see others, but he didn't purchase any. In-stead, he bought an exquisite heart diamond necklace and the matching diamond earrings.

The second store was Harry Winston. He had her try on more

engagement rings. Again, he purchased jewelry, no engagement ring.

They continued down the rest of the street to Moussaieff, Chaumet and Tiffany & Co. He had her try on a few more rings, but nothing popped out at him.

"Austin, why do you have me trying on all of these rings?" she curiously asked.

But he didn't respond. He just winked at her as other jewelry was purchased.

They finished up at Chatila and Rolex. However, she saw Prada, Gucci, Dolce & Gabbana and Alexander McQueen and had to stop.

After leaving the Jewelry District, there was one more place he wanted to take her. The driver passed their hotel and stopped a couple blocks down at Harrods.

Harrods was the most famous, upscale department store in Europe. It was also the largest with over 200 departments inside. This iconic Edwardian building located on Brompton Road sat on more than four acres of land and carried items from clothing, shoes and fragrances to produce, household items and pets. Needless to say, they shopped again.

When they returned to the hotel, they stopped by the restaurant for a bite to eat. They were starved. Then, they went to their suite to smoke and relax.

"I have a big day planned for us tomorrow," said Austin.

"More shopping?"

"No."

"Ok."

She didn't ever think she'd be shopped out, but she was.

~Chapter 31~

London
Friday

Austin woke Angelica up around 9:00 a.m. They got dressed and went to the airport. They boarded a private jet for an hour flight to Amsterdam.

He rented a black stretch limo to take them to a well-known area where pretty much anything went, the Red Light District. It consisted of sex shops, peep shows, prostitution and coffeeshops where marijuana could be purchased and smoked.

They stopped in front of a four-story brick building with a tan awning that said "GreenHouse City Coffeeshop". It was located along the Haarlemmer Straat. This spot supposedly had the best cannabis in Amsterdam. That was where they wanted to be.

They walked in with the anticipation of trying different kinds. They started with some Haze Weed. Then tried Hydro Weed and Exotic Hash. They sat at a corner table getting high as hell.

"You know…I saw that female looking at you like she wanted to jump your bones," said Angelica talking about work.

"Who?"

"Gloria."

"Gloria who?"

"The female consultant that we met with."

"I saw her, but she doesn't matter. Baby, she can look all she want, but I belong to you," he said looking at her.

"You sure about that?"

"Yes."

"Ok," she said kissing him.

By this time, the munchies had kicked in and they were ready to eat. And although the coffeeshop sold food, they wanted something different. So, they asked around and heard lots of suggestions. They decided to try somewhere else.

Austin told the limo driver to drive around. Although he was hungry for food, he was feeling frisky and wanted to eat Angelica out in the back of the limo first. It felt so intense from being so high. Once she came, she pleasured him. He held her hair as she sucked him up. Austin trembled as he popped. It felt amazing and was the best head he'd ever had, according to him.

They stopped at the Pancake Bakery. Breakfast food sounded really good…or they were just high.

Angelica got an omelet with bacon, cheese, tomatoes, mushrooms and spinach with a side of apple and banana pancakes. Austin got an omelet with bacon, ham, onions, cheese and tomatoes with a side of Grand Marnier pancakes.

Angelica told Austin about an exclusive member's only club in London. Claudia became a member after she attended two years ago. It was supposed to be like nothing they'd ever seen before. He was willing to go, if they could get in. So, Angelica called Claudia. Because it was last minute, she would have to pull some strings to get them added onto the guest list, which was by invitation only.

They spent the next two hours in the Van Gogh Museum, which housed a collection of his paintings. They visited both buildings and bought several keepsakes from the gift shop.

It was almost time to go back to London. So, they stopped at another coffeeshop to get real high before flying back.

As they rode back to the hotel, Angelica received a text message from Claudia confirming their invitation to the club. She sent all of the information they'd need in order to get in. Claudia also told her how to dress. These two lovebirds had an exciting night ahead of them.

The club was called The Platform. It was an affluent adult partier's paradise. Another world existed in this 20,000 square foot, five-story building located in Soho Square.

The exterior of the building looked like an ordinary steel and brick building with tinted windows. But the inside…that was where it all went down.

Angelica walked in on Austin's arm wearing a floor length, white mink coat. He wore an Armani suit.

"Hello and good evening," said a tall white man with a British accent.

"Good evening," they both said.

"Code name, please."

Angelica gave him the code Claudia texted her.

There were two doors behind the host, one straight ahead and one to the left. They were asked to go to the left and wait for their female attendant, who immediately approached them.

She handed them a glass of champagne as they were asked to sign confidentiality statements. It protected everyone in the club.

Next, they went to the cashier's booth where they were issued gold club cards with their choice of lanyard. Austin's credit card was linked to these gold cards. This was the only way to pay for anything in the club. He would receive an itemized receipt for all products and services rendered at the end of the night.

Last, they were required to leave all personal belongings in a mini storage closet that locked. No purses, cell phones, coats or other electronic devices were allowed inside. The only two items they could carry were the gold card and the closet key, which went on the lanyard provided. They were searched and wanded before entering to make certain they followed the rules.

Angelica wore a black strapless, see-through lace dress with a skimpy gold thong that barely covered anything. She had on gold Louboutin heels with gold and diamond jewelry. So she couldn't hide much anyway and Austin left his suit jacket in the closet.

As they walked into the lounge area, a woman approached them and escorted them to a table where she explained the operation of the club. She also explained the available drugs, services and entertainment for the night, but these luxuries didn't come cheap.

After selecting their services, Austin swiped his card to pay for them. Then, the woman attached another key to his lanyard. She also reminded them that they could add other services at any time throughout the night.

Austin and Angelica were led to a drug kiosk by the elevator. They received a complimentary drug of their choice for the services selected. Angelica chose the strongest strain of cannabis.

Once they entered the elevator, the door closed behind them. Then, another door on the opposite side opened. What they saw was incredible.

The first floor was known as the Blue Room because the entire room was lit up in blue. There were blue ceiling lights and spotlights that reflected against the walls. Also, there were twinkling blue lights centered on the stage area that featured a stripper pole.

As they stepped into the room a little further, the stench of marijuana radiated across the room and clouds of smoke blurred their vision. They could hardly see the drug kiosks that sat in every corner and the S & M stations all around.

As they smoked, they walked around checking things out. People were everywhere doing whatever they wanted to the bass of the music. Waiters and waitresses served drinks in the nude. People were snorting cocaine, smoking weed and doing the drug of their choice on the blue sofas around the stage. Nude staff members performed private dances or were having sex on the blue-colored booths lined against a wall. And women were with other women, men were with other men and couples were with other couples on the beds covered in blue satin sheets that lined another wall. It was just one huge orgy and anyone could join in for the right price.

"This is some crazy shit," said Austin.

"I know," said Angelica winking at him.

Austin and Angelica explored every floor. It was pretty much the same way, with the exception of the room color. The second floor was green, the third was purple and the fourth floor was the psychedelic floor. It was predominantly white with rotating, colorful lights everywhere for those rolling on X.

The fifth floor was their destination spot. This was the Red Room where everything was decorated in red.

They sat in the lounge area smoking more weed and getting higher, if it were possible. Then, they went to their room.

Austin used the key he received to open a door to a 15' x 15' space with tinted windows and a movable, wooden harness. This harness had straps to tie hands and feet and metal handles on the sides for climbing.

Austin took off his clothes and then undressed Angelica. He fastened her to the harness and then blindfolded her.

He began by feverishly kissing her and pulling on her nipples.

Angelica's hips started moving. Austin knew she wanted more. So, he wet two of his fingers and slid them inside of her, fingering her. She went wild as he sucked on her breasts. After she came, he tilted the harness back and climbed on top of her. He wanted his dick sucked and Angelica obliged.

As she choked on chocolate, she felt a mouth spread her lower lips apart. "Suck it…eat that pussy," was all she heard Austin say. So, she knew it wasn't him, but didn't care. It felt so good. Not long after, she came again.

Austin got up. Seconds later, Angelica felt the harness spread apart, widening her legs further. She felt her clit being rubbed on as a giant dick penetrated. Then, she felt a presence over her sucking on her breasts. Angelica quickly realized it was another woman when the woman's strawberry flavored pussy touched her lips. She just went with the flow.

"Ay, Papi…qué rico," came out of Angelica's mouth as she was getting piped down. "Dámelo, Papi…así…duro!" purred Angelica wanting that dick deep inside of her, begging for more. She wanted it rough and fast to make her cum. So, Austin pounded her guts. Angelica kept screaming Austin's name. She guessed right 'cause Austin wasn't letting anyone other than him tap that ass.

After she came multiple times, it was Austin's turn. She restrained him to the harness and blindfolded him.

Angelica began by whirling her tongue around his cock. She sucked and pulled on him trying to stretch him as far as he could go. His hips moved like crazy. She crept down to his nuts and hummed with them in her mouth. This really drove him mad.

"Oh yes, Baby! Right there! YES!" screamed Austin wanting more.

Then, she stopped. He heard the clacking sound against the metal. He knew someone was climbing up the handles on the harness.

"Suck it," said Angelica.

Angelica climbed up the harness and sat on his face. She wanted to feel the hotness of his tongue licking on her. At the same time, a warm, wet hole began sliding up and down on his dick. It moved faster with every moan he let out. This made Angelica gyrate faster on his face as he was being sexed harder. He wanted to get loose to fuck the person back real good, but it wasn't happening. Angelica was in control and would have it her way.

Angelica climbed down after she came. Austin heard the click of a bottle cap open. Suddenly, he felt a cold liquid gel being poured on his dick. After a few strokes, he felt a warmer, tighter hole. It slowly moved up and down until his dick was all in. Then she went buck wild, making him go crazy. His moans got louder as Angelica talked nasty. But he didn't know it was because another man entered the room and was pleasuring her.

After Austin came, everyone left and he was freed. He couldn't believe how down Angelica was. This made him more attracted to her. He wasn't letting her go.

They got more refreshments and did whatever they wanted to do.

Their phenomenal sexual experience ended at 4:00 a.m. when it closed. They only had five hours to sleep before heading back the States.

~Chapter 32~

New Position

Angelica walked into the office Monday morning exhilarated and full of smiles.

"Good morning, Cherry," sang Angelica.

"Good morning, Miss Angelica. Are you ok?"

"I'm fabulous!" raved Angelica.

Angelica had a fantastic week. She was lost in love and on cloud nine.

Cherry followed her into her office as she normally would. She updated her on everything that went on while she was away. She gave Angelica all her messages and went over her schedule.

Angelica received a phone call from Marla. Austin called an emergency meeting with his executive staff. He had an important announcement to make.

"I called this meeting for two reasons. First, I've created a new position…Sr Vice President of Human Resources. This position will oversee all aspects of HR in the U.S. and Europe. Also, the incumbent will report directly to me. Marla will e-mail the application instructions to those interested. It will be open for two weeks. However, I'd like those that are interested to email your names to Marla by this afternoon. With the upcoming expansion, I plan to move quickly on my decision," said Austin receiving questions. Then said, "And the second reason is to inform you that the consultants from Europe will be here in a couple of weeks. More information to follow. Thank you."

After the meeting, Austin asked Angelica to stay. He needed to discuss business. However, he was dry, churlish and back to his normal arrogant self, as if the "I love you's" they shared never happened. This pissed Angelica off. She wondered what kind of game he was playing.

Damian invited Angelica to lunch and she accepted. They went to Olive Garden by Northlake Mall.

"I saw this and thought of you. I missed you so much," he said handing her a diamond bracelet with a pink butterfly on it.

"Thank you. It's nice. And I missed you too, Baby," she said sounding dreadful.

"Damn, Baby. It doesn't sound like it. What's wrong?"

After some hesitation, she said, "I have something to tell you." She wanted to come clean about her feelings for Austin. Even though she was mad at him, the feelings were there.

"What is it?"

Just as she was about to spill it, his phone rang. There was an emergency at work and he had to get back. So, they got their meal to go, but he promised to go by her place later to talk.

Angelica went back to her office. She thought about Austin and his behavior. She figured it was because of work, but was annoyed at how quick-tempered he was towards her.

Then, she thought about Damian. She had to figure out what to do with him. She kind of lost all momentum for him.

She stopped thinking about the men in her life and emailed Marla her name for the new position. Marla immediately emailed her back with the instructions and required action items that she'd have to present.

Angelica got started right away. She walked over to the Distribution Center to get ideas for one of the action items. As she looked around, she heard sex moans coming from the other side of the back wall. She remembered the room Thad told her about where Shana and Matt meet for their rendezvous.

She peeped around the corner and couldn't really see anything. Then, she saw them through an open blind. Matt had his back to her, but she liked how he handled Shana. With one swift move, Angelica saw his profile. She was amazed at how big he was too. Thad and his brother were well endowed for some white boys. She recorded their session giving her some ammunition.

After work, Angelica was walking to her car when Austin drove up on the side of her.

"Get in," he said unlocking the car door.

"And he speaks," she said a little irritated.

Austin tried talking to Angelica during the car ride, but she was short with him. So for the most part, they rode in silence. He wondered what was wrong with her.

"What are we doing here, Austin?" she asked as they drove up the driveway to the house in the Tillwell subdivision in Huntersville.

Austin didn't say a word. He just escorted her inside.

This beautiful home was hers. He had all of her desired renovations and upgrades done while they were away and all of the artwork he purchased while in Atlanta were displayed throughout the house.

"Here, Sweetheart…these are yours," he said handing her the keys.

"I can't believe you did this," she said hugging him so tight.

"I love you."

"I love you, too," she said kissing him all over his face.

Then, he led her to the garage. There was a white Benz SL500 sitting inside.

"Do you like it?" he asked.

"Do you really have to ask?" she said excitedly sitting in the car.

"I knew you needed your own place and I knew you liked this house, so I got it for you. I took the liberty of having it decorated. Everything is in your name. The paperwork is in the kitchen drawer," explained Austin.

As she listened to him, Angelica remembered why she was mad at him. She couldn't figure him out. So, she just walked away.

"What's wrong?" he asked stopping her in the kitchen, confused about her reaction.

"You!"

"What did I do?"

"You bring me here and give me all this stuff, yet you don't say two nice words to me at the office today. You were rude, mean and acted like you didn't give a fuck about us," she said fuming.

"Angelica…Sweetheart," he calmly said. "I apologize if I came across that way, but I was trying to make sure I showed no emotion towards you. In light of recent events, we can't be associated as a couple. I knew you were going to apply for the new position. In fact, I was counting on it. I need someone like you over my HR Department. I primarily had you in mind when I created it. You've proven yourself time and time again. But I'd hate for you to be prohibited or possibly disqualified from applying because of our relationship."

"I understand and you're correct. But where's the communication, Austin? I knew we couldn't be all over each other, but I didn't think we'd go back to how it was when we first met."

"Well, maybe you took it that way 'cause you looo…ovvv…ve me," teased Austin, making her crack a smile. "Sweetheart, I wouldn't go out of my way for you if I didn't give a fuck about you. I meant everything I said when we were away. Again, I apologize if I was harsh with you today, but it's hard on me, too. Now I have to be aware of my behavior at work. I don't want to raise suspicions about us. I have to watch myself and what people see."

Angelica understood and agreed to keep their relationship hush-hush for now.

"I know what's wrong with you," he said seating her on top of the kitchen counter. He lifted her skirt and removed her panties as he gave her second pair of lips mouth-to-mouth resuscitation.

Afterwards, he took a shower for a meeting he had to attend. He opened his garment bag and took out a suit. He got dressed, sprayed some smell good and brushed his teeth.

"Where are you going?" she asked curiously.

"I have somewhere I need to be."

"Mmm Huh" muttered Angelica kind of jealous 'cause she didn't get any dick.

"I'll see you tomorrow, Dear. Love you," he said giving her a kiss.

"Love you, too."

"Enjoy looking around the house," he said smiling.

That's exactly what she did. She walked around her new house cheesin'. She couldn't believe what Austin had done. Everything surpassed her expectations, especially the placement of her artwork. She really had her own house.

Damian texted that he'd be at the condo in an hour. She wasn't sure she wanted him over, but knew she had to deal with the situation. So, she left in her new Benz.

~Chapter 33~

Damian's Decision

Angelica was on South College Street, heading towards the EpiCentre. She was picking up dinner on her way to the condo. There was a lot of commotion in front of the Charlotte Plaza. So, she went around the cars that were holding up traffic. As she passed by, she saw Austin's car in the middle of that commotion. So, she got back over and parked at the very front of the street. It was the only open space available. She looked in her rear view mirror trying to get a glimpse, but couldn't see anything. So, she got out and stood on the side of a building, peeking around the corner.

A beautiful older woman got out of Austin's car. She didn't think anything of it until the woman kissed him on the mouth. He didn't pull away either. He actually kissed her back and held her by the waist as they went inside. She assumed they were going to

Royce's Restaurant. Angelica couldn't believe it. She was highly pissed off.

She was so mad that she skipped dinner and drove back to the apartment in tears. Her eyes were so watery she could barely see. She was so angry that she cursed him out in English and Spanish. She didn't know what to think anymore. He professed his love, took her on those trips, bought her a house and a car and introduced her to his best friends. Then, he leaves her for another woman. She couldn't understand.

As she sat in her parking spot, it hit her. Austin was never going to change. She believed he liked her, but not enough to settle down. He wasn't ready to be with just one woman. This was hurtful and disappointing.

Twenty minutes later, there was a knock at her door.

"Hi," she said answering the door for Damian.

"Hi. I brought dinner," he said waving food in front of her.

"Great."

Angelica wasn't that hungry. She was too upset. Instead, she grabbed her pipe and went to the balcony. Damian followed her.

"So are you gonna tell me what's wrong?" he asked as she smoked.

"Just have a lot on my mind," she said avoiding the question.

"Babe, talk to me."

"Damian, why are you here? What do you seriously want besides sex?"

"Whoa…wait a minute! Where's all of this coming from?"

"Don't you think I deserve someone to love me and just me? Someone I don't have to share?"

"Yes, you do."

"That's where all of this is coming from. I want to be the only woman a man loves. I'm enough."

Angelica took something out on Damian that was meant for

Austin, but she couldn't help it. She was speaking from a hurt place. However, it made Damian feel compelled to explain himself.

"Angelica…I never lied to you about Shana. I've been honest with you since the very beginning. But I will admit you're the first woman that I've opened up to…that I actually think about more than my wife. I want you so bad that I don't want to be home anymore. Ever since we've been together, she doesn't satisfy me."

"I bet."

"I don't mean just sexually. I mean she doesn't put a smile on my face, I don't want to share anything with her and I don't desire her anymore. It's getting to a point where I want to leave."

"Do you trust your wife?"

"I don't know."

"What do you mean?"

"I mean I'm not sure. I think she's capable of messing around with someone to pay me back for cheating on her, but I haven't seen it. Who knows…she probably has."

"So why stay?" asked Angelica.

"Because I cheated and have a guilty conscious. Besides, it's easier."

"That's stupid."

"Maybe…but it's easier to stay and deal with the bullshit I'm used to dealing with rather than dealing with new bullshit."

"That's such a cope out."

"Let's be realistic. You never know what you're gonna get when you start messing around with someone new. The first few months…everything is great. The relationship is great. Sex is great. Women put on a front. Afterwards, they show their ass and it gets bad. So at least I know what I'm dealing with if I stay."

"I agree. Women work to get a man and then stop working once they have him. Then, they wonder why men cheat."

"Exactly!"

"But you still shouldn't cheat. Just be single and do all of that stuff."

"It's not that easy, Angelica. There's a lot invested when two people get married. You can't just walk away."

"Well cheating isn't the answer either."

"It's not. But if a man cheats, he usually cheats up or nasty."

"What's that?"

"Usually a man will find someone more accomplished, more beautiful or more of something than his wife to cheat up with. He's not going to cheat with someone like her. He can stay home for that."

"Ok," said Angelica.

"Now the cheat nasty is when a guy has the best, but she won't get nasty sexually. She acts too classy for the stuff he wants or just won't do it. So, he gets him a ghetto girl, a stripper or someone like that to be downright nasty with," he said animating slapping a girl's butt.

Angelica laughed and then said, "Listen…I get that. But do you know how many times I've heard married men say they want to leave their wives, but won't because it's easier to stay. So, these good men are ruined by these witches. It pisses me off. I don't understand why a man wants to live in misery rather than be happy."

"That's because you've never been married. No one prepares you for after the honeymoon. The normal, routine life," said Damian.

"I don't agree. I think it's more work to keep a spouse, not less."

"It's true, but most women don't understand that."

"It's not just women though…men, too."

"You're right."

"Men stop the gifts, the flowers, the compliments 'cause now they're too busy working or cheating with the nasty girl," said Angelica laughing.

"You're right."

Then she asked the question, "So which one am I?"

"BOTH! Girl…you're definitely a cheat up and a cheat nasty!" he said standing up animating sexing her.

Angelica busted out laughing.

She felt a lot better. Damian made her completely forget about Austin. He made her laugh so hard that she couldn't stay angry. Besides, she wasn't really mad at him.

Angelica got up and fixed their plates. Then went back out onto the balcony.

"So tell me about your ring," said Angelica.

Damian's great-grandfather gave his grandfather a ring that symbolized strength, courage and determination. This ring survived slavery, racism, war, cancer…you name it. It also had an inscription inside: *A scared man is a weak man.* He didn't believe men were made to be afraid and fearful of other men. "Only fear God" was his motto.

When he passed away, the ring was given to Damian's father. He decided to replicate it for each of his boys and his uncles did the same for their sons. It was a reminder to overcome struggles and fears through strength and courage. It was something held in high honor amongst the men in his family.

"Touching story," said Angelica.

Damian even got teary-eyed, realizing something as he told the story.

"You know what?" he said.

"What?"

"If I truly believe in myself, I can't be afraid to let go. I have to do what's in my heart. I can't care about losing material possessions. I can get those back. It's about what I'll gain and that's you. I choose you Angelica."

"What do you mean?"

"I'm staying here with you tonight and every other night you'll have me. I'm not going to be afraid to go after what I want anymore. I'm gonna ask Shana for the divorce tomorrow. There's no sense in waiting. Things haven't been good between us for a while. You're my happiness and I don't want you to have part of me. I want you to have all of me."

Angelica laughed, but not in a cruel way. It was cute.

"Damian, you're sweet. But the truth is that you're still married and we can't walk around like you're not. We still have to be careful. I don't want the rumors at work. Besides, don't get a divorce because of me. Do it for you. Do it even if you could never be with me again. Have the strength and courage to do the things you want to do."

"I don't get women! I make a choice and still get pushed away," said Damian irritated.

"I'm not pushing you away, but your situation won't be over in a day."

"I know, but at least I made the choice. That's the hardest part. Now, I just have to show you."

"Come here," she said holding out her hand.

Angelica kissed him passionately. Then said, "Do whatever you want. I'll be here." She was calling his bluff.

They had sex all night like it was their first time again. The feelings for Damian were still there.

~Chapter 34~

Busy day for Angelica

There was tension flying around the building by the end of the week. Shana and Damian had been arguing in Shana's office, Cherry was pissed about her male friend and school and Austin hadn't seen Angelica since he showed her the house.

Austin barged through her door and said in a low, but aggressive tone, "You're coming over tonight!"

"No, I'm not. I have to finish packing. The movers are coming tomorrow."

"Maybe you didn't hear me clearly. I expect you at my house at 7:00 tonight. And you better be there!"

"Excuse me…" she started to say, but he left.

Angelica was numb and indifferent to his antics. She was emotionless, so that little incident didn't bother her. She had a plan and refused to let him or anyone else deter her from it.

Twenty minutes later, Damian came rushing into her office.

"I need to talk to you," he said angrily.

"What's up?"

"Why does it seem like you're avoiding me? I tell you I want to be with you and I don't hear from you the rest of the week."

Angelica didn't say a word. She calmly got up, locked her door and closed the blinds. She pushed him against the door and engrossed him with her delicious kisses. His hands touched her back, pulling her closer to him. She slid her hand down his chest and unzipped his pants. He took deep breaths, anticipating her next move. With his pants around his ankles, she began massaging his dick. All of his anger left the building. He rocked his hips back and forth, engaging in the foreplay.

All of a sudden, there was a knock at her door.

"Angelica…its Shana."

Damian couldn't believe his luck.

"Give me a sec," she yelled as she fixed herself.

Damian hid behind a partial wall that was behind the door.

"Hey Girl. You ready for our 11:00?" asked Shana standing at the door.

"No. I need to push it back to this afternoon…like 1, if you don't mind. My boss is on his way down right now. There was some kind of an emergency."

"Ok. Just call me when you're finished."

"Ok…thanks."

Cherry looked at her confused. Max wasn't on his way down. Then, it hit her. Damian was still in her office. She just shook her head at Angelica. Angelica winked at her and locked the door.

She got completely undressed and stood in front of Damian in her birthday suit. His clothes were off just as fast.

"You're so beautiful," he said kissing her.

Angelica wrapped her legs around Damian as he picked her up

to sex in the corner. She was wet and warm just like he liked her.

"Baby, this is what I needed," he said lustfully in her ear.

"I know, Baby. And I'm gonna feed my dick," she whispered back.

"It's yours, Baby. It's all yours."

"It better be."

Angelica threw that thang at him, showing no mercy. Damian was lovin' it. Then, they heard Austin's voice.

"Cherry…is Angelica available?" he asked.

"No, sir. She's on a very important call with Florida. I know because I transferred the call myself," she said nervously and saying too much.

"Well, I need to speak to her. It'll only take a minute," he said reaching for the doorknob.

"Mr. Zachary…Wait! Sorry for yelling, but I have these very important documents that need your signature," said Cherry stopping him from trying to go in.

Cherry went line by line explaining. He wound up taking the documents with him and asking Cherry to have Angelica call him once she was available.

Angelica and Damian, on the other hand, continued doing the nasty. They actually moved from the corner to her desk. Austin didn't stop a thing.

"Am I going to see you tonight?" asked Damian, as they got dressed.

"Probably not. I have to finish packing. The movers are coming tomorrow."

"I can't wait to see your new house."

"It's beautiful."

Damian put his arms around her waist.

"Angelica talk to me. What's going on with you? Why are you dodging me?"

"Honestly, I've been busy doing what's required for the new position. But Damian, I'm trying to let you do what you need to do. I'm not going to hound you or pressure you. I'm giving you space to handle your business like you said you would. I need to see what you're truly about."

"So what does that mean? I can't see you or we can't talk until then?"

"No. We can talk…I mean we have to. We can even hang out. But the sex stops now until you're ready for me."

Damian didn't like it, but understood. This gave him more of an incentive to resolve his issues.

Angelica called Cherry into her office after Damian left. She thanked her for what she did with Austin. Cherry admitted she was nervous, but wanted to hear all the juicy details. Angelica confided in her. She told her about their trip to Philly, New York and Chicago. This was Angelica's chance to see if Cherry would talk.

However, Angelica really needed someone to talk to that she trusted and knew her situation. So, she invited Thad to lunch.

"Thad, are we good?" asked Angelica checking to make sure he was okay after what happened between them.

"Yeah…we're straight. I know the deal with us. I'm cool," he said smiling. "I just can't wait to collect," he said laughing.

Angelica laughed and said, "Soon." After a slight pause, she asked, "Can I talk to you about Damian and Austin?"

Thad didn't mind.

First, she told him about Damian and asked his advice. Thad was very honest with her. Damian really loved Angelica and had every intention of leaving Shana. Nonetheless, he was still married and would be for a while. Getting a divorce was a process and it wasn't looking pretty between them, especially since Shana was being evil with splitting the marital assets.

Then, she talked about Austin. She commented on what happened earlier in the week regarding the other woman he was with. Thad knew who she was talking about and told her it wasn't what she thought. It looked bad for Austin, but he was actually cleaning house. She should be patient with him and forgiving. He loved her and thought he was the better choice.

"So, how about the night Damian stayed with you…I was over his house with Shana," said Thad laughing.

"What?" yelled Angelica. "Damian told her he was with you. Is that why they've been arguing?"

"Man, I told you she was no good. That's part of it. She knew before I went that he was with someone else and not with me."

"So, why did you go?"

"She said it was important. When I got there, she was in lingerie and looking nice. We started drinking and one thing led to another and…"

"I don't get it. If she loves your brother, why is she after you?"

"Have you ever heard of Steve Vaughn, the Pro Golf Player?" asked Thad.

"Yeah…he was the best. He recently retired."

"That's my father."

"Damn!!!!"

"Yeah. And I know you've heard of Dana Taylor?"

"Yep! Who hasn't? She was the famous model."

"Yes…well, that's my mom. She goes by Dana Vaughn now."

"She's an interior designer now. She has that show on cable."

"Yes…well, my point is Shana smelled money and dug her claws into Matt since I wasn't having it."

"She tried you too?" questioned Angelica.

"She tried me first, but Damian was my boy. I couldn't do that to him, even though I fucked her a few times. But what she's trying to do is make sure she doesn't go without when things go down with Damian. You know she slipped and told me about the divorce papers she already had drawn up."

"Did you tell Damian?"

"No. But after she told me where they were, I moved them. I put them in his dresser drawer like she was trying to hide them. He found them the next morning."

"So, that's why they've been fighting so much lately."

"Yeah and she's trying to take him to the cleaners while digging into Matt. But I'm not letting that shit happen to either one of them."

Angelica still didn't mention the bet between her and Shana.

"Speaking of siblings, I met your sister," said Angelica.

"I know. She told me. She really likes you and thinks you're the perfect one for Austin. That's all she talks about."

As Thad continued talking, he gave her more ammunition without even knowing. He also mentioned how obsessed Shana was about the Tennessee property.

Angelica went to Shana's office that afternoon for her meeting. They strategized and went over numbers for Angelica's project ideas.

Afterwards, Angelica wanted to update Shana on her progress. So, she showed her the video of Damian spending $1,500 in Chicago and let her hear the voice recording of him telling her he loves her.

"Two down…two to go," said Angelica.

"You're good."

"I told you. In fact, I warned you."

"Well, this means I just need to hurry up with my plans," said Shana being arrogant.

"Oh you mean this…" said Angelica showing her the video of her and Matt.

Shana looked dumbfounded.

"Oh I know all about you and him. I know who Matt is and who his parents are. I know you're trying to dig your grubby claws into him to make sure he takes care of your financial needs after Damian."

"Who told you…Thad?" asked Shana.

"Thad knows, too?" yelled Angelica acting shocked. "So, your husband's best friend knows and hasn't said a word to Damian? Wow! That's fucked up!" She slightly paused and then said, "No, it wasn't Thad. I found out about his parents on the Internet. It's a tell-all resource. Besides, I'm having him investigated. I know you. You'll go with anyone who gives up a dollar…and I mean a dollar," she said lying about the Internet. She didn't want Shana suspecting Thad told her anything.

"You're such a BITCH!"

"Tomato…tomoto. Minor details."

"What do you want?"

"Leave Damian alone and change the stipulations of the divorce. He leaves with equal or more than you. He's worked his ass off all these years too and deserves something besides an ex trifling ass wife."

Shana assumed Damian told her and had nothing further to say. So Angelica left.

~Chapter 35~

Over Angelica's

Ding Dong.

"Didn't I tell you to be at my place at 7:00!" yelled Austin barging his way through Angelica's door.

"And I told you I had to finish packing!"

"What the FUCK is your problem? What kind of games are you playing?" exclaimed Austin heated.

"I'm not playing any games, ASSHOLE!" she said walking towards the kitchen.

"Now I'm the asshole?" he asked following her.

"Yes, you are!"

Austin grabbed her and said, "Was this a joke to you? Was your master plan to fuck me over?"

Angelica reached in the kitchen drawer and grabbed her Glock 9. She pointed it dead in his face and said, "Let this be the last fuckin' time you think about putting your hands on me."

Austin immediately let her go. "It's not loaded," he said being cocky.

She grabbed the magazine and inserted it. "It is now."

Austin stopped fooling around with her. He saw a look in her eyes.

"Stop playing, Angelica. Put that thing away. I just want to talk."

"Now you want to talk…and I'm not the one playing games! I wasn't the one that bought me a house, a new car and ate my pussy before going on a date with another woman!"

Austin didn't say another word and calmed down.

"I saw you that night after you left me. You were at the Charlotte Tower in Uptown with an older, beautiful woman. I saw her kiss you and you kissed her back. Then, grabbed her by the waist and went inside. So don't fucking come over here talking about playing games when you crushed me…You FUCKIN' ASS-HOLE!!!"

Austin put his head down. He had no idea she saw that.

"And before you think I was following you, I wasn't. I stayed at the new house for a while looking around. Then, I decided to pick up dinner at the EpiCentre on my way here. As I was going around traffic, there you were with that woman. So, I parked and got out. I wasn't going to think the worst of you at first. She could've been anyone. But then when I saw all of the kissing and touching, I was sick to my stomach."

"Angelica…I'm sorry. I'm so sorry. Please…you have to forgive me."

"No, Austin…I don't and I won't. We just had the time of our lives. You opened up to me, you told me you loved me and that you wanted to be with me. And not even 24 hours later you're with another woman. So no! I don't have to."

"It wasn't what you think. I didn't sleep with her. I didn't do anything with her. I actually broke it off with her. That's what that dinner was about."

"It didn't look like it to me."

"It's the truth."

Austin had been dealing with this older woman for a while. They were really good friends aside from lovers. He told Angelica the truth about what the other woman meant to him and explained that what she saw was their normal behavior. That was until he broke it off with her. She cursed him out in the restaurant and threw a drink at him. He even had to pay for the dishes she broke.

"It's whatever, Austin. I've decided to concentrate on me and what I want, like getting this new position. You can do whatever you want."

"No! Angelica…you can't do this! We've come too far."

"You did this Austin! You! I was perfectly willing to give us a fair chance! But now I don't trust you...again! Now my walls are back up! And to tell you the truth...you don't deserve me!" she said tearing.

"Baby, please…" he said hugging her. "Don't do this to us. I swear I didn't do anything. And I promise I was trying to make things right. I was trying to do right by you and get rid of all of my female friends that I'd been dealing with. I want you and only you…I want only us."

"You should've told me," she said breaking free and lighting a blunt.

"I was trying to do it on my own. I was trying to prove to you how serious I am about this relationship."

She stayed quiet and just looked at him. Then said, "That's why Paris and London were so great. You didn't worry about people. It was just us. You held my hand, took me sightseeing and ate lunch in public. No rules or restrictions. Freedom!"

"I'm not ashamed of you, if that's what you're getting at."

"I don't care anymore, Austin."

Austin heard and understood every word she said.

"How do I make it better? How do I fix it?"

"I don't know."

"Please look at me," he said softly turning her face towards him. "I love you and I promise I'm looking out for us. The only reason I haven't screamed that I'm in love with you from rooftops is because of work. I know how hard you've been working. But if you don't want that, please let me know. I'll withdraw your name right now and announce us to the world."

She was tired of hearing that same story, even though she knew it was true.

Austin continued, "Sweetheart…you also have to remember that we agreed early on that our private and professional lives would be separate."

"You know what, Austin? You don't get it. Something inside of you should've clicked to where you didn't want to act your normal way with her. I should've come to mind…something," said Angelica.

"Baby, I'm sorry. I was just thinking hurry up and tell her so I can get it over with."

"I'm tired of love coming into my life with strings attached. It doesn't seem like it can ever just be. There's something that prevents it from fully blossoming into this great experience that I know it to be."

"I understand. But you tell me what you want. If you want the position, this is how it has to be for now. If not…Baby we can do all kinds of PDA in the office, in the car, at the mall, wherever. But it's your decision. Tell me what you want and I'll do it."

Angelica thought about what Thad said earlier. She trusted

Thad.

"I don't want you to do anything. Just leave things alone. I guess it'll work itself out."

"I'm not with anyone else, Sweetheart. I've spent this week getting rid of what doesn't fit into my new life with you."

She wanted to believe him.

"Let's go," he said.

"Where?"

"Does it matter?"

"No."

"So, you'll go anywhere with me?" he asked expecting sarcasm.

"Yes."

"Why?"

"Because I know you'll take care of me."

Austin grinned from ear to ear. He loved her response and she was right.

They went to a restaurant in Uptown. They walked in holding hands. He knew he had to prove himself.

He spent the next two hours making her laugh and trying to get back into her good graces.

When they got back to her place, they smoked and finished packing. They didn't have sex.

~Chapter 36~

Consultants Arrive

It was Wednesday morning and Austin scheduled a tour of the facility for his international guests. The European consultants arrived on Monday and were headed back to Paris that evening. They had a rigorous couple of days with back-to-back meetings hashing out details and cost. Business had gone well so far and Austin was pleased with the results.

It was also the day Angelica was going back to Miami for Memorial weekend. She was planning to leave work early.

All of the executives joined Austin on the tour. The very friendly female consultant, Gloria, had her arm securely wrapped around Austin's as they walked through the Distribution Center. She enjoyed flirting with him. Angelica didn't say much because she figured Austin was being polite, but she was getting tired of the closeness and the hand touching.

Two hours later, they all met in a conference room one last time. Business was finalized and contracts were signed. It was time to celebrate over lunch.

Austin reserved a private room at Chapman's Restaurant. Gloria sat next to Austin as everyone was seated. She placed her hand on his lap, being fresh and he went along with it. However, Angelica was done. She excused herself and apologized for leaving so abruptly, but she had a plane to catch.

Austin caught her outside before she left.

"Hey!" he yelled.

"What?"

"What's with the attitude?"

"I'm tired of watching her flirt with you and you not saying anything about it. I get you want the deal, but at what cost?" she asked getting in the car. "Have fun. I'm out," she said driving off in her Benz.

She was mad at Austin, so she called Damian.

"Baby, come to my house. I want to see you before I leave," she said disregarding what she said previously.

"I thought your plane left at 5?"

"It does."

"I'll try to come, but I have a 2:00 meeting."

"Forget it, Damian. I'll see you when I get back," she said and hung up the phone.

Angelica took her anger out on Damian once again when the person she was really mad at was Austin. She didn't mean to. That's just the way it was.

She made it home by 12:30 that afternoon. She started smoking to calm her nerves. She blasted some music that made her get pumped about her trip. After a few hits and a few songs, she was excited. She was going back home and got into "fuck it" mode. She buried all feelings for everybody in a matter of seconds and thought about herself. She was going to let loose and be wild.

As she got out of the shower, she heard the doorbell. It was Damian. She answered the door wearing a towel.

"Why do you do that, Angelica? Why are you so impatient with me?" he asked mad.

She didn't say anything. She just walked back towards her room.

She dropped the towel and tried putting her clothes on, but he kept snatching them away. So, she answered his question.

"Because I want what I want when I want it."

"I didn't appreciate you hanging up on me."

She didn't have a care in the world. She was high and in a different mindset.

However, Damian couldn't stay mad at her for long as he lusted after her body.

"The reason I said that was because I was trying to surprise you. I bought you a gift."

He handed her a jewelry box. She passed him the blunt as she opened it. It was a gold chain with a cross pendant. It was nice.

"Thank you, Baby. And I'm sorry," she said giving him a kiss.

"I took the afternoon off to take you to the airport."

"I got the car service to come get me."

"Cancel it."

"Ok."

With her back to him, he put the chain around her neck. Then, he kissed her neck and played with her breasts. Her head rested on his shoulder as she became aroused.

"Baby, I expect you to have some decisions made by the time I get back," she said.

"Ok."

He kissed her all the way to the bed. He laid her down and ate her pussy real good. He wanted to make sure she thought about him while she was away. And he knew he was succeeding when she started talking in Spanish. But then, she pulled out some tricks of her own while having sex, making him beg for more. He even got a little aggressive, grabbing her hair and slapping her ass.

After their moment of passion, it was time to go. Damian put her carry-on in the car while she checked to make sure she had everything. She checked her wallet for her license, credit cards and cash. She couldn't find her license. She emptied her purse, checked her bedroom and both cars, but couldn't find it.

Then, she recalled leaving it in the top drawer of her desk. She called Cherry to confirm it was there. It was.

"Baby, I'm gonna miss you," said Damian as they drove to the office for a quick pit stop.

"I'm gonna miss you, too. And don't be fucking your wife."

"I can't even think about her after what you just did. Girl, you got my brain all twisted."

Angelica giggled innocently. "I just want you to know what you have."

"Shit! I can't forget."

Damian stopped in front of the corporate building while she ran upstairs. He didn't care who saw them.

"Thank you, Cherry," said Angelica as Cherry handed her her license.

"You're welcome, Miss Angelica. Have fun."

"I will," said Angelica leaving. "Have a great weekend!"

She went towards Austin's office to say good-bye. She was partially over the whole Gloria thing.

"Austin…I just wanted…" she started to say, but couldn't finish after what she saw. "Sorry. Have a great weekend," she said slamming his door shut.

"Angelica!!! Wait!!!" he hollered.

By the time he opened the door, she was gone.

Once again, Austin was caught kissing another woman…Gloria. And even though she could tell Gloria was all over him, he did nothing to stop it.

Angelica didn't get mad. She loved on Damian more and thought about Miami.

Damian stopped at Cookout before taking her to the airport. She wanted a chicken strip tray with Cajun fries and a corndog. She also wanted one of their world-famous milkshakes, strawberry cheesecake.

He parked in front of the terminal and helped her with her suitcase.

"Here…open it on the plane," said Damian handing her a little box.

"Ok."

They kissed before she walked off.

As she boarded the plane, her phone rang. It was Austin. She turned it off. She wasn't dealing with him.

She sat in her seat and opened the box Damian gave her. It was a picture of them from their trip in Chicago with a card. Inside the card was a letter expressing his feelings. Angelica smiled after reading it. It was sweet, but she wasn't trying to hear none of that. She was ready to be back home.

~Chapter 37~

Miami

"I'm in Miami Bitchhhhhh!!!!"

Angelica excitedly recited the words to LMAFO's song as she drove south on US-1 from Fort Lauderdale airport in her rental car. She was back home and pumped up. Her first stop was her parents' house in Hollywood.

"Fuck you, Bitch!" yelled Angelica to a woman who cut her off. The woman flipped her the bird, so Angelica flipped her off in return. She forgot just how rude people were in Miami. They were always in a hurry to go nowhere. But she loved her town and being there made her realize just how much she missed home.

She turned right on N 14th Avenue and then made a left on Fillmore Street. She drove up to her parents' home and jumped out of the car.

"Mami, papi, abuelita, abuelito…" she yelled walking through the door. "I'm here!"

"Angelica?" said her dad, Alfredo, with a strong Spanish accent.

"Si, papi. It's me!"

She ran into the kitchen and hugged him. She kissed him so many times on his forehead, cheeks and nose.

"Ay mija, I missed you so much," said Alfredo almost in tears.

"I missed you too, papi," she said hugging him tighter. Once she let go, she noticed some changes. "Mami changed the curtains, didn't she?"

"Yes, you know your mother."

Her parents lived in a stunning two-story, six-bedroom home located in Hollywood Lakes. They recently renovated and finished all of the upgrades, including new tile floors; a gourmet kitchen with granite countertops, coffered ceiling and black appliances; a new roof; stone and concrete exterior with a concrete driveway; and a refinished pool.

"And what's abuela cooking? It smells so good in here," said Angelica lifting the lid off the pot.

"Ropa vieja con arroz blanco y tostones," replied her dad.

Traditionally, Latin grandmothers liked to cook. So, they were often in the kitchen cooking for their children, no matter the age. So, Angelica's grandmother wasn't any different. She had the house filled with the aroma of a traditional Cuban dish, ropa vieja. It was flank steak shredded and cooked in tomato sauce with vegetables like onions, bell peppers, peas and topped with pimentos. It was usually served with white rice and in this case, fried green plantains.

"Where is mami? At the hospital?" asked Angelica.

"Yes, but she should be here any minute. She can't wait to see you."

Her mom worked as a head nurse at Joe DiMaggio Children's Hospital. She has worked there ever since Angelica can remember.

"Where is everyone?"

"They're out back."

As she passed through the family room and the sun room, she heard music coming from their backyard.

The backyard was their little oasis with large palm trees, a jungle gym/swing set in the corner of the patio attached to a tree house and an outdoor BBQ area. And there was still plenty of room for entertaining.

"Familia!!" yelled Angelica busting through the back door.

Everyone yelled and cheered when they saw her. She saw plenty of people back there, too. It was her three sisters, Falio with about ten of his friends, Colin and his best friend and the kids: Nina, Angelo and Ricky. Nina was Asila's daughter and Angelo and Ricky were Falio and Ariana's two sons.

Angelica went around greeting everyone the usual Spanish way…with hugs and kisses. She glanced at Falio and it was like life entered the atmosphere. Ariana hated it.

"Sis…I missed you," said Asila.

"I missed you too, lil' sis."

Then, Angelica screamed as Falio snatched her up from behind and swung her around. He hugged her so tight.

"I need you to come by my place after we leave here," she whispered in his ear.

"I'm already there," he said nodding, putting her down.

Angelica played with all of the kids chasing them around, tickling them. She had Nina and Angelo pinned to the ground. Ricky came up from behind trying to get her, but Falio grabbed him and tickled him. They were all playing together.

"Mija!!!" yelled her mother, Alicia, at the back door.

Angelica ran to her and hugged her tight. Tears fell from both of their faces. Angelica missed her mom so much.

They all sat outside updating Angelica on what had been happening in Miami.

Alfredo's business was doing well. He was a pharmacist with his own pharmacy across the street from Joe DiMaggio Children's Hospital. Her mom was up for another promotion. Falio bought his mom a bigger house in West Miramar. Asila was still struggling and having problems with Nina's father. And Alina got engaged over her birthday weekend.

"Let me see," Angelica said to Alina referring to her engagement ring. "It's beautiful."

"Thank you," said Alina smiling.

Colin purchased Alina a 7-carat diamond platinum ring. The center stone was a flawless 5-carat Princess cut diamond with smaller round diamonds surrounding it. The band had rows of diamonds on each side.

"And thank you for my birthday trip. Aruba was very romantic and special," she said wiggling her ring finger.

"You're welcome. I'm still sorry I wasn't here."

"You made up for it big time, so no worries," said Alina hugging Angelica. Then, Angelica hugged Colin and congratulated him.

Colin Mendoza was dreamy. He was Alina's 29 year-old Cuban fiancé that stood 5'11", seductive brown eyes and short black hair that he wore slicked back. His smile was perfect with the deepest dimples ever. His body was incredibly fit and lean, but muscular with great abs. He was model perfect and was often mistaken for Mario Lopez.

Next, Angelica updated them on everything going on with her. She told them about the new position she was trying to get and showed them pictures of her new house and new car.

Then, she told Asila to think about going back to Charlotte with her. A fresh start was what she needed and could give Nina a better quality of life.

Last, they talked about Nina's birthday. She was turning three on Memorial Day, but Asila was celebrating it on Sunday because Angelica had to get back to Charlotte.

"Why didn't you tell me? I would've sent you money," said Angelica.

"You already do enough by sending us money every week."

"So! You can still ask me."

"Yeah, but he should be doing something for his daughter."

"Fuck him!"

Angelica was pissed because Asila hadn't planned very much for Nina. She was waiting on her sorry ass baby daddy to give her some money, but he hadn't come through yet. So, Angelica took care of everything and suggested having a huge party in their parents' backyard. There was plenty of space for a bounce house, cotton candy machine, sno cone machine and buffet tables filled with all kinds of food.

"Nina! Come here, Mama," said Angelica.

Nina came walking.

"I missed you."

"I miss you," said Nina in toddler talk.

"You have a birthday coming up."

Nina nodded.

"Who do you like Mama? You like Dora? Or Tinkerbell? Little Mermaid?" asked Angelica.

"Little Mermaid," she whispered being silly.

"Then, you're gonna have the best Little Mermaid party ever," she told Nina giving her a kiss and squeezing her tight.

"Tomorrow we're gonna do everything for the party, Asila. Ok?" said Angelica.

"Ok. What time 'cause I have school in the morning."

"You know me. I'm going out tonight. So, probably around 2 or 3 in the afternoon."

"Ok.

"So, tonight…design the best Little Mermaid party you can dream of. Write down everything you want. I mean everything! I'll call Marina now and have her meet us here after you get out of school."

"Ok."

Angelica called her friend, Marina, who was one of Miami's top party planners. She had an impeccable reputation and was popular amongst the famous. Her work was amazing and she could transform anything to life.

"Ok. All set. She'll be here tomorrow at 2. I told her the theme, so she'll bring all of her ideas and I'll pay for it tomorrow," said Angelica.

Asila hugged her sister so tight. She was so grateful for Angelica and Angelica knew it. That was the reason she helped her with everything.

Angelica loved all three of her sisters. They all had weird but mostly functional relationships.

Asila was the baby. She was 24 years old and stood 5'8" with long, straight chestnut brown hair, blue eyes and full lips. She was a little like Angelica with her feistiness. But overall, she was the sweetheart. She always tried to see the good in everybody and didn't like confrontations. She was all about love and romance, however it seemed like men used her because she was so caring. That was the reason Angelica was so protective of her. Asila didn't have anyone taking care of her like the other two. So, Angelica and Asila were the closest because Angelica felt she needed the most guidance.

Alina was 26 years old, 5'9" with green eyes. She had long, straight black hair with a burgundy tint and was the sadity sister. Her friends were mostly white and she hung out with the most prominent people in town. Her dream job was being a lawyer, which was why Angelica helped pay for her education. Like

Angelica, she loved the finer things in life and considered herself upper class. When it came to men, she refused to end up like Ariana. No man would control her, rule her or treat her any kind of way. She was a bit of a hard ass and could hold her own, which Angelica admired about her.

Ariana was 28 years old and stood 5'8" with blue eyes and long, black hair like Angelica's. Ariana wanted so badly to be like Angelica, but didn't want to work. She wanted everything handed to her, so living that life came with a price. She had everything she wanted except a husband who loved her.

All of the sisters had bad ass bodies, booties and were in shape. They got it from their mama.

"Mami, papi…I'll see you tomorrow. I have people to see and parties to attend," said Angelica giving her parents a hug and a kiss.

"Mija, be careful," said Alicia.

"I will. Bye y'all. See you later," she yelled.

She ran and kissed all the kids. Then, she looked at Falio. He nodded. He knew what that meant.

~Chapter 38~

Home Sweet Home

Angelica finally made it home. She missed her place so much and couldn't wait to get inside. But she went to Claudia's first.

'Charlotte is making me sappy' she thought to herself as she knocked on her door. They screamed and hugged once they saw each other.

They went to Angelica's place to catch up. She told Claudia everything, including what Austin did again.

Just then, Austin called. She didn't pick up. She didn't plan to talk to him while she was home. She wanted to let her hair down, party and do her. She was gonna make sure she had a fabulous weekend, indulging in some of her bad habits.

Victor texted her that he was in town for the weekend and wanted to meet up later for drinks. She agreed.

A few hours later, Claudia left to get ready for Nico while Angelica freshened up. It was so humid outside, even at 10:00 at night.

She left her front door cracked open after the concierge called to tell her that Falio was on his way up.

"Angelica!" he said out loud knocking on the door.

"Come in!" she yelled from the room.

She finished applying her make-up and then went out to greet her guests.

"Hey!" yelled Angelica coming around the corner.

Falio's eyes popped out of his head.

She came out in these white ruffled booty shorts and a lavender strapless baby doll top. The bra was sparkly and covered in rhinestones while the rest of it was see through. Her hair was down and loose. She had on diamond bracelets, two fat rings, 4-carat diamond studs in her ears and a diamond anklet.

"Damn, girl!" he said picking her up.

"Hi Miguel…hi Carlos," she said greeting his friends.

"Hey, Angelica," they said one after the other.

"Where's Nico?" she asked.

"Next door," said Falio.

Falio kissed her as he carried her to the kitchen. She saw the bottle of Patron sitting on the counter. He knew that was one of her favorites. So, she grabbed some shot glasses and took the bottle into the living room.

As she poured everyone a shot, they sparked up two blunts. Angelica sat on Falio's lap as they smoked.

Miguel asked for a glass of water, so she brought both Miguel and Carlos a glass.

"Where's mine?" asked Falio.

She headed for the kitchen with Falio behind her. As she reached for a glass, he pinned her arms up against the wall.

"You're so beautiful. I missed you, Mami," he said really close to her face.

"I missed you, too, Papi," she said sticking her tongue out and softly licking upwards on his lips.

"Don't play with me, Angelica. You know I want you bad as fuck."

"I know, but I only want what you got for me."

"I want what you got for me, too"

"Give it to me, Papi," she said messing around with him.

"You get it. I put it in a safe place," he said looking down at his dick.

He let her arms loose. She slid down and stopped when her face was in front of his genitalia area. She slowly unbuckled his belt and unzipped his pants, allowing them to fall to the floor. His dick imprint through his boxer briefs was growing. He got harder and harder as she rubbed it feeling for her package. Then, she pulled his underwear halfway down. His big, fat Mandingo sprung out. It was harder than a jaw breaker. She massaged it and squeezed his head before sliding his underwear all the way down. A quarter ounce of weed fell out.

"I love the package," she teased.

"Which one?" he asked not sure if she was talking about his dick that hung like horse or her weed.

She got up with the weed in her hand. "This one, of course," she said smiling.

Falio wouldn't let her move. They stood there playing the staring game.

"Miguel, Carlos…go to the store," he told his boys who sat on the couch watching the show.

"You want something, Angelica?" asked Carlos.

"A BIG bottle of Ciroc," she said emphasizing on the word big while still starring at Falio.

"Ok. Be back," said Miguel.

"Thank you, gentlemen," said Angelica.

"Oh and the rest of it is on the table," said Carlos referring to the blunt.

Falio stripped down to nothing. This made it difficult for Angelica since her nemesis was pretty boys with big sticks.

"I see you still have my name on you," she said referring to his tattoo.

"Hell yeah! It ain't going no where. I'll get a bigger one if you want me to."

"You're crazy."

"So, what you gon' do with me now?"

"Nothing," she said trying to walk away.

"Why not?" he asked grabbing her.

"Don't do this, Falio," she said trying to enjoy her high.

"Do what? Want you, desire you, love you…which one?

"Yes…all of it," she said moving him out of the way and went to sit on the couch.

"Well, I can't forget that you were mine first. It was you and me before your sister came along. You're my girl and it'll always be that way. We're supposed to be married right now, not me and your sister."

Angelica knew the story all too well.

Falio stopped talking and pulled her on his lap, facing him. She was in perfect position to ride him, but didn't. She just pushed his hardness towards the front and laid it on his stomach.

With his hands in her hair and their eyes locked, he said, "Mi Angel…you're my everything and you know that."

She kissed him, teasing him some more. But he knew what she was doing and stopped her. He got really serious.

With a smoldering look and in a low tone, he said, "Baby, I've changed. I'm not the same person I was when you left. I know what I was doing wrong. I just couldn't see it while you were here, but I don't want to make those same mistakes."

She couldn't believe her ears.

"But I want you to do something for me," he said.

"What?"

"Baby, love me…just for tonight. Be back in love with me like you used to be. Let me give you the world."

"Why Lilo? You know what that always leads to," she said.

He didn't want to hear that, so his lips softly kissed her neck. He pulled her top down and eased his tongue down to her breasts. At the same time, his fingers massaged her clit. She tried to resist, but he knew where her spots were. He knew that body inside and out.

"Stand up," he whispered. "Feed me."

Angelica's body responded to his every touch.

"Lilo, we can't do this," she said breathing heavy about to cum.

So, he took his hands off of her.

"I can't make you be with me, Angelica, so I'll stop. But all I want to do is be with you and I want you to WANT to be with me, too."

Angelica couldn't believe he stopped. He even asked her to get up so he could put his clothes on. This attracted her to him more.

"Ok, Lilo. I'm yours…right here, right now. I want to be with you," she said kissing him.

"Mi Angel," he said carrying her into the bedroom.

He took her clothes off and laid her down. His tongue licked every inch of her body to ecstasy. He explored her neck, breasts, stomach and center. Her hips moved in small circular motions as he fed off the sweetness of her addicting nectar. He flipped her over so she could ride his face. After she came, he slid her down so she could ride him.

"Dámelo, Mami!" he said as she sat all the way down on him. "Give it to me, Baby."

Angelica made him feel as though they were the only two in the world. She made him feel wanted, cared for and loved. She really missed Falio at that very moment and he savored it all. He felt like the luckiest man in the world.

They spent the next two hours giving in to their sexual appetites.

"Thank you," he said lying next to her afterwards.

"You're welcome. Thank you."

"You're welcome."

They called everyone back over while they got up.

Angelica and Falio went into the living room where she poured them another shot and lit another blunt.

"I love you," he said brushing her hair away from her face.

"I love you, too, Falio. And I always will," she said winking at him.

In no time, the others were at the door. Miguel and Carlos came back with a bunch of snacks and more bottles of liquor: Nuvo, Bacardi, Ciroc and Voli. Claudia and Nico were hand-in-hand. And they all knew Falio had finally gotten some from the way he held Angelica.

"Let's go to Mango's…my treat," suggested Falio. "I know Angelica wants to see Vivian and Jaime."

"Let's go," said Angelica.

Angelica went to her bedroom to change. Falio followed.

"I know you're paying for Nina's party tomorrow, so here..." he said counting out $5,000. "And this is for you," he said counting out another $5,000.

"Thank you, Papi…but it's ok."

"Let me do this for you…please."

"Ok."

"And is it us tonight? Or just you?" he asked wanting to be clear who she was spending her time with at the club.

"Us."

"Cool," he said reaching for her hand.

She changed into a cream-colored, haltered crochet top that tied around the neck and back with a short jean skirt. She wore her large crochet hoop earrings and her crocheted Manolo Blahnik heels. A Swarovski crystal-embellished and gold embroidered clutch by Marchesa finished her look.

South Beach was crowded for a Wednesday, but it was Memorial weekend. So, it was to be expected.

"Hey!!!!" Angelica yelled to Jaime, who was behind the bar.

"Angelica!!!!" he screamed jumping over to hug her. "When did you get into town?"

"Today."

Then, she heard a scream over the music.

"Bitch! When did you get into town?" screamed Vivian.

"Today," said Angelica laughing and hugging her.

They were all immediately seated in VIP. Bottles were brought over and everyone ordered more drinks. Falio even called Paula and John to come out for a while.

Falio sparked up more blunts. Angelica called over a few her female friends to hang out with Miguel and Carlos. Everyone was enjoying themselves.

"So when did this happen?" asked Paula as she watched Angelica and Falio behave like they did when they first met.

"Tonight," said Angelica kissing Falio.

Paula nodded in agreement.

A song came on and Falio took his angel to the dance floor.

"Thank you for tonight, Papi," she told him, looking into his eyes. "It feels really good being with you."

"You're welcome and I love you, mi Angel," he said holding her closer.

"I love you, too."

They were inseparable the rest of the night. It warmed Claudia and Paula's hearts to see them together. His boys were especially happy for him.

Everyone left the club around 4:00 a.m. Miguel and Carlos left with Angelica's friends, Nico went to Claudia's and Falio went home with Angelica.

They were at it all over again.

~Chapter 39~

The Party Continued

Angelica and Falio woke up around 1:00 the next afternoon to his phone ringing.

"Hello," he said sounding groggy.

"Where the fuck are you?" screamed Ariana.

He just hung up on her and turned his phone off. He wasn't going to let her spoil the only moment he may ever have again with Angelica.

"Call her back," said Angelica turning away from him.

"No. She needs to chill out with all that bullshit."

"She's worried about you."

"No, she's worried about who I'm with. She knows this is my money making weekend. She knows she won't see me until next week sometime…maybe."

Angelica stayed quiet. She wasn't getting in the middle of that.

"You hungry?" he asked.

"Yes…starving."

"Let's go."

He went to his car and got a change of clothes. Before they left, he told her to bring one of her big purses. She knew what that meant.

They hopped in his silver Cadillac CTS V-coupe and headed south on the Turnpike. Angelica had no clue where they were going, but she didn't care. She smoked and enjoyed the scenery as they passed Kendall, Homestead and then merged onto US-1. They were headed to the Keys.

He made a few phone calls on the way, including the restaurant they were headed to, Garcia's. He wanted the food waiting on them, not the other way around.

Garcia's was located on one of the many beaches in Key Largo and served the freshest seafood in the world, according to Falio. This small, quaint restaurant had a small outdoor patio and the best ocean view.

"You're crazy, you know that?" she said.

"Why?"

"We're in the Keys for lunch. Only you," she said laughing.

"I wanted to bring you to my favorite spot."

"Thank you, Papi…I appreciate it."

There was a buffet of food sitting on the table, awaiting them.

"This is insane," she said covering her mouth.

Falio pulled out her chair and served her glass of champagne.

They both loved seafood. So he had Garcia, the owner, prepare different platters with his special seasoning. There was crab legs and lobster tails in a butter garlic sauce, crab stuffed lobster tails, fried shrimp, large lump crab cakes, fried oysters, fresh oysters with fresh lemon, scallop shooters and a whole Red Snapper fried. It was served with hush puppies, French fries and garlic bread.

Angelica was in heaven. The food tasted so good. She even took a picture and sent it to Cherry. She knew how much she loved food.

"So, I'm trying to get Asila to come back with me," she said sparking up a conversation.

"She needs to. She's doing bad right now."

"I know. I can tell."

"She's a sweet kid, but she falls for the wrong guys. Did you hear about the recent one Richard caught her with?"

"No…who?"

Asila was dating some kid who was apparently was using her for her car. When Richard found out she was dating, he scared the kid off and threatened to take Nina. He wasn't serious though. Richard made empty threats all the time. Besides, no one could know about him and Asila…let alone Nina.

Then, Angelica's phone rang. It was Marina. She forgot about their appointment. So, Marina agreed to meet Angelica at her office at 8:00 p.m. They'd discuss the final details and payment.

"So, you ridin' out with me today? Or are you leaving after this?" he asked.

"I'll ride out. I'm on vacation. I don't have any plans," she said having a good time.

He paid for their meal and then went to one of his houses in Kendall. When they walked in, Carlos and Miguel were there taking care of business. Falio handed them some food and went to the back room with her purse. When he came back out, he told his friends to follow him somewhere.

Miguel and Carlos jumped in the Cadillac while Falio and Angelica jumped in his blue Yukon Denali. He told her to look inside her purse. It was full of money. She knew they were headed to Dolphin Mall.

The first stop was the Coach Factory Store. He purchased four extra large suitcases and four large bags that he planned to fill up for her.

Each of them, Carlos and Miguel included, pulled a suitcase and a bag as they entered different stores. If she mentioned something was cute, Falio bought two or three of the same item in different colors. If she liked something, he bought it in different styles and shapes. She saw some boots for $700 and he bought three pairs without blinking an eye. She saw a couple of coats she liked, he bought those and a few others. He bought her handbags and shoes like crazy. Angelica came out of there with at least thirty-five pairs of shoes, including heels, boots, sandals and sneakers. Poor Miguel and Carlos…they were the ones constantly running to the truck putting the stuff away.

By 7:30 p.m., Angelica not only had all of the suitcases and bags filled, but Falio bought five more suitcases that he filled up as well.

Carlos and Miguel went to handle business while Falio took Angelica to her appointment with Marina.

"I had fun today," he told her lighting a blunt.

"I did, too."

"Do you remember the first time I filled your purse with cash?"

"Yep. It scared me. I wondered where you got all that money. But you took my hand and told me everything was going to be ok."

"You were my angel then and will always be."

Angelica smiled at him with such sincerity. "What happened to us? I mean I know what happened, but how did we get to that place where I didn't even want to be around you?"

"It was a lot of things, but I know I didn't make it easy. I was so obsessed with you that I didn't realize I was pushing you away. Plus, you started seeing other people and getting exposed to different things," he said pausing. "It was only when you left that I realized I had to change and be like my old self again but better. I had to be the man you fell in love with in the beginning, not this pyscho dude that chased you everywhere," explained Falio.

"I like the changed you. I can relate to you much better," she said holding his hand.

They arrived to Marina's office in Downtown Miami. Marina showed Angelica all of the things Asila wanted. She also shared some of her ideas, but Angelica wanted more. She wanted over-the-top.

"Use the black card I gave you," said Falio.

"Are you sure?" asked Angelica. "I have cash."

"Yes, I'm sure."

She took out the black AmEx card with the initials "F.R." on the back, which stood for Falio Rodriguez. Marina swiped it and received her $12,000 payment. Angelica spent a little more for expedited services.

The concierge in Angelica's building used a cart to take her stuff upstairs.

"Thank you for everything, Papi," she said once they got up-stairs. She gave him a hug and a kiss.

"Thank you for letting me do this for you. You know how much this means to me."

"I know. And I really had a great time."

"Me, too," he said hugging her harder.

She surprised him by pulling his pants down to get a quickie in before he left. However, that quickie turned into an hour.

"Are we hanging tonight?" he asked before leaving.

"Yes. You can come back and get me. I'll go wherever you take me."

He was so excited. He kept kissing and hugging her.

After he left, Angelica called Claudia over to show her all of the stuff Falio bought. Claudia wanted to know what the deal was between them.

"I don't know, Claude. It's like when we first met. I guess the space between us did him some good," said Angelica.

"I see that. You two are inseparable."

"We're going out tonight…again."

"Again?" yelled Claudia.

"Yeah, but just us."

Angelica told her how things felt so right. Falio was kind, gentle and sweet. He was more understanding and she could talk to him without him blowing up. They made each other laugh and had a good time being together. Claudia was happy for her friend. She hoped that meant she'd move back.

Falio was back within the hour. He went to get his clothes and trade cars. He came back in his black on black Bugatti Veyron. He was taking his favorite girl out on the town and showing her off.

He wore a black Tom Ford suit with black Gucci shoes, a Rolex and a 20-carat diamond men's bracelet.

Angelica wore a white sleeveless, high neck Gucci gown with bronze detailing. It was tight-fitting with a thigh high split and a train. She wore bronze jeweled Miu Miu heels with a Lauren Merkin clutch. And her sparkle for the night was chocolate diamonds.

They had a very romantic and private candlelight dinner at Nobu on Collins Avenue, which was known for its world-renowned Japanese cuisine. Afterwards, he took her to LIV nightclub. They spent the entire night in each other's arms, even when they got back to her place.

~Chapter 40~

Friday

Angelica spent most of the day at her parents' house. She talked to her mom about all of her men. She told her about Shana and Damian, the bets made, falling for Austin and the past couple days with Falio. She was really close to her mother and could tell her anything.

First, Alicia addressed Shana and Damian. She told Angelica to be careful because he would be the one hurt at the end of it all. She understood and really wasn't trying to hurt him. Angelica liked Damian, but he wasn't available.

Her mom didn't like the bets made, but knew Angelica always did what she wanted to do.

Then, they talked about Austin, who Alicia favored. He was single and available. It sounded like he loved Angelica, but didn't have time to clean up his single life before jumping into a relationship with her. So, things weren't going as smoothly as they could have. However, she admired him for putting her daughter first with regards to the new job.

Last, they talked about Falio and her sister.

"Angelica, try to leave Falio alone. Mija, you know your sister," said Alicia.

"I know, ma, but I wanted to do it and I did. Falio has really changed. He's like the person I fell I love with. It's been about us these past couple of days and I'm having a great time."

"What do you mean us? Angelica…don't tell me you're getting back together."

"No, but it's not a bad idea.

"Please, Angelica…"

"Sometimes I think it's her punishment, ma, for what she did to me."

"I know, mija. That girl is so hard-headed and defiant. I don't know where she got that from."

"Yeah, well…"

"How is Falio? Poor thing…I'm sure he's fallen for you all over again," chuckled her mother.

"Yeah…he wants us back together, but hasn't pushed the issue. And he took me to the Keys for lunch, took me shopping, gave me money and even paid for Nina's party."

"Mija…he's crazy about you and will do anything for you. That's the type of man you should be with. One that loves you and will protect you. One that will take care of you no matter what. Like your father…he's still like that 'til this day."

"I know."

"And your father and I love Falio. We just don't like the situation."

Angelica and Falio's relationship had that deep, intense passion that Angelica desired. The chemistry and fireworks between them was indescribable. Their kind of love was rare. That was the reason she blamed Ariana for ruining her happiness.

Her mother didn't like her "locuras", which meant crazy escapades. But Alicia understood her daughter and knew she had a heart of gold. That was the reason men went crazy for her. She was so beautiful, smart and thoughtful. Any guy that captured her true heart would be lucky. Alicia hoped it was Austin because Falio's situation was complicated even though he loved her very much.

"Hey, sis," said Asila coming in the kitchen where they were talking.

"Hey," said Angelica giving her a kiss on the cheek. "So are you coming back to North Carolina with me?"

Asila wasn't sure, but Alicia loved the idea because she wouldn't have to worry about Richard trying to take Nina.

Asila was nineteen and a virgin when she got mixed up with Richard. She was in her second year of college and doing well. Richard made her stop going to school, got her to start drinking, was very controlling and he even hit her a couple of times. Then, she became pregnant. That was when they found out he was married with two kids. It sent Asila into a depression, but she came out of it after the birth of her daughter. She decided to get her life together for Nina and be strong. Angelica hated him and Alfredo was ready to shoot Richard, if he ever saw him again. The only thing everyone was grateful to him for was Nina.

"You can live with me, go to school full time, Nina can grow up in a better environment. Think about it. You should come," said Angelica.

Asila promised to think about it.

Soon after, Angelica left to get ready to cruise South Beach.

Memorial weekend on South Beach was also known as Urban Beach Week. Over a quarter of a million people packed the streets of Miami during this time to floss in the most exotic cars, party with A-list celebrities, drink at the most hottest clubs, see the livest performances, sex beautiful people and experience once-in-a-lifetime adventures.

Angelica drove her motorcycle down Washington Avenue to maneuver her way through traffic. She saw Erotica's neon sign and decided to visit her old friends. It was a popular and upscale strip club on Washington Avenue and 15th Street.

Angelica looked smokin' hot in her black, strapless corset that laced up in the front with her boy shorts and thigh high, black boots. She had smoky eyes and wore a diamond floral neck choker with the matching bracelet and earrings.

"Gary!!!" yelled Angelica as she approached the bar.

"Angelica!! My God!!! Where have you been?" he asked giving her a hug.

She ordered a shot of Patron and talked to Gary and the bartender. She laughed at Gary's corny jokes and cheered on her stripper friends that were still there.

Just then, a waiter went up to Gary and whispered something in his ear. Gary turned towards Angelica and said, "Someone wants a private dance from you in the attic."

"What? I don't work here anymore," she said looking confused.

"No, but he recognized you from a long time ago. He's willing to spend some serious money on you, girl."

"Who?" she asked looking around.

"All he said is that he's waiting for his Queen Madame in room six."

Angelica laughed once he said that name. She knew exactly who it was. There was only one person who knew her by that name.

She took her last shot of Patron and went upstairs.

The attic wasn't really an attic. It was the top floor of the building with only six rooms on the floor. Each one usually rented for

$225 for twenty-five minutes of sexual pleasures. However, Gary raised prices for Memorial weekend to $400. And every room came with the option of sexual intercourse, a panic button for protection and a security guard in case things got out of hand.

When she got to the room, she stood in front of the door.

"Hey, Vince," she said to the security guard as she finger brushed her hair back and wrapped it in a bun.

"Hey, Angelica. How are you? Long time no see."

"I know. I'm good and you?"

"Great," he said smiling. "Just like old times, huh?" he asked laughing.

"Yes, it is," she laughed as he opened the door.

The room was very dim. Her face went from a smile to mean. All she could see was a gentleman's silhouette standing in the dark corner.

"Sit down," she demanded, instructing him to sit in the recliner next to the window.

She circled around the chair, checking him out. She took off her shorts and straddled him. She immediately slapped him.

"Unlace my top," she demanded.

As he went to do it, she slapped him again.

"With your teeth," she said.

He did, exposing her breasts.

"Suck on them," she whispered.

As he did what he was told, she pushed his head back and slapped him.

"Slowly."

So, he slowly moved towards her chest and did as told.

"Stop," she said.

She climbed on the chair, standing on the arms and holding onto the back. She crouched down, waving her nookie up and down in his face. When he opened his mouth, she slapped him.

"You can't taste yet."

She turned to the side and cocked one leg on the back of the chair while the other one stood between his legs.

She slowly squatted in front of him, putting all her goods in his face. He couldn't wait anymore. He ripped her panties off and went to work as he reclined the chair all the way back.

"Falio!!!!"

"You know that shit turns me on," he said as he proceeded to handle his business.

"You're not playing right," she barely said between moans and groans.

They got a quickie in after he made her cum. Then, they got dressed and went back to the bar.

"You know when Gary told me that someone wanted to see me upstairs, I looked at him crazy," Angelica told Falio.

"I know. That's why I told him Queen Madame."

Falio and Angelica used to role play when she worked there. It helped her gain confidence in herself and her sexiness. It also kept their sexual lives fun and interesting.

"Gary!!!" yelled Angelica.

"Yes, Sweetheart."

"Do you still keep new sets of panties in the back?" she asked showing him what Falio did.

"Yes...I'll get one for you," he said laughing.

"So how did you know I was here?" she asked Falio.

"Shit!!! Who didn't know you were here, walking in wearing that," he said pointing to her outfit.

She laughed.

"Naw...me and my boys came in about a half hour ago. We just came to chill out and relax. I was going to call you when we were headed to the club, but then Miguel noticed you. I was talking to Nico and he kept tapping me, telling me to look. And when I did, to my surprise, there you were."

After she changed, he rounded up his troops and they headed to Elecktra Nightclub. Again, they found themselves hanging out together and having a good time. Her friends from the other night were still out with Miguel and Carlos.

They left at 4:30 a.m. and went to his 2-story Rooftop Suite at the Z Ocean Hotel. He was staying there the entire week.

This expansive two-bedroom suite had soaring ceilings, Turkish marble flooring with a mosaic tile design, hand-painted art everywhere and floor-to-ceiling windows that offered an exceptional 180-degree view of the beach. But the best feature was the oversized rooftop terrace. Just off the balcony was a spiral staircase that led guests upstairs to a private paradise complete with native palms, stainless steel railings, a hot tub, wet bar, lush landscaping and surround sound. There was also a remote controlled private awning and retractable shade that created the perfect hideaway.

He invited her to stay and she did. They made love on the rooftop with a rising sun over the ocean as the background.

~Chapter 41~

Club Mansion

He only slept for like four hours before his phone rang off the hook. It was business.

"I see business is good," she commented.

"It is. I made back what I spent yesterday in ten minutes."

"Damn!"

"Yeah, but Baby I have to go and take care of something."

"Be careful, Lilo."

"I will. Stay as long as you want. Whatever you want is on me. I don't know how long I'll be gone, but I hope you're here when I get back."

"Ok."

They kissed and he left.

She slept for another four hours. Then, got up and put on one of the bikinis Falio had there for her. She went to the rooftop to sun bathe. She called her friends who were still in Carlos and Miguel's suites and invited them up. She ordered food, drinks and turned up the music.

An hour later, the fellas came back with a slough of bottles and more weed. Falio was so happy she was still there and having a good time.

After they got good and high, Angelica whispered in his ear, "I didn't want to leave without feeding you first."

It put a smile on his face. "Good 'cause I'm starved," he said. "I want it right now."

Falio didn't care who was there. He laid back on the lounge bed and told Angelica to ride him. So, she did while the other two girls were also pleasuring his boys. Everyone got their freak on in the beaming hot sun.

Angelica went home and thought about the past few days. Then, she thought about Austin. She was ready to face him and knew exactly where it would take place.

Club Mansion was throwing a star-studded event with Austin as one of their celebrity guests making an appearance. It was all over the radio. So, she had to look her cutest.

Angelica invited Asila to go out with her and Falio. Then, she texted Falio and told him to go extra deep. She had a funny feeling about the evening.

Asila chose whatever she wanted out of Angelica's closet.

"Sis…I'm scared I'm going to run into Richard tonight."

Angelica assured her that he'd get handled if he did anything.

The streets of South Beach were once again in full swing. Thousands crowded the streets to partake in the festivities.

Angelica, Asila, Falio and all of his boys walked into Club Mansion. They were immediately escorted to VIP and given the royal treatment. Falio received much respect walking in with Angelica on his arm. And Asila looked hot wearing a turquoise, strapless mini dress walking in on Carlos's arm.

Everyone sat down and started drinking. Angelica started smoking and gave some to Asila. She didn't smoke like Angelica, but she wasn't a newbie to smoking weed either.

A group of them went to the dance floor. Carlos and Asila danced most of the night. He was seriously feelin' her and she was very attracted to him. Falio and Angelica were getting their groove on as well.

Then, the DJ announced the celebrities.

"Look who just walked in…AZ! For those that don't know, NFL player Austin Zachary is in the house!"

The crowd went crazy and women bum rushed him.

Ten minutes later, she and Asila left for the bathroom.

"He's here, isn't he?" asked Asila.

"Yes."

She freshened up and made sure she looked FABULOUS!!!!! They stopped by the bar where he stood with three women. Angelica and Asila scooted in beside him.

"Can I get two shots of Patron, please?" asked Angelica.

When he saw her, he moved those women out of the way.

"Angelica…Baby," he said trying to get her attention.

"Hello," she said cold.

"Where have you been? I've been trying to call you."

"I know."

Angelica and Asila toasted and tossed the shots back.

"Two more please," said Angelica.

"Hi," he said to Asila.

"Asila this is Austin. Austin, this is my sister Asila," said Angelica introducing them.

They shook hands.

The ladies took their second shots and turned around to leave.

But he stopped her.

"Please, Angelica…can we talk?"

Before she could answer, Richard walked in with another woman on his arm. He immediately noticed Asila and asked the woman to find a table while he went to get drinks. He scooted right next to Asila and whispered, "Bitch, you better go home and take care of our daughter. Stop walking around here looking like a whore like your sister before I whoop yo' ass."

Angelica knew he didn't say anything nice by how frightened Asila became.

"Come on, Asila," said Angelica taking her by the hand.

Richard didn't like that and grabbed Asila by her hair. Austin jumped up and grabbed him.

"Man, are you crazy?" yelled Austin in his face.

But Falio and twenty of his boys, including Carlos, were front and center.

Falio grabbed Richard by the throat and said, "Apologize to her."

"I'm sorry, Asila," he said choked up.

Then, Falio leaned in and whispered in his ear, "If I see you next to her again, I'll kill you. Do you understand?" Falio showed him his gun.

"Yes."

Falio reached for Angelica's hand. She grabbed it and left with Falio. Carlos took Asila by the hand as they returned to their area. Angelica wasn't going to let Austin ruin her good time.

Angelica pulled Falio to the side and told him what she wanted to do so that Richard would leave Asila alone forever. She waited for this day for a long time. Falio was game.

Angelica went back to the bar while Falio made some phone calls. He had to get his people in place for what was to come. She asked her bartender friend to prepare a real stiff drink and have it sent to Richard, who was busy looking at Asila and Carlos.

~Chapter 42~

Revenge

Thirty minutes later, Angelica went up to Richard and whispered in his ear. He told the woman he was with that he'd be right back. As they walked out, Angelica nodded at some of her friends.

Richard walked with Angelica towards the parking garage behind the club.

"I've always wanted to fuck you. Your sister is good, but you're a bad bitch," said Richard slurring.

She just smiled and kept walking. He didn't even notice everyone behind them.

Then, she said, "But it's not free, Sweetheart."

She was trying to get him to talk about how much money his wife just won in a recent settlement. He'd been bragging to Asila about it. But yet, didn't feel the need to take care of his daughter.

"Oh, I got money," he said slurring and barely able to walk. "I got over half a million dollars."

That's what she wanted to hear. "Where? I don't see it," she said trying to keep him talking.

"It's in my bank account dumb ass! I'm not gonna walk around with it on me," he said digging himself into a deeper hole.

They finally made it to the elevator where Falio's boys caught him before he collapsed. The drug added to his drink had finally taken affect.

Richard was placed in the back seat of his Cadillac Escalade and striped naked. Money and drugs were spread all around him making it look like he was partying. Then, lots of provocative pictures were taken of him with two of Angelica's transvestite friends. They showed body parts and captured different positions and angles to make it look so wrong. They even made it look like Richard was taking it from behind with lipstick on.

Angelica took the $2000 in cash from his wallet and gave Falio his bank card and three credit cards. Falio made more phone calls and put their plan into action. After he hung up, he gave Angelica the thumbs up. That was her cue to get him dressed. Richard was left by the elevator with an envelope attached to his clothes. Angelica took his truck key.

Twenty minutes later, Richard was back in the club and in VIP.

"Asila, I'm sorry for all the hell I put you through. I promise to leave you alone."

Asila just looked at him strangely. He'd never apologized for any of his actions, let alone in front of a bunch of people.

As he walked away, Angelica and Falio escorted him downstairs. She had him sign a release form giving up all parental rights to Nina. He also signed a restraining order agreeing to stay at least 500 feet away from Asila and Nina. If he didn't, Asila could have him arrested.

Richard was beyond pissed, but there was nothing he could do. The envelope attached to him had his phone inside with those pictures on it. Also, there was a letter that stated if he apologized publicly and signed the forms, he would receive the camera's memory card with all of the original photos.

"Here is the envelope as promised," said Angelica smiling.

"Dirty Bitch!" said Richard furiously as he snatched it and left.

Falio wanted to choke him for cussing at her, but Angelica stopped him. Instead, they watched as he read what was inside the envelope. Asila wondered why everyone was laughing. So, Angelica told her what they did after they saw him scream and swipe a glass off the table, breaking it.

Richard received a blank memory card and was told he'd never get the original photos that were taken. He was also informed that one hundred thousand dollars was transferred into a trust account for Nina using his bank card. Asila was keeping his $2,000 cash and the $16,000 from his three credit cards that they maxed out. Lastly, he not only signed the paternity rights release form and the restraining order, but he also signed the title of his truck over to Asila, gifting it to her. They warned him that if he called the police, they'd release the photos of him with the drugs, cash and women at his wife's job and children's school. Angelica would tell his wife about Asila and Nina. Then, she'd press charges for attempted rape and domestic violence, ruining his political career.

Asila hugged and thanked them both. They continued to party and had a great time 'til around 4 a.m.

As they were walking out, Falio had his arm around Angelica's waist. Austin tried grabbing her arm, but Falio quickly pulled out his .357 Magnum, long barrel revolver from behind his back and cocked it, pointing it in Austin's face before he could blink.

"Don't you ever disrespect her like that! What if this was my wife, my sister, my mother…that's not how you handle a woman," said Falio.

Angelica stopped him.

"It's cool, Lilo. Please…give me a sec."

"Ok," he said tongue kissing her. She kissed him right back.

Once he left, Austin yelled, "What the fuck was that? You're with him now?"

"Don't worry about that."

"Angelica, we need to talk."

"Why?"

"I need to apologize. I get it. I understand. Even if we can't be in public together, I need to stop being disrespectful and behave like a man in a relationship. It won't be long before the world knows about us anyway."

"Us?" she questioned with a face. "Last I recall you were kissing another woman in your office. That's not "us" behavior," she said doing the quote sign.

"I love you, Angelica. I really do and I was wrong. I know that, but please can we talk…please?"

"I love you, Austin. I really do. But I can't and won't be with someone that cares more about their reputation rather than genuinely taking care of the one he loves. It's like you won't face the truth about being in love and finding someone that is worth settling down with."

"I know…I know…but I don't want to lose you."

"I'm worth a man saying no thank you to every other woman that approaches him once I have his heart, but you don't get that. You prefer flirting with Gloria, making club appearances and hanging out with women, still trying to be THE MAN. I don't want that," she said, walking away.

Everyone went to Failo's room to party on the rooftop. Meanwhile, Angelica sat in a corner. Falio saw her and went over to her.

"That was him, huh?" asked Falio.

"Him who?" she asked making a face.

"I'm not stupid, Angelica. Any man willing to lose his life for you besides me is my worst nightmare."

"Falio, just hold me."

So, he did. But he saw the look in her eyes and knew their fairy-tale romance was coming to an end.

"I love you, mi Angel," he said looking into her eyes.

"I love you, too Lilo."

He excused himself for a moment. He sent Asila over with a blunt and a drink.

Angelica told her what happened with Austin. Asila was sorry to hear that things didn't go well. Then, she told her she was moving to Charlotte. Her and Nina would leave with her on Tuesday morning. This cheered Angelica up and made her so happy.

Falio came back for Angelica.

"Come with me," he said reaching for her hand.

"See you later, sis...and use condoms with Carlos," Angelica told Asila.

"I will," said Asila shaking her head.

Asila didn't have sex with everyone she dated, but she was seriously feelin' Carlos.

When they got downstairs, there were so many candles lit and rose petals everywhere. Slow music played as he asked her to dance.

"I know you're leaving and I know this is probably our last night together..." he said to her.

"The room looks nice," she said avoiding the comment.

"I had it planned since yesterday."

"Thank you, Falio…for everything," she said as a tear fell down her face.

He picked her up and carried her to the bed. He took his time and they didn't rush. They made love for hours.

~Chapter 43~

Nina's Birthday Party

It was eight o'clock in the morning and they hadn't slept yet. She was tired from messing around with Falio.

She got dressed and went up to the roof where Falio was leaning against the rail smoking.

"Lilo…" she said approaching him.

"Don't say it, Angelica. I don't want to hear it."

"Please let me say what I need to say."

He turned and looked at her. His eyes were so watery from crying.

"Falio, I love you. I love you very much and thank you for everything you've done for me. I had a really good time with you. You made me feel special."

He hugged her and held her tight. "You are, Angelica. Never forget that."

"I won't," she said as they both cried.

"You're the love of my life. I love taking care of you. I love feeling like your man. You've made me the happiest man alive this weekend. You deserve what I gave you and much more."

She smiled and hugged him tighter. They kissed like it was the last time. They kept it about them and didn't discuss problems. But Falio knew it was over.

"See you later," she said leaving him hunched over the rail looking out onto the ocean.

Angelica went home and got some sleep. She slept until 3:00 p.m. She woke up to the sound of Asila screaming at her through the phone, wondering where she was. She called Claudia and told her to get ready as she quickly got dressed.

When Angelica asked for over the top, she received over the top.

As they approached the house, they saw dozens of Little Mermaid balloons floating high in the front yard. There was a seven-foot poster of Nina dressed as a mermaid with her name in large balloon letters above it with tons of streamers hanging down. Little Mermaid cut-outs, sea creatures and shells were in mini swimming pools. Birthday signs with the different characters were posted everywhere displaying birthday messages. And on the side of the house was a Little Mermaid balloon arch with streamers that created an entryway to the backyard.

Angelica and Claudia headed back and felt like they'd just entered Little Mermaid world. Paper lanterns, lights and sea animals made of tissue paper were strung across the different trees. The pool had large floating Little Mermaids with boats, seaweed, seashells and a bubble machine nearby that made it look like an ocean. There were two Little Mermaid bounce houses, an eighteen foot tidal wave water slide with pool and a sno cone, popcorn and cotton candy machine. The candy station had fun-shaped sweets like starfish lollipops, clam cookies, rice Krispy sushi bars, goldfish and gummy shell suckers. The gift bag table had purple and green tutu purses for the girls and goodie boxes shaped like Sebastian for the boys. The piñata was a huge Ariel mermaid with candy, toys and little trinkets inside. The tables were dressed in green and orange linens with chair covers and sashes to match. Large castles with sand, glittered mermaids and fish bowls with real fish were used as centerpieces to decorate the tables. The plates, napkins and cups had Ariel's face plastered all over them. And all the characters from the Little Mermaid walked around, greeting the kids.

Nina looked too cute. She wore an orange pleated skirt with a sparkly green bikini top made of shells. She also wore custom made Little Mermaid sandals. Her hair was down and she wore a tiara. Angelica gave her a gold necklace with her name on it and gold bangles.

More than twenty five kids showed up. They were very entertained playing games, dancing, face painting and in the bounce houses. They all munched on fish-shaped sandwiches, pizza, chicken nuggets, burgers, hot dogs and chips from the mini buffet. And many tried to get a taste of Nina's three-tiered, green and orange cake with Ariel's face on top. However, some succeeded at grabbing cake pops and cupcakes that were near the bottom layer of the cake.

Angelica got a text from Austin. It said, "I'm sorry. I get it. Turn on the radio." She ran inside and turned on the radio in her mom's room. Asila, Alina, Ariana, Claudia and Alicia all sat with her listening. Austin was doing a radio interview at Power 96.

The female DJ asked Austin questions about retiring from the NFL, his current business ventures and his personal life. Austin admitted that he was in love, but never said a female's name. He admitted that he messed up and hoped that by telling the world how he felt it would make things right. He told the listeners that

he was ripping up his player's card. She congratulated him and
his lucky lady, whoever she was. Then, she promoted the club
on South Beach where he'd be making a guest appearance and
warned the ladies that he was officially off the market.

"What are you going to do?" asked Asila cheesing.

Before she could answer, her phone rang. It was Austin. He
asked if he could see her. She agreed and gave him her parents'
address.

An hour later, he came with flowers for Angelica, her three sisters, Claudia, her mother and Nina. He also got Nina a $500 Toys
R'Us gift card for her birthday. Then, he met her father. Alfredo
was super excited about the box of cigars Austin brought him.
Both of her parents liked him.

Angelica left Austin talking to her parents while she played a
game with the kids. It gave them a chance to get to know him a
little better. If they were going to be serious, her parents had to
approve.

Halfway through the kids' party, Angelica slipped away to talk
to Austin. He immediately apologized about Gloria. He shouldn't
have done what he did. He should've been more professional and
conducted business rather than allowing the flirting and kissing.
She accepted his apology.

He also apologized about the women at the club, the woman at
the restaurant and every other incident that got him into hot water.

Then all hell broke loose. One of Angelica's uncles came to the
party with his mistress. His wife was there with his ex-wife, who
was Angelica's aunt. The two wives were cool because of the
kids, but the current wife got up and chased her husband around
with a baseball bat. Then, another one of Angelica's uncles saw
the mistress and called out her name. An argument started because it turned out that the mistress had been sleeping with both
uncles and they didn't know. She didn't even know they were

related. So, she got out of there quick.

Falio and his crew walked in with a big gift box. When he saw Angelica, he got mad. He looked at Austin like he wanted to hurt him.

"Tio! Tio!" yelled Nina running to him.

"Nina! Nina!" screamed Falio smiling, picking her up.

They exchanged hugs and kisses. She was happy because he bought her a bike.

Angelica and Austin tried to talk, but there were too many interruptions. So, she agreed to meet up with him later. Besides, he had to go get ready for his last club appearance.

After a while, the kids' party turned into an adult party. The DJ played salsa and merengue to get the crowd moving. Angelica danced with her father as Colin danced with Alicia. Alina thought it was so cute. Ariana tried dancing with Falio, but he got as far away from her as possible.

By 10:00 p.m., the clean-up crew was there to tear everything down and take all of the props. That was Angelica's cue to leave. Her and Claudia kissed her parents bye and she told them she'd be by the next day.

Falio followed them to the car.

"Hey," he said getting Angelica's attention.

"Oh my God! You scared me," she said with her hand on her chest.

"I'm sorry, Baby."

"What's up?"

"Stay with me tonight…please."

"Falio…"

"Just think about it. I'm not going to pressure you. I'll be waiting for you at the hotel. Miguel and Carlos can handle business. I'm not going out. I'll be there all night if I have to Angelica," he said kissing her lips and left.

~Chapter 44~

A Night to Remember

Angelica and Claudia discussed Falio all the way home. After talking things through, Angelica knew what she had to do.

Angelica took a cab to South Beach to avoid parking. She told the driver where to drop her off.

"Falio…" she said walking up to the rooftop.

"Baby, you came," he said hugging her tight.

"Yo', I'm out man," said Miguel. "Hey, Angelica."

"Hey, Miguel."

Falio told him what to do before he left.

"Thank you for coming," he said caressing her face.

"Falio…we have to talk."

"I know," he said as they sat down.

"You've been a big part of my life, even when I pushed you away. You're a very important person to me and I need you to believe that."

"I do, but why does this sound like good-bye?"

"Because in a way, it is."

Falio stood up and walked over to the railing.

"Sweetheart, I'm giving him a chance...a fair chance. That means one without you."

"Does he deserve you?"

"Yes. For the first time since us, I've found someone I can picture myself marrying. So, I want to be right for him."

That was a hard pill for Falio to swallow.

"He's a lucky man."

"I'm a lucky girl."

"Why won't you give us another try? And don't say Ariana. I'll divorce her right now."

"You know she won't give you a divorce and this whole situation is hard for me."

"And you don't think it's hard for me?"

"You're married to my sister. Then, there are my nephews… they deserve to have their mother and father."

"No! They deserve to see their father with someone he loves. We can provide a healthier home and family life for them."

"That might be true, but there's just so much. We're complicated while being intense and passionate at the same time. I want simple and he can give me that."

"I'm happy for you. I really am. But don't ask me to let you go. I can't do that."

"And I can't stay."

He pulled her close to him. They just hugged each other.

"How long do I have you for?" he asked.

"Until the morning."

Then her phone rang. It was Austin. She told him she was taking care of some important business and would see him tomorrow.

"Angelica, what am I going to do without you? I've never pictured my life with you not in it."

"I don't know. I never pictured my life without you either. And to be honest, I was going to try us again on my 30th birthday."

"So, get rid of him and stay single for the next six months. I'll marry you then or right now."

She tapped his leg, laughing. "I can't do that."

"I need to know something," he said.

"Yes."

"Do you honestly blame me for what happened to us?"

"No. But it was hard accepting you and my sister."

"Can I be honest with you?"

"Yes."

"This is going to sound weird, but I've never slept with Ariana sober. Both times I was fucked up."

"You mean you haven't slept with her in all these years?" Angelica asked surprised.

"Fuck no! Why do you think she's so jealous of you? And why do you think I have other women? I will not sleep in the same bed with her. She's not my woman. You are."

"Falio, I don't know what to say."

"Say you'll stay with me. Choose me."

She kissed him.

"I got you something," she said walking to her purse.

She came back and handed him a jewelry box. When he opened it, he saw a gold Cuban link chain with a cross pendant made of diamonds. There was a ribbon stretched across the front that said, "I love you".

"This is nice," he said.

"Turn it over," she said.

It read, "Falio & Angelica" with the date.

"Thank you," he said giving her a kiss.

They went to the bedroom where he made love to her with everything left in him. He was going all out if it was truly their last time and she let him. Falio had always been the love of her life. So, she made sure they had the most passionate and sexy night.

Around 8:00 in the morning, she texted Claudia to pick her up. He saw her texting and went back up to the rooftop.
"Hey…" she said trying to get his attention.
"What's up?" he said a little agitated.
"I'm about to go."
"See ya. Have a safe trip home."
"Can I get a hug?"
"No."
She thought he was joking and tried to get one. He extended his arm out, preventing her from touching him. She turned around and walked away, but he chased her to the stairs and grabbed her. He hugged her so tight he almost took her breath away.
"I love you, Angelica…and I can't let you go! I can't! My brain can't think about not ever being with you again," he said balling his eyes out.
"I love you too, Lilo," she said as tears rolled down her face.
"Stay…don't go!!"
"I have to go."
"Please, Angelica," he begged getting on his knees.
Angelica got down on her knees and kissed him. She hugged him tight one last time before running out of there. It was too much for her to take.
As she collected her things from the room, she heard him kicking furniture, breaking glass and yelling at the top of his lungs on the rooftop. She wanted to go back upstairs and calm him down, but she knew it would only make matters worse. So, she bolted out of there as fast as she could so she didn't have to hear his pain.

After his rampage, Falio balled up in a corner crying like a baby. He knew she was gone. He had just lost the love of his life. He felt like he couldn't breathe. Angelica was his air and he was suffocating without her. He couldn't fathom living his life without her in it. It hurt so bad.

He saw the necklace and picked it up to throw it over the balcony, but his fingers wouldn't let go of it. So, he held on to it as he cried some more.

About thirty minutes later, he cleaned himself up. He put the necklace on and decided to never take it off again. It would be a constant reminder to get her back. He wasn't letting her go. He couldn't. He wasn't prepared to let go of a love like theirs. He was now more determined than ever to marry her. So, his first step was divorcing her sister.

~Chapter 45~

Austin's Condo

Claudia dropped Angelica off at Austin's.

Knock knock.

Austin opened the door and was glad to see Angelica. And by the way she hugged him, she was glad to see him too.

"Are you ok?" he asked.

"No," she said crying.

"What's wrong? Look at me," he said lifting her head.

Her eyes were red.

"You hungry?" he asked.

"Yes."

"Ok."

Austin ordered breakfast while she went to take a shower.

While showering, Angelica slid down the wall and balled up in the fetal position with the water hitting her, crying her eyes out.

She hadn't realized what a stronghold Falio had on her. He had always been there and she could always count on his love. She wasn't sure if she was ready to release him, but she had to in order to be happy with Austin. It saddened her.

She put on one of his t-shirts and a pair of boxers. She walked out to the dining room where he sat waiting for her.

"Are you ready to talk?" he asked.

"Yes."

But just then, the doorbell rang. It was breakfast.

He ordered pancakes, eggs, sausage, bacon, breakfast potatoes and toast. He took their food to the balcony where they sat as she told her story.

Her parents came from Cuba at a very young age. They met at a mechanic shop where her dad used to work. They dated and eventually got married. They had two girls, her and Ariana, back to back. It wasn't easy as they barely made ends meet while her mother attended nursing school. They all stayed in a studio apartment in a not so nice neighborhood. Then, her mother became pregnant again with Alina before graduating. Her father started school to be a pharmacist. Already strapped for cash, they had another baby…Asila. However, things finally started looking up once both her parents were working at the hospital.

But after seeing their struggle, Angelica learned early that she wanted a better life for herself and felt she needed to help her family being the oldest. So, she did well in high school in order to get a free ride to college.

In her freshman year, she was a bit of a mess. She described how she looked.

In her sophomore year, she was a little better. She changed her look and got noticed by one particular guy. They became really good friends, yet they flirted a lot and hung out with each other all the time.

By her junior year, she was fully transformed. Her and the guy fell madly in love and she lost her virginity to him. They stayed together even through their senior year. He always made her feel safe and secure by protecting her, even when she worked at the strip club to earn extra cash. She was describing Falio.

Angelica and Falio were inseparable. They planned out this beautiful life together. So after graduation, he started making money hustling. He got them their first apartment and they moved in together. He proposed and they were supposed to get married.

She didn't think much about his career choice until the first time he filled her purse with money and took her shopping. That was when she knew he was deep in the game. But the plan was for him to quit after they got married, which never happened because of Ariana.

One night, Ariana went to see Angelica, but she hadn't made it home yet. So, Ariana kept Falio company while waiting. She fixed them some drinks and smoked with him. Falio felt really drunk fifteen minutes later and went to lie down. Ariana waited a few minutes and then climbed into bed with him. She pretended to be Angelica. When Angelica finally got home, she saw Ariana naked in the bed with her man. Angelica snatched her up by the hair and drug her to living room where they fought. She beat up her sister pretty bad and then threw her out naked. Angelica called her mom and dad and told them what Ariana did.

Through it all, Falio didn't budge. It was like he blacked out. When he came to, he saw the apartment messed up and Angelica bleeding. She told him what happened, but he couldn't remember anything. Ariana told everyone about her amazing night with Falio, but he couldn't remember a thing. He was so apologetic, but it was too late. The damage was done and Angelica left him.

Weeks later, Ariana found out she was pregnant. It had to be Falio's because she was a virgin prior to that night. He hated

Ariana for what she did and her family became so divided and dysfunctional for a while. Angelica didn't speak to her sister the whole time she was pregnant. Falio blamed Ariana for ruining his life. Angelica was supposed to be the mother of all his children, not her.

After that, Falio dove deep into selling drugs. It was his way out. Her family pressured him into marrying her, so he did. But he was never home…occupational hazard.

Later on, they found out that Ariana drugged Falio to get him to sleep with her. That's why he blacked out and couldn't remember what happened. That's when Angelica forgave Falio and they became cool again. But she beat her sister up again for what she did.

Ariana found a way to drug him again. That's how she became pregnant with their second child. Even after finding out about being drugged, Falio never left Ariana because of his kids. Besides, Angelica wouldn't take him back. So, he stayed. But Ariana made his life impossible and constantly threatened him with the kids if he tried to divorce her.

However, Falio never left Angelica's side. He worked twice as hard to get her back as they remained friends and sometime lovers. He always made sure she was taken care of. Ariana couldn't stand it, but he didn't care. Whenever she was ready to have him, Ariana was out and she knew it. Angelica had always been his priority and he was her first and only love until now.

"That's fucked up what your sister did. I mean real fucked up! I would've been mad as hell if that happened to me," said Austin understanding Falio's attitude. "Now I understand him."

"Yeah…he's been there…like we've been through so much shit together. He takes care of my parents, my sisters and me. He paid for my parents' home and all of their renovations, helped me put Alina through law school and bought Asila a car. He even bought my condo and car for me."

"I'm sorry for what happened, but I would've been mad as HELL!" said Austin repeating himself. He couldn't believe her story.

She took a breather and stopped crying.

"Austin…I love you, but that's why I won't play these games anymore. You're the first person since Falio that I've completely opened to and actually pictured having a life with. I want to get married and have kids, but not to someone who's going to break my heart."

He reached his hand out and pulled her onto his lap. "I understand. I want the same things you do and I'm ready to let go of my past. Are you?"

"Yes."

"I've never met anyone like you. So, I feel like I have to fight for us."

"What do you mean?"

"I fell in love with you and your feistiness, your confidence, your sex appeal, your sex game. Definitely, the sex," he said making her smile. "But, I also know you aren't with me 'cause of my money and you won't take my shit."

"True."

"And that's the thing, you'll put someone in their place and not care. Yet, you're sweet, thoughtful, smart and beautiful. I'd be a total dumb ass if I let you go."

"Ok…so don't. Just hold me tight and no more lies or games."

"Ok," he said holding her. Then said, "But I do need some time as far as work goes. We can't go in there saying we're together yet."

"I know and understand, but my concern is the disrespectful behavior with other women and having that playboy reputation just 'cause we can't be seen together."

"Not anymore. I'm done with that. Promise!"

She felt better after their talk.

Angelica was so tired, physically and emotionally. She laid down and he cuddled next to her.

"Oh…I forgot to tell you. Asila's moving to Charlotte," said Angelica. "She's coming with me tomorrow."

"Really?"

"Yep. She needs a fresh start."

"I'll call the moving company and have them pick up her stuff tomorrow afternoon."

"Thank you."

"Use our card for their plane tickets or whatever else she needs. I'll take care of it."

"Thank you, Baby," she said smiling. "Our card, huh?"

"Yep, ours…me and you," he said kissing her.

~Chapter 46~

VP Announcement

On Wednesday morning, Austin called an all staff meeting to make the official announcement for the new Sr. VP position.

"Good morning, everyone. I hope you all had a great Memorial weekend," said Austin pausing to listen to their responses. "Well, I called this meeting to announce the new Sr. Vice President of Human Resources. Please help me congratulate Ms. Angelica Zambrano."

Everyone cheered and clapped as she went to stand next to Austin.

In the midst of it all, Marla softly made an inappropriate comment.

"Do you care to repeat what you just said, Marla?" Austin asked sternly.

"I said it figures since you want to screw her," Marla boldly stated.

The entire room got quiet. They couldn't believe she actually repeated that out loud. She must've had a death wish.

"Excuse me," said Angelica.

Austin immediately intervened.

"Esta puta no me conoce," said Angelica under her breathe.

"So, you think I gave Ms. Zambrano the position because I want to sleep with her? Is that correct?" asked Austin verifying the allegations.

"I only said what others were thinking," Marla said confidently.

"Ok. Who else feels this way?" he asked looking around the room.

No one responded. She called out some names, but they looked at her crazy and denied the accusations.

"Well then…let me explain why Ms. Zambrano was selected."

First, Austin explained the educational and work experience requirements, which she met. Then, he explained the three assign-ments each applicant had to complete: improve and replace three company policies to fit corporate's new image; acquire an ongoing legal case and make recommendations and/or resolve the case; and select a country where they weren't doing business and create a proposal from a HR perspective for doing business in that coun-try. As a bonus exercise, each applicant had to come up with ideas to increase profits by 20% and demonstrate the affects on Human Resources.

Last, he commended Angelica for the way she utilized the com-pany's resources. She consistently met with the Financial Direc-tor (Shana), two board members, the attorney (Lance) and the IT director for information. She read existing policies, procedures and financial records. All of the executives corroborated his story.

Angelica came up with three new company policies that had to do with vacation accrual, personal time off and disciplinary actions. They would be implemented beginning July 1st.

She not only made recommendations for her legal case, but resolved it. Austin partially explained the case, how long it had been pending and what she did. Through vigorous negotiations, the case was settled out of court. The employee and all parties involved came up with an amicable solution.

Angelica chose Brazil as her country and presented a detailed report for doing business in that country from a HR perspective. The report had colored charts, laws and all the information required showing the impact it could have on the company.

For the bonus exercise, she stepped out of her field of expertise and came up with so many ways to increase the bottom line. She felt the company should target women by selling more home good products like small kitchen appliances, home decor, bedding, bathroom scents, more women wear and customized women trinkets. She suggested adding a few more sports that catered to the different regions, such as fishing, mountain climbing, skiing and surfing. She strongly recommended adding FIFA to the professional sports list. Soccer was huge in other countries. Then, Angelica brought it home with suggesting the stores add college sports wear to their inventory. It had equal importance as professional sports.

Austin showed enthusiasm because adding college sports wear to the stores would open up a whole new demographic, including students, parents, coaches, players…the colleges themselves. It also meant more employment opportunities from a HR perspective.

Angelica would start her new role effective immediately. He explained the company was going through a complete overhaul and her first assignment was the restructuring of the company's table of organization.

The last thing he discussed was the Fourth of July company picnic. He needed suggestions where it should be held this year.

Marla publicly apologized for her outburst. Angelica reluctantly accepted her apology, but Austin fired her anyway. He would not tolerate her behavior or disrespect. Then, he met with those individuals Marla named and issued reprimands. He demonstrated zero tolerance for gossip.

After the meeting, Austin called a quick meeting with Shana, Matthew, Thad and a few others to discuss a serious matter happening in one of the Atlanta stores. It required their immediate attention, so Austin wanted them there by Friday afternoon.

Meanwhile, Angelica saw Marla heading towards the bathroom and followed her.

"I'm sorry, Ms. Angelica," said Marla crying.

"I know," responded Angelica.

"Huh?" asked Marla with a disturbed look on her face.

"I said I know. I know you're sorry. You're a sorry ass woman that Austin doesn't want. What did you honestly think you were going to gain out of that? Austin?" asked Angelica laughing. "You may have fucked him a couple of times and felt magic, but you weren't nothing more than a piece of ass. Your inadequacies and insecurities as a woman are far too great for a man like him. He needs a real woman…one that knows how to conduct herself as one; one that demonstrates professionalism; one that is smart rather than pretends to be; and he definitely needs one that can keep her mouth shut and not act like a jealous thirteen year old little girl."

"You can't…" Marla started to say.

"Shhh!!" said Angelica putting her finger over her lips. "Sweetheart. No need for words. I think you've said and done enough. And I just want to reiterate that I know what he needs, especially in the bedroom," said Angelica slapping her own butt. "You just don't matter, Sweetheart. Never did."

Marla cried even harder at Angelica's mean and cruel words.

"Oh and just a little piece of advice…the next time you feel like opening your mouth and accusing people of sleeping together… DON'T!" said Angelica walking out of the bathroom.

Angelica was in her office when Damian came in ecstatic. Shana was leaving for the weekend, so he invited her over to his place. He mentioned having a surprise and she instantly felt bad. She'd forgotten what she told him before leaving. And now she had to find a way to tell him they were over.

Then, she received a phone call from her lawyer. He wanted to know how she wanted to proceed with the investigation Angelica had him conducting. She asked for ten minutes to call him back.

Angelica went to see Shana with a sincere heart, wanting to call a truce regarding the bet. Angelica's feelings towards Damian had changed. She found someone she wanted to be with, but didn't say who. She didn't want to play the game anymore because too many people would end up hurt.

Shana stood up and laughed like she heard a joke. Angelica didn't understand her reaction. But Shana wasn't having it.

"Too fucking bad, Bitch!" said Shana turning her smile into anger. "You've walked around here being hurtful, manipulative and down right nasty acting like yo' shit don't stink. You were so ready to have my husband 90 days ago. But now…because you have a man of your own, you want to dump mine like he's yesterday's trash. Well, too fucking bad! I will collect on the deal if you walk away now. Besides, it'll save you the embarrassment of waiting a week since that's all you have left."

"Shana…are you serious right now?"

"Angelica…we're done here. You can get the FUCK out of my office!"

Angelica was steaming.

"You're right, Shana. We're done here and I'm leaving, but

know this…you will NOT get one Mutha Fuckin' dime from me! See what I thought was a friendly little competition, turned out to be a devised exit plan for you and your marriage. You want to go play house and lay up with Matt because of his family's millions, but you won't get that either. I'll make sure of it! You ain't nothing but a five dollar hoe. Always have been and always will be! Just be ready to pay up because this bet is over on Friday. With your footprints fresh out the door, mine will be fresh in, fucking your husband in yo' bed and winning the bet. And I will collect… BITCH!!!"

Angelica walked out and then returned.

"Oh and one more thing…my shit don't stink," said Angelica winking at her.

Angelica went to Damian's office and told him to get ready for the night of his life. She was going to make him never want to leave her. He got excited.

Angelica called the lawyer back and told him to proceed with force regarding their plans. Then, she invited Thad over for dinner.

~Chapter 47~

Thad meets Asila

"Asila! Nina!" screamed Angelica walking through the door.

"Hey, sis," said Asila with Nina in her arms.

"Ti ti," said Nina going to her.

Angelica took her and gave her a big hug.

"How was work?" asked Asila.

"I have so much to tell you. But first what smells so good?"

Angelica put Nina down and walked over to the pots on the stove.

"I'm making carne asada con papas, moro y maduros," said Asila. (Cuban-style pot roast with black beans and white rice cooked together and sweet plantains).

"You need my help?" asked Angelica.

"No, thanks. It's almost done."

"Oh…I invited a friend over for dinner. I think you'll like him," said Angelica giggling like a matchmaking teenager.

"Angelica! I just got here!" said Asila.

"So!"

Asila shook her head and changed the subject. "My stuff came today."

Angelica went to the garage to check out the whip.

Tuesday morning before leaving Miami, they went to DMV and changed Richard's vehicle into her name. Asila was now the proud owner of a white 2012 Cadillac Escalade.

"Good. Now we can go real grocery shopping," said Angelica.

They sat down to talk before her guest arrived. Angelica told her about Shana not letting her off the hook. So, she planned to take Shana to the cleaners for being a hard ass.

"Angelica, I can't believe you," said Asila.

"What?"

"That was an easy bet for you. Why did you take it to begin with?"

"I let my curiosity get the best of me. I liked Damian in college, so I wondered what it would be like to sleep with him."

"And what's going to happen to him when this is all over since you're with Austin now?"

"I don't know, Asila. That's what worries me. Damian really is a great guy. He's just been mind-fucked by Shana for too long." Then she quickly apologized for cussing around Nina.

"I think it's messed up that Damian will be hurt."

"I do too. I honestly feel bad, which is why I tried to get out of it. Austin and I are finally in a good place. I don't want to mess that up. But if I don't go through with it, I'll owe that Bi…scuit eater a lot of money."

Asila laughed because Angelica was working hard to avoid cussing in front of Nina. Then, Angelica told her how much money was involved. Asila couldn't believe a wife would do that to her own husband.

"I don't know, sis. That's a lot of money. Are you willing to give it up for Austin?"

Before she could answer, there was a knock at the door.

"Hey," said Angelica giving Thad a hug and a kiss on the cheek.

"Hey," said Thad.

"Come in. I want you to meet someone."

Angelica drug him into the kitchen, but Asila was gone.

"Asila!" screamed Angelica.

"Coming!"

Moments later, she appeared.

"Hi," said Asila who changed and fixed herself up a bit.

"Asila…this is Thad. Thad…this is my sister, Asila," said Angelica introducing them.

"Nice to meet you, Asila," said a stricken Thad shaking her hand.

"Likewise," she said smiling.

"And this little princess is my niece, Nina," said Angelica introducing Thad to Nina. "Say hi Nina."

"Hi, Princess. How are you?" Thad asked Nina.

"Fine," she said with a face making them laugh.

"She's beautiful like her mother," he said making Asila blush.

Angelica was setting the table when she heard the doorbell.

"Hi, Baby," said Angelica to Austin.

"Hey, Beautiful."

"Thad is here," whispered Angelica.

"I know," he whispered back.

Austin told Thad about them, but he admitted he already knew. So, they didn't have to hide in front of him. She was glad considering Thad would be over more often if her plan worked between Thad and Asila.

"Hey everyone," said Austin walking into the kitchen.

Asila greeted him with a hug and kiss on the cheek. "How are you?" she asked.

"Good, thanks and you?"

"Good."

"Hi, Nina," said Austin waving.

"I'm jealous now," Thad told Asila. "I didn't get that when I came in," teased Thad.

So, she gave him a hug and kiss on the cheek, too.

They all sat down to a scrumptious dinner. Thad was impressed with Asila's cooking. Angelica informed them that they learned from the best…their mother.

"You can cook?" Austin asked Angelica surprised.

"Yes!" she said laughing. "And don't say it like that."

"I mean I'm always the one cooking."

"Because you want to. Besides, you never asked."

Austin talked about Angelica's promotion. Asila was happy for her, but wondered why she didn't tell her. Angelica forgot because she was talking about Damian and Austin.

"Thad…I need a huge favor. I have to work late tomorrow. Can you take Asila to the grocery store for me?" asked Angelica.

"Yeah, sure. I'm actually off tomorrow." Then, he looked at Asila and said, "I can come early, take you to the store and then show you around, if you want?"

"Thanks. I'd like that," said Asila smiling.

Angelica started talking about Asila going back to nursing school. She was following in their mother's footsteps. So, she needed to find a school in the area. Thad made some recommendations and offered to take her to sign up. Austin even offered her a job at Sportie Fans in the meantime to earn income. Thad mentioned good schools for Nina and some activities to do around the Charlotte area. Asila appreciated it and would think about everything. But at the moment, she was trying to grasp the move to North Carolina. Angelica understood better than anyone.

After dinner, Angelica and Austin took Nina to her room and put her down for bed. They made her brush her teeth and read her a bedtime story. This gave Asila and Thad a chance to talk.

"So what do you think of the city so far?" asked Thad.

"It's ok. It's just different. Now, I know what Angelica felt when she first moved here."

"I hope you don't give up on us and leave. I hope you stay."

"I am. There's nothing for me in Miami and I have to give my daughter a better life."

"Good. I think you just need to get out and see the city. And I'm willing to be your tour guide."

"I'd like that."

They talked about Richard, some of her problems and her dreams. Thad told her about his past relationships, his love for motorcycles and his desire to settle down. Asila also wanted to settle down. She wanted Nina to have a stable home life like she had.

Angelica gave Austin an air high-five as they peeked in on them. She thought Thad was perfect for Asila and would take care of her and the baby. Besides, he was a hot looking white boy with a big dick.

Angelica and Austin left them and went to bed.

~Chapter 48~

Friday Night at Damian's House

Angelica came downstairs wearing some dark blue low rider jeans, a hot pink fishnet bra top with a Swarovski crystal bra underneath, hot pink Bella Dama peep toe pumps and a hot pink clutch. She wore chandelier diamond earrings, an 8-row diamond ring and a 2-strand diamond belly chain.

"Titties," said Nina laughing, referring to Angelica's breasts popping out.

Asila, Angelica and Thad laughed.

"Damn, sis…you look hot!" said Asila.

"Thank you."

"He ain't gonna know what hit him," said Thad.

"He sure isn't," said Angelica.

"I talked to Damian today and you'll be surprised," said Thad.

"Thanks for the head's up," said Angelica. "Hey, when do you leave?"

"I'm on the last flight out at like 10:00 tonight."

"I thought you had to be there early?"

"I was supposed to be, but I'll just work all day tomorrow."

"Cool. Well have a safe trip," Angelica told Thad walking out the door with a blunt in her hand.

Thad stayed talking to Asila. She asked if he was uncomfortable seeing Angelica half nude. He didn't want to lie to her, so he told her about them sleeping together. He explained the whole story and why they had sex. It only happened once he assured her, but it didn't bring her comfort. Asila was kind of upset, but understood. She was more concerned with him wanting Angelica, but he reassured her that they'd become good friends. He was more like her trusted confidant because he knew about Damian and Austin. Asila knew men couldn't resist Angelica, so she made him promise to let her know if he changed his mind. He promised he wouldn't and sealed it with a kiss.

Then, she asked his opinion about the bet between Angelica and Shana regarding Damian, assuming he knew. But he didn't know what she was talking about and made her spill it. So, she told him everything. Thad couldn't believe Shana and felt bad for Angelica. She was in a tough spot.

Angelica lit her blunt as she drove towards Ballantyne. She thought about what she was going to do. She needed proof of what was about to go down.

She stopped at the nearest Rite-Aid after existing the highway. She came up with a brilliant idea and needed to get some things.

Before getting to Damian's house, she hit the blunt a few more times. She wanted to be super high for this session.

Damian's eyes popped out of his head when he saw her.

"Damn, Baby! You look sexy as hell!" he said sticking his tongue down her throat.

Damian had the house dim and romantic with candles lit. He led her to the dining room where he prepared a candlelight dinner for two. He handed her a dozen of roses and pulled out her chair. Then, he served them dinner, but she didn't eat much since she had other things on her mind.

The whole time she was sitting there, she thought *'he has no idea what's coming'*. Shana fucked him and he didn't even know it.

They adjourned to the family room where she positioned her mini camcorder towards the sofa. She purchased it along with three 16 GB memory cards when she stopped earlier. Angelica planned to record their entire evening so Shana wouldn't miss a thing. However, Damian assumed she was being a little kinky.

"Here…open this," said Damian handing her an envelope.

It was his divorce papers. Shana left them for him to sign, which he did.

Next, he took off his ring and reached for her left hand. He slid it onto her ring finger. Angelica took lots of pictures with it on and was glad it was recording.

"I love you," he said. "And I'm willing to give you everything I have."

"I love you, too."

"You're my strength. I feel like I can do anything by your side," said an emotional Damian.

Officially, Angelica won the bet. She could've taken off running without compromising her relationship with Austin, but she didn't. Instead, she really wanted to give Damian a night he wouldn't forget.

Angelica played the Dominatrix role. She took off her clothes and sat on the couch. She pointed to the floor, gesturing he get on his knees. She opened wide and pushed his face in her pussy. She was a bit rougher than usual. This excited him as he became more aggressive.

After she came, he sexed her in so many different positions. She also rode him so good that he screamed like a bitch. She showed no mercy.

Then, they made their way to his bedroom. She faced the camera towards them as she put on a show. She made him do things like suck her toes, eat more pussy and lick ass.

After their session, she was starved. So, Damian went to the kitchen to warm up her food. He came back with her plate and one for himself. Angelica lit her blunt while they ate and talked.

Before she left, she asked for the divorce papers. She told him she wanted to hold on to them until Shana got back so they could tell her together. He didn't mind and allowed her to take them. Then, she kissed him good-bye and left.

When she got home, she told Asila all about what happened. She even showed her the divorce papers.

"Sis…your pussy must be made of kryptonite cause… DAMN!!!!" shouted Asila.

"I crushed that BITCH like a bug!" Angelica proudly ranted.

She grabbed her laptop to show Asila some of the footage, but Asila closed her eyes at what she saw. Angelica laughed as she e-mailed Shana parts of the video, especially the important parts like divorce papers and the ring. Shana had until the close of business Monday to pay her debt. No excuses!!

"Sis, I need to talk to you about you and Thad," Asila told her.

"He told you?" asked Angelica.

"Yes."

"Ok."

Angelica explained her side of the story, which sounded exactly like Thad's version.

"Asila, I promise that me and Thad aren't sleeping together. It was one time," said Angelica.

"I know. He told me the same thing."

"Please believe us."

"I do."

"I would never purposely hurt you by setting you up with someone that I'm interested in."

"I know. It's just I think I like him and I don't want him lusting after you."

"Oh Sweety…it's not like that at all. He and I have become more like brother and sister. He's just a really great guy and I think he'll be good for you."

Asila told her about the kiss. Angelica was happy things were progressing and convinced her to give Thad a chance. She agreed as long as Angelica didn't get mad at her for telling Thad about the bet between her and Shana. Angelica didn't get upset. She was glad she told him.

~Chapter 49~

The Big Payday

This particular Monday morning brought joy to Angelica's heart. It was a beautiful day in Charlotte.

Angelica was moving to a bigger office, so the movers were there bright and early. Cherry was moving as well since she was promoted to Senior Executive Secretary. She would remain Angelica's assistant, which included a nice raise.

"Here you go, Miss Angelica. This just came for you," said Cherry handing her an envelope.

Angelica reviewed the contents and became overjoyed, if it were possible.

An hour later, Shana visited Angelica in her new office.

"Congratulations, Angelica. A bet is a bet," said Shana handing her a cashier's check for $20,000.

"Thank you," said Angelica smiling.

"Also, here are the certificates for my shares of stock."

"So gracious of you."

"Now with regards to the property in Tennessee, there's been a little hiccup."

But Angelica didn't let Shana say another word.

"No, there has not been any hiccups. Just deceit. See, I knew you were going to try and pull some bullshit about this real estate. I saw how important it was to you. So, I had my lawyer on it since we made the bet. And would you like to know what I found out?"

"What?" asked Shana crossing her arms.

"I'll tell you. See last week you tried to record a quick claim deed and convey your property to Matthew Vaughn. But what you hadn't realized was that I recorded the initial bet so I used it as evidence to put a lien on the property."

Shana gave her a look.

"Yes, I recorded that conversation because I knew you would try something like this. So, you see…you were knowingly and purposely trying to transfer property that had a claim against it. Didn't you know that's against the law? Here…I'll read the Tennessee law to you," said Angelica reading the following:

Any person who transfers land by execution of a deed with knowledge of outstanding liens, mortgages, deeds of trust or other claims against such transferred land with the intent to defraud, commits a Class E felony.

"So, technically, there are no hiccups, Shana. There's just intent to defraud."

"No because technically I didn't know you put a lien on the property."

"Shana…Shana…Shana…you agreed to the bet. That meant you knew there was a claim against it. Just because it was verbal doesn't mean it wasn't legal."

Shana looked disgusted as Angelica made her sign the release forms transferring the title into Angelica's name.

"Oh and Shana…I'll see you tonight," said Angelica winking at her before she stormed off.

Angelica was in such a good mood that she went to Austin's office and locked the door. She closed the curtains and crawled under his desk. She gave him the best head ever. He didn't know what he did to deserve it, but he wanted to continue doing it.

Afterwards, Angelica split her legs apart on the edge of his desk so he could give it to her.

"What did I do to deserve that?" he asked afterwards buckling his pants.

"I love you and I'm in a good mood."

"Well, we need to keep you that way. That head was the BOMB!"

"Shut up," she said laughing. "Dinner is on me tonight. Let's celebrate."

"What are we celebrating?"

"Love," she said waving her hands in the air, walking out.

Austin didn't know what had gotten into her, but he was happy that she was happy.

Damian left the office a little early. He was meeting Angelica at his house to break the news to Shana.

When he got there, Angelica's car was already there parked behind another car in front of his house. He sat in the driveway looking at the exterior of his home. He thought about what he was getting ready to do. Doubts ran through his mind about ending his marriage to Shana for Angelica. Then, he thought about Shana and Angelica alone in his house and got out of the car.

He stood at the front door listening for them yelling. It was quiet, so he proceeded with caution. He carefully and quietly opened the door. He wanted to try and sneak up on them to hear what they were talking about.

As he entered, he tripped on a pair of men's shoes that were by the front door. No one heard him 'cause of the music playing. He was also flabbergasted that the house smelled like a pound of weed. He immediately frowned wondering what the hell was going on.

As he crept down the hallway, he faintly heard male and female sex moans.

"Suck it…yes…right there," was what he heard as he drew closer to the family room.

He really wondered what the hell was going on.

"You like that?" asked the male voice.

"Yes…take it all," Damian heard as he continued creeping.

He followed the sounds, which grew louder with every step. He couldn't believe what he was hearing. It sounded like Angelica.

"Suck it…I'm about to cum…suck harder. I want to cum in your mouth!"

He stormed around the corner.

"WHAT THE FUCK???" he yelled.

He saw Angelica butt booty naked on the couch with her legs spread open yelling, "I'm cuming" as Shana was on her knees eating Angelica out. And what Damian heard was Friday night's video of him and Angelica. That male voice he heard was his own!!!

~Chapter 50~

Truth Revealed

After his unmitigated shock wore off, Damian was told the truth. They started from the beginning.

"Do you remember my friend, Alice?" Shana asked Damian.

"No."

"From college. FIU? Miami?"

"Are you serious right now? College? What does that have to do with anything?"

"Think back."

"I don't know…maybe."

"Remember when you played that trick on Shana and her friend, Alice? You pranked Alice and fucked Shana?" Angelica chimed in.

"Yes! Alice was the ugly duckling," laughed Damian.

"Well…" Shana started to say, but Angelica stopped her.

"Did you know that Alice was in love with you? Like really in love with you?" asked Angelica.

"No. I knew she liked me, but that was it," responded Damian. "I thought Shana was the one 'cause of how she acted."

"Did you know that Shana went after you knowing that Alice was in love with you?"

"No. I never knew that."

"So, you didn't know that Shana plotted on you while lying to her best friend, Alice?"

"No! And why do you keep talking about Alice? And how do you know those things about Shana?" he demanded.

"Hi…I'm Alice," said Angelica.

"What!!! You do NOT look like Alice! She was weird looking."

Angelica explained the whole story, including Shana's deceitful ways.

"So, I don't understand…was this revenge for what I did to you in college?" Damian asked Angelica mad.

"Yes!" yelled Shana.

"Really, Shana? You're gonna lie like that to my face?" asked Angelica.

"No…it wasn't revenge," said Shana.

"I went to Shana's office my first day because I recognized you two. After confirming who you were, we sat there talking. She wanted to tell you who I was, but I asked her not to. She thought it was because I still wanted you and told me to stay away from you. But the truth was that I wanted to surprise you. I assured her I didn't date married men."

"Well that was a lie," he said angrily.

"No, it's not a lie! I usually don't, but Shana sought me out saying something about problems between you two and wanting me to tempt you to cheat."

"What!?!" yelled Damian. "Why would you do that?"

"Because she said she could have you if she wanted," yelled Shana.

Angelica explained the context in which she said it. It wasn't meant for a bet or to hurt him. She was simply talking to Shana. And even though Angelica said no and refused to "help" as Shana called it, Shana wouldn't let it go. She insisted they make a bet and began offering things in exchange. Angelica didn't realize how serious she was until her eyes lit up when they discussed Angelica purchasing some land in Tennessee if she lost.

"You sold me up a river for some damn real estate?" Damian shouted to Shana. "I want to know all the details of the bet."

Angelica told him everything.

"Why did you agree in the end? Was money and property going to justify what you did?" Damian asked Angelica.

"No! I did it because of you. I didn't know I still liked you until I saw you in the conference room the first day at work. You still gave me butterflies when I heard your voice. But I wasn't going to touch you because you were married. I kept telling Shana that, but she thought I would try and sneak off with you…" Angelica was saying.

"And you would've, Damian! I know you! You cheated on me before I let Angelica sleep with you! You've always been a cheat!" screamed Shana.

"One time, Shana! Just once and you supposedly forgave me for that!"

"There was another woman too!"

"Give me a name!"

"I don't know her name!"

"You're always coming up with these crazy assumptions!" yelled Damian not admitting the truth. "You're always accusing me of fucking someone else! Maybe if you were fucking me, you wouldn't have to worry about someone else doing it!"

"I am fucking you!"

"That sorry ass pussy! I take it 'cause you're my wife, but I know what you're capable of. And you haven't fucked me right in a while now."

"Fuck you, Damian!" said Shana.

Damian looked at her and said, "Oh…I get it. You're fucking someone else, aren't you?" It was like a light bulb went off.

Angelica made a face as she sat down to watch the fireworks.

"So there lies the answer. You wanted Angelica to distract me while you fucked around too. And you didn't think I'd leave because of the baby situation you keep holding over my head. Does that sound about right?" asked Damian.

"I didn't think you'd leave me. You weren't supposed to actually want a divorce," said Shana crying.

"How could I not after Angelica?"

"I just didn't think she could pull it off in 90 days," re-iterated Shana.

"Angelica's an amazing woman and obviously a woman of her word. You don't know half her skills. She knows how to take care of a man and please the hell out of one. She's also funny, beautiful and sexy as hell…how do you think a man could resist her if she makes the effort to get to know him?" Damian asked Shana.

"You were supposed to!"

"I'm a man, Shana! And you let your husband roam free. What did you think could happen? You're stupid!"

Angelica snickered.

"What I want to know is why the hell were you eating her pussy…and like a pro I might add," Damian asked Shana.

Angelica told him about Shana's lesbian experience in college. The girl's name was Samantha, but she went by Sam. Shana just wanted to see what it was like. However, Angelica used to tease her so Shana swore she'd never do it to her.

"That turned out to be a lie," laughed Angelica.

"So, who is he Shana?" asked Damian, wanting to know who she was sleeping with.

"Well, I'm leaving," said Angelica. "You two need to work this out."

"What about us?" Damian quickly asked Angelica getting close to her.

This was Angelica's chance to end things with Damian.

"There is no us."

"Oh…so you got what you wanted and now I'm nothing?"

"That's not it, Damian…"

"Whatever! You can leave, too…Trick!"

"Trick? You Stupid Ass Bitch! You owe Thad $3,000!"

"No, I don't! For what?" he asked and then shook his head.

Angelica knew that he realized she knew about the bet he made with Thad.

"Yeah, Bitch! I knew about the bet you made with Thad," she said.

"How did you know?"

"After you left my office the day we got back from Chicago, I went for a walk. I was near the patio when I overheard you and Thad talking. You betted I'd be wrapped around your finger, remember? You were supposed to have both me and Shana…remember that?" she asked.

"Yes, but…"

"But nothing! You bet on me right after we got back from an amazing trip. I really believed the things you told me. I really thought I had a chance to be with you. But after hearing you talk about me the way you did…I was done. I checked out by that point and concentrated on the monetary portion of mine and Shana's bet," explained Angelica.

"But you already had a bet on me!"

"Yeah, but to keep you, to be with you, to love you, to marry you. I told Shana that you were going to be MY husband. I was going to be the luckiest girl in the world with the finest man on Earth by my side," she said making him feel bad.

"Yeah right! You had a boyfriend! Remember that?" questioned Damian.

"No, I didn't! I lied. You looked so uncomfortable at the restaurant that night so I said that to put your mind at ease."

"Then who were the flowers from that day in your office?"

"Victor! My friend from the club!" she exclaimed, lying and thinking quick on her feet.

Damian felt like a total dumb ass.

"I'm sorry, Angelica. I really am. I didn't know," said Damian.

Angelica grabbed her things.

"You both deserve each other! You're both losers! You bet that Damian wouldn't love me and he does," she told Shana. "And you bet that Thad couldn't fuck me, but he did. And just to let you know…that white boy has a big dick. Ask your wife! She knows about him and his brother who is the proud owner of those shoes," said Angelica kicking them as she walked out.

~Chapter 51~

Double
Date

It was early July and Austin and Angelica were on a double date with Thad, Asila and Nina. They were celebrating Asila's 25th birthday. They were also celebrating hers and Thad's one month anniversary.

They went to Rouley's in Uptown Charlotte. This upscale restaurant was very romantic with its black and white themed dining room. It had large windows with silk curtains, black leather booths and candlelight centered on each table. The bar had a grand collection of liquor for any kind of drink and jazz played in the background.

Thad surprised Asila with many gifts, including the sparkly rose gold-colored cocktail dress she was wearing. It had vertical and horizontal sequin patterns with a deep V-neckline. It was sexy, but classy. Her hair was down and wavy and her make-up was flawless. She looked beautiful.

Asila wanted to look good for Thad. It was a special night. She planned to have sex with him for the first time.

"Austin Zachary," said a woman approaching them.

Austin looked and said, "Lacey."

"How are you, Austin?" asked Lacey going for a hug.

He pushed her away and asked her to step back.

"Hi, I'm Angelica…his girlfriend."

"Yeah…well, it was nice seeing you Austin," said Lacey totaling dismissing Angelica.

"Can't say the same, Lacey," said Austin rolling his eyes.

She left to sit with a gentleman who appeared to be waiting for her.

Lacey's antics didn't faze Angelica because her and Austin's relationship couldn't be more perfect. Austin stopped all of his games and got serious with Angelica. And after the whole bet ordeal, she settled with Austin.

"Wow. She was rude," said Asila.

"Sorry about that. That was my ex. Things didn't exactly end well," said Austin.

Then, Angelica's phone rang. It was Claudia. She excused herself to speak with her outside. When she came back, she told them about going to Miami. Claudia needed help with preparations for her engagement party.

"So, what kind of engagement ring would you like, Asila," Thad randomly asked.

"I'm simple unlike Angelica and Claudia. I love hearts, so maybe a heart ring and a simple band."

"Oh no! I want big bling and extravagance," said Angelica.

Austin just shook his head.

Nina was sitting on Thad's lap when dinner arrived.

"Papi…" said Nina calling Thad dad in Spanish.

"Yes, mija?" Thad responded without hesitation.

Everyone looked at them in shock.

"Nina! He's not your…" Asila started to say, but he put his finger on his lips motioning her to not say anything.

"Papa!" said Nina excitedly about the food arriving.

Angelica didn't say a word. She was in utter shock.

Throughout dinner, Lacey wouldn't leave well enough alone. She kept sending Austin inappropriate text messages and pictures with Angelica sitting right beside him. This pissed Angelica off. She even had the audacity to call him, but Austin didn't pick up. Angelica knew what to do to fix her.

On their way out, Angelica told Thad and Asila to wait outside. She didn't want Nina to see what was about to happen. So they left, but best believe they were looking through the window.

Angelica grabbed Austin's hand and walked over to the booth where Lacey and her date were sitting. She stood there kissing Austin, making sure Lacey saw plenty of tongue swapping. Then, she rubbed all over Austin, grabbing his dick. Angelica wanted Lacey to see what she couldn't have. Angelica indiscreetly put his hand in her panties to get his fingers nice and wet. Out of spite, she took that same hand and rubbed Lacey's bottom lip. Lacey was pissed and jumped in Angelica's face. Angelica waved her hand in her face and then poked her in the forehead. Austin immediately grabbed Angelica and left.

Austin and Thad couldn't believe Angelica's boldness. Asila wasn't surprised. She knew what Angelica was capable of.

"Be good, mija with ti ti…ok?" Asila told Nina.

Nina nodded.

"Can papi have a kiss?" Thad asked Nina.

She left Angelica's arms and went to Thad. She gave him a hug and a kiss. Then, she went back to her aunt who was babysitting for the night.

Once they got to Thad's place, Asila went off on him.

"Listen, Thad! I appreciate everything you've done for me, but you can't tell my daughter that you're her father. She has one," Asila said pacing the floor.

"And where is he, Asila? I don't see him spending time with her everyday like I do!"

She slapped him.

He grabbed her and hugged her tight.

"I'm sorry, Sweetheart! I shouldn't have said that," he said very apologetic.

"I don't want her thinking you're going to be in her life forever, Thad."

"Is that so bad?"

"You might get tired and leave."

"I'm not going anywhere, Asila. You're the one I want."

"You say that now, but who knows."

"Asila…look at me," said Thad looking into her eyes. "Don't compare me to your past relationships. We promised not to do that to one another, remember?"

She nodded.

"Give me a chance to show you what I want and who I want," he said.

"Thad, it scared me when she said that. She's never said that to anyone other than my father."

Thad picked her up and carried her to the bed. He undressed her and then took his clothes off. While lying on top of her, he said, "I understand you're scared, but I love you both and I want to be her father."

Asila cried as she made love to Thad all night.

~Chapter 52~

Uh-Oh!!!

The following weekend Angelica left to Miami. She and Claudia had been running around making the necessary preparations for the engagement party. But Angelica missed Austin, so she called him.

"Hey, Baby."

"Hey, Sweetness. How's Miami?" he asked.

"Hot. What are you doing?"

"Flippin' through the channels. What about you?"

"Calling you. I miss you."

"I miss you, too."

As they talked, he thought he heard a noise at his front door. He got up to check, but there was no one there. So, he sat back down and continued flipping through the channels. Then, he screamed.

"Austin! What's wrong?" Angelica asked concerned.

"Nothing, Baby. I thought I saw a rat."

It was a rat alright. It was Lacey standing in front of him naked with his spare key in her hand.

"I see your spare key is still in the same spot," she said using her inside voice.

Austin muted the phone as she spoke. He kept motioning for her to leave, but she shook her head in disagreement.

"Baby, can I call you back?" he asked unmuting the call.

"Wait…" babbled Angelica, still talking.

Austin took the phone away from his ear and told Lacey to leave. However, the response was always the same.

Then, he drug her to the door, but she screamed.

"Austin…what was that?" asked Angelica.

"The television, Baby."

Austin muted the phone while Lacey stood there laughing. She saw Austin getting pissed off. So, she decided to calm his nerves.

"Lacey get out!" yelled Austin, but she wasn't listening.

Lacey tried to unzip his pants, but he pushed her away. She kept trying until she backed him onto the couch.

"Yes, that's nice, Honey," said Austin unmuting the phone trying to listen to Angelica.

Lacey sat on him and went to unzip his pants again. But he covered it with his hand. So, she slid her vagina up and down on his hand, making herself wet. She began moaning, so he quickly put his hand over her mouth. She wanted him to do that so she could unzip his pants. Then, she reached for his dick, but he stopped her. She used her other hand, but he rested the phone on his shoulder and stopped that hand. She got in his face and licked his lips.

"No!" yelled Austin.

"No, what?" asked Angelica.

"Nothing, Baby."

Austin couldn't take it anymore and stood up making her fall.

He attempted to fix himself, but she snatched his pants and underwear down, exposing what she wanted. When he tried to pick them up, she was already between his legs, sucking his dick.

Austin pulled her by the hair, but she clamped down with her teeth. He immediately let go. She spit on his dick and sucked on it some more. Austin was losing the battle 'cause it felt so good. She slowly pushed him back onto the couch so he could really enjoy it.

Lacey sucked up and down and moved her head all around. She went as far down as she could go, deep throating. Austin pushed her head down too trying to choke her. She didn't mind.

"Baby…can I PLEASE call you right back?" asked Austin still trying to get off the phone.

But Angelica had one more thing to say.

By this point, Austin was naked since she removed his pants and he didn't have a shirt on to begin with.

She pulled his finger down to her clit. He moved it. She bit down using teeth again and placed his finger right back. This time, he massaged her clit.

With Angelica in his ear and him playing with ex-girlfriend's pussy, he didn't know what to do. But he knew it was so wrong and it wouldn't end well.

Then, Lacey decided not to play fair anymore. She was tired of being nice.

"Rub her faster," she said, but he shook his head no.

"Who is that?" asked Angelica.

"No one, Babe. It was the TV," said Austin trying to mute the phone again.

"Make her cum…" she said a little louder, but he covered her mouth.

Austin did as he was told to shut her up. This made Lacey suck his dick harder and faster. She twisted his nipples, exciting him even more. Austin finger banged her until she came.

"Austin…Austin!" screamed Angelica trying to get his attention.

"Yes…I'm here," he said very distracted.

"What are you doing? And who is that talking?"

"Nothing Baby…no one. "

Lacey got up and straddled him so she could ride him. He kept trying to push her off, but she wrapped her legs around him where he couldn't even stand this time.

"Stop!" asserted Austin.

"What the hell is going on, Austin!" yelled Angelica. "Who's there?"

Lacey rocked back and forth, creeping up so his dick could slide in. She almost made it.

"Baby! I have to call you back," yelled Austin.

"Yeah, Bitch! He has to fuck me now. Bye!" yelled Lacey before he hung up.

"What the fuck is wrong with you?" he asked grabbing Lacey.

But by the way he grabbed her, she rocked once more and…

Stay tuned for what happens next in...

The Betting Game 2